Maxwell's Reality

ALSO BY M.J. TROW

SCHOOLMASTER MYSTERIES

MAXWELL'S REALITY

M. J. TROW

A Schoolmaster Murder Mystery Book 22

JOFFE
BOOKS

Joffe Books, London
www.joffebooks.com

First published in Great Britain in 2025

Cover art by Cherie Chapman

ISBN: 978-1-80573-002-6

For Ann,
who knows Maxwell better than I do

CHAPTER ONE

'What do I know about reality TV?'

DI Jacquie Carpenter-Maxwell looked up sharply at her husband. She had been concentrating on a report she needed to deliver the next morning and had been miles away. Perhaps she had misheard.

'Next to nothing, I would imagine.'

Peter Maxwell, scourge and saviour in equal measure of schoolchildren the length and breadth of Leighford and beyond, blew out his breath in relief. 'Thank goodness. I was a bit worried for a moment there.' He turned his attention back to the folder on his lap and, after a while, his wife could bear it no longer.

'Why do you ask?'

He looked up. 'Hmm? Ask what?' He reached for his glass of the amber nectar and sipped from it, looking startled when it proved to be empty.

'What *is* that you're reading?' Jacquie was concerned. Her husband was that strange creature, a man who could multitask to an almost Olympic standard. She had seen him deal with Mrs B, cleaner, IT guru and now neighbour, answering her scattergun questions without breaking a sweat. He had once even fed two cats and a child three different

1

things for breakfast and they all got the right bowls. She had seen him watch an episode of *The West Wing* while writing cover notes for a lesson on the British constitution and not miss a beat, whatever President Jed Bartlet was whiffling on about. So — what was in the folder? She made a lunge for it, but he held it over his head.

'It's plans for next term.'

Now she was really worried. 'Plans? Whose plans? You don't make plans.' Her eyes were big and anxious. Change came, of course it did, but she liked to be able to ambush it on the road when she could, feel its collar, work out what it was planning to steal or otherwise bugger up before it arrived on the doorstep.

'Senior Management Team.' He looked up at her. 'Only for some reason they call it Senior Leadership Team . . . clear sign they don't know them very well. Where was I?'

'SMT.'

'Right, yes. Apparently . . .' he turned to the front of the folder, 'apparently some company called Fly On The Wall Ltd,' he turned it to face her, 'look — it's got capital letters and everything. On every word, bless them, but they probably can't help that. And a little fly, look, instead of the "e".' He pointed. 'I'm off at a tangent again.'

'Some company.'

'Yes. This company, which apparently is called FOTWL for short.' He mouthed it silently, trying to make it into a word and failing. 'I think I will just call it "Fly" for short; anyway, Fly has identified Leighford High School as a perfect candidate for their upcoming series of *Fly on the Wall* — did you see what they did there?' He raised his eyebrows at her and almost smiled. 'Fly-on-the-wall documentaries. Which is why I asked you if I know anything about reality TV.'

'They're not going to do it, though, surely?'

He flicked some pages and shrugged. 'Hard to tell. I recognise the cold hand of County Hall in this. I expect there is money changing hands somewhere. It used to be two thousand quid a day for location shooting, which is why the Carnarvons, owning Highclere as they do, are still richer than God. Think *Downton Abbey*.'

Jacquie would rather not.

'I've read this so many times it is coming out of my ears and it's totally without detail. Have you seen any of the stuff by this crew?'

Jacquie wrinkled her nose, thinking. 'I suppose it might have been on in the canteen at some point if I was there late. It's the kind of thing we have on for wallpaper when it's a quiet night. But not consciously, no. Will you have any say?'

'Me, specifically?' He chuckled. 'I will be saying stuff, but whether that will count as having a say, as such, is doubtful.'

She laughed too. 'Of course, *you'll* be saying something. I took that as a given. I think I meant, though, will the staff have a say? Surely, they can't make you be on TV without permission?'

Maxwell flicked through the pages, muttering, 'I saw something . . . yes, here it is. To paraphrase, we can refuse to be on film, but this will be only for, and I quote, "good reason". Umm . . . drone, drone, blah, blah . . . "The school and governors would be most appreciative if staff could not withhold permission without good cause, as it will make the filming schedule difficult."' He looked up. 'That means that it is a done deal, don't you think?'

Jacquie nodded ruefully. 'Sounds like, I'm afraid. Who will refuse, do you reckon? Apart from you, I mean.'

'Let me see. Helen, for one.'

'Any particular reason?' Jacquie had got to know her husband's Number Two in the Sixth Form hierarchy quite well. 'She has never struck me as being very much of a rebel.'

'No, indeed. She isn't. But she does worry about her bum looking big in almost anything and apparently the camera adds ten pounds. There are another couple of staff who will be thinking along the same lines, I would imagine. Oh, oh.' He bounced in his seat, his finger in the air. 'I would bet good money on the new bug in Business not wanting to be on camera.'

'Do I know him? The new boy?'

Maxwell had a think. 'Dunno. At the Christmas do at the Ferret and Weasel, do you remember the rather . . . well, appropriately enough rather weaselly bloke who was knocking them back like there was no tomorrow?'

'I thought he was Don from Maths. I hope it was, I phoned it in when I saw car keys in his hand, I'm afraid.'

'Oh, that was you, was it? Well grassed, Parkhurst. I did wonder. Everyone blamed Thingee Two. No, not him. The one at his table. The one with the dyed hair and the big lapels.'

'Oh, *him*. I remember *him*. Who wouldn't?' Jacquie pointed a rigid finger and looked over the opposite shoulder.

'Yes. John Travolta, the kids call him. They have long memories, filmically, at Leighford, bless them.'

'Some things go on forever,' Jacquie said. She had been married to an historian for long enough now to know what to say when.

'They do, they do indeed. Well, anyway, his name is something like Kirk or Lee or something . . . I've got it, Doug Harvey.'

'Seriously, Doug Harvey. And you remember it by Lee and Kirk?' She shook her head. The map inside her husband's head would have taken anyone on a wild and wonderful ride.

'Hmm?' He looked at her for a moment then chuckled. 'Oh, yes. Do you know, I hadn't really thought of it that way. Anyhoo, everyone calls him JT since that Christmas do and he doesn't seem to mind.'

'But why would he not want to be filmed, do you think?'

'It's just a feeling I have. He's been at the school since September, but we know no more about him now than when he came. We don't even know where he was before, and that's usually a given. But there is no real gossip conduit from the SMT now that everyone has moved on.' He looked a little pensive for a moment. 'I can't say that any of them were exactly ornaments to the profession, but you get used to people. Over the years, you know. Legs. Bernard. Even dear old Dierdre. Where are they now, I wonder?'

'Well, Dierdre is all over the South Downs, as I remember. Scattered on a particularly blustery day.'

'Oh, yes,' Maxwell smiled. Bernard Ryan had done the honours, wearing a black Crombie, outdated even then, and he had ended up with a grey layer of Dierdre all down one side when the wind changed. 'It's what she would have wanted.'

'I wonder if he ever quite got rid of all of her?' Jacquie smiled. Poor Dierdre. She had had her moments, but Jacquie knew that she had been fond of Maxwell, deep down in what Dierdre would probably have called her soul.

'Well, I still wake up screaming sometimes,' Maxwell said with a straight face. 'So, I'm guessing not.'

'Does anyone hear from Bernard?' she asked. She really had had a soft spot for Bernard, the deputy headmaster who actually wanted to be a butterfly. Once scandal had set him free, he had gone off into the sunset with the love of his life without a backward glance.

'No,' Maxwell said. 'I don't think anyone thinks ill of him, it's just that he wanted out — and out he got. I think if you look very closely in some audience shots, you can catch a glimpse; I suppose his SO gets him . . .'

Jacquie raised a hand. 'Let me stop you there,' she said. 'SO? Who are you and what have you done with my husband?'

'Sorry. Too much time with Ten Are Zed. They seem to speak in just letters and I'm getting quite adept. SMH took me a while, but I didn't think, like Lord David Cameron, that LOL meant lots of love, at least.'

Jacquie put her own file aside and walked over to the sideboard. She held up the bottle of Southern Comfort and waggled it at him. 'SC?'

'NMH.'

She looked at him oddly. 'NMH?'

'Nodding my head,' he said, leaning over with his glass to be topped up. 'You are my BFF, IMHO.'

'DS!'

Maxwell rummaged in his pocket, got out his wallet and consulted a dog-eared piece of paper folded in the back. 'No, you've got me. What's that?'

'Damn straight!'

'I'm adding that to the list,' he said, producing a pen from somewhere behind his ear. His hair was still as mad as it had been when Jacquie had first clapped eyes on him and for all she knew he had a desk and a couple of sandwiches hidden in there as well.

'So,' Jacquie said, 'apart from a couple of also-rans, that just leaves Legs.' It had taken her a while to call the Headmaster James Diamond by his nemesis's favourite nickname, courtesy of the Ray Danton gangster movie of yesteryear, but now he had gone on to greater glories at County Hall, it seemed all right to do so. 'Is he still with the authority?'

'Ha!' Maxwell stowed the pen back behind his ear. 'He never had any authority as far as I remember.'

'Education, I mean.'

'Nor that. But yes, to answer your question, he is indeed still with the powers that be. To be fair to him, he spreads himself thin enough not to be a bother. But any moment he might suddenly appear like Banquo's ghost and scare the bejesus out of us. Thingee has nightmares, apparently.'

'Which Thingee?' Although Maxwell lumped the two together, Jacquie always felt it was important to know.

'Afternoon Thingee, of course.' Maxwell clicked his tongue. 'Morning Thingee has a hide like a rhino, as everyone knows.' He flicked through the file again. 'I wonder if he has anything to do with this Fly thing? It's just his kind of cock-amamie plan.'

'Why not ring him and ask?'

'I don't have his number.' He looked at her and let a few beats pass. 'Although, of course, like everyone else, I *do* have his number.'

'It's on your phone.'

'What's that got to do with anything?'

'It means you can ring him.'

'No, it doesn't. Don't be so silly. By the way, talking of phones, you know Plocker has a phone?'

As Plocker was their son's BFF, this was rather important and she was really rather shocked. 'No, really? I'm shocked. I thought his mother had more sense.'

Maxwell was less sanguine about the mental acumen of Mrs Plocker, but let it go. 'Well, he has. Apparently, his grandmother gave it to him for Christmas, wanting to get down with the kids, no doubt, knee replacement notwithstanding. It's for emergencies, so Nole says.'

'Emergencies as in . . .'

'Sonic the Hedgehog and Minecraft.' Maxwell chuckled. 'You can play them both offline, I am reliably informed.'

Jacquie smiled and twirled the lemon in her gin. 'Sometimes, you know,' she said, fondly, 'you almost sound as if you know what you're talking about.'

'I *do*, don't I?' Maxwell said proudly. 'I also sounded as if I knew what I was talking about when I told Nolan that he could have a phone when Hell froze over.'

'And . . .'

'And so he whined, sulked, flung himself on the sofa and said I was the worst dad in the world.'

'Really?'

'No. We negotiated for a while and when he has proved he is responsible enough, he can have a phone.'

'That sounds a pretty open arrangement,' she said. 'When will that be?'

He smiled at her, and they spoke in concert.

'When Hell freezes over.'

Behind the sofa, curled in the warm spot just under the radiator, Metternich, black-and-white behemoth, nudged the tabby curl that was Bismarck, his BFF. They snickered, as cats will. They really did own the best humans on the planet, lucky them.

CHAPTER TWO

Maxwell was in a bit of a cleft stick over half-terms. In one respect, of course, like all teachers, he relied on them to keep him just a little bit sane. Without a week off from the chalk-face — which hadn't seen chalk for what seemed like hundreds of years — every six weeks or so, they would all go stark staring mad. Some of them did that anyway, but it would come sooner without half-terms. But the other side of the coin was that they broke what momentum they had been able to gather with classes of all ages and abilities. It was extraordinary that something dinned into reluctant heads over a six-week period could be nevertheless completely forgotten over a mere nine days. How could anyone, for example, forget the Convention of Cintra? So, he tended to think of half-terms as Marmite — good enough in their way, but very easy to have too much of a good thing. The half-term which they had just enjoyed (or endured, delete as appropriate) at Leighford High was the one he hated the most. Cold and wet, for the most part, coming in the dead time of year when you are still finding pine needles in the carpet but haven't as yet succumbed to a vase of daffs on the sideboard. The laughingly named 'Spring Term' half-term holiday.

Another Marmite moment was that the first day back was only a first day back for staff, the students having another day off because the staff were having 'in service training', known for short as INSET. Maxwell was old enough to remember when they were called Baker Days after a former Minister of Education whose name has now been forgotten. Maxwell at least comforted himself with the fact that it was pronounceable, unlike FOTWL, a set of initials he was pretty sure everyone would be sick of before the day was out.

Nolan's school had no truck with such wimpy ideas as INSET. The Private Sector, he had once been reminded by the headmistress — no headteacher nonsense for her — provided training for staff at times convenient for parents (in other words, in evenings and weekends) and so there would be no namby-pamby days off in term time. Maxwell only managed to refrain from snapping back that as they had at least four weeks' extra holiday a year this was rather moot by Jacquie's simple expedient of stamping hard on his foot. So Nolan was safe in the bosom of the Plockers, his home from home, the Maxwell boy no doubt eyeing his mate's phone with envy.

It was a quiet lobby that Maxwell trailed across that Monday morning in February, leaving behind him slightly grubby footmarks and the odd skeleton leaf. Leighford, he had to admit, didn't look at its salubrious best at this time of the year. He had parked White Surrey, his faithful bike, in the usual spot reserved for the school minibus and popped his cycle clips into his pocket.

Morning Thingee was already hard at work watching the photocopier while buffing her nail extensions and he gave her a cheery wave. The Thingees, One and Two, were under the impression that he knew nothing about them at all and that to him they were just a face behind the glass. They would have been surprised to learn that he knew more about them than any member of the SMT did — for the simple reason that he cared. Also, if one of them ever went missing — not unprecedented, after all — he would like to be able to at least provide their eye colour and approximate height to the police. Thingee One waved a hand and went back to her buffing, in unavoidable rhythm with the copies shooting into the tray. It all made work for the working woman to do.

Up in Maxwell's office, the sixth form tutors had gathered in a mob, not angry, as such, but a bit miffed. Not a thing to create headlines, but unusual enough for Maxwell to pull himself up short in the doorway. They were, to use the cliché, a motley crew, generally detested by everybody else because their tutorial charges were at least nominally sophisticated and relatively intelligent, whereas the hoi polloi among the staff had to deal with Seven Haitch Pee and others who were barely hominids.

'Hello, chaps,' he said, throwing his coat into one corner and his briefcase into another, his pork-pie hat onto his desk. 'Something up?'

Maxwell was aware that calling women chaps could get him up before the beak these days and he had mulled over not doing it once or twice, while up in the night for a pee, a time when he did his best thinking. But he had decided against it — someone had to take a stand against puerile snowflakery and for once the SMT had taken the sensible course of making sure that he was not given a teacher straight out of training, with the woke still wet behind her ears. When a government had been known to have a Minister for Common Sense, it was sometimes a good idea to employ some. So no one sniffed, sobbed or rent their garments. Instead, as one, they all looked at Don from Maths, as the man would now be in Maxwell's mind from hereon in.

Don had not so much stepped forward to volunteer as been a bit slow at stepping back with the rest of them. He looked helplessly at his colleagues and turned to Maxwell like a rabbit in the headlights.

Maxwell helped him out. 'Don?' he said, with a smile, tipping his head sideways in a helpful gesture.

'Max,' the Maths teacher replied, and then found his mouth had gone completely dry.

'Don,' Maxwell repeated, but could suddenly see a whole morning slipping by this way, so headed him off at the pass. 'I assume you are not here to wish me a belated Happy Groundhog Day or an almost on time Happy Valentine's Day. So, what seems to be the trouble? Come on, we're all friends here.'

'Well,' Don from Maths said, looking behind him at his colleagues, who didn't meet his eye, 'it's this *Fly on the Wall* thing.'

Maxwell decided to go for sarcastic; it had served him well over the years but sadly he had forgotten he was dealing with a mathematician. 'Well, goodness, Don,' he added 'from Maths' silently in his head, 'I can't imagine what could possibly be the problem there. Nice people with cameras dogging your every footstep. Agendas and attitudes and a script written by the studio cat. Following you home from time to time, wouldn't be surprised — the cameras, that is, not the cat.'

Don's shoulders began to stiffen and there were stifled giggles from the back of the room.

Maxwell drew himself up to see past Don — not that difficult, as the maths whizz was something of a short-arse. 'Helen, dear heart. Is something funny back there?'

'No, no, Max. Nothing.' His Number Two turned to look out of the window, her shoulders shaking with the effort.

'So, Don. Spit it out. What about the flies on the wall? Apart from the obvious?'

'Obvious?' Don felt that the day was getting a bit brighter. Could it be that this was going to be something of a slam dunk after all?

'Well, yes. The obvious fact that we don't want all of the above, any of us. That it is totally inappropriate to film children in a classroom setting which many of them already find almost insupportably stressful. That controlling a roomful of herberts bent on social unrest at the most basic level is enough to make a strong man weep, without some spotty oik with a hamster on a stick leaning over your shoulder. And any of the other hundred damned good reasons to say "no" you can think of.' Maxwell beamed around his team. 'Does that sum it up, more or less?'

Don's wind had left his sails. 'Um, well, yes . . .'

'Good. Well, don't let me keep you, people. It's been fun. Did you all have a good half-term?' He held the door open and began to usher people out. 'Family round, bit of gardening, short holiday . . . hmm mm, yes, indeedy. Not you, Mrs Maitland.' He held his arm out. 'I could do with a word.'

Helen stepped back and waited. She had the kopi luwak coffee on the go, her special treat for them both at beginnings and ends of terms. She just hoped he never realised it had been through a civet before it reached his special mug, or her days were numbered.

Maxwell sat back on his rather worse-for-wear couch. It had seen laughter, it had seen tears. It had even once seen Maxwell leap over the back and land heavily on Legs Diamond, but that was in another country, and besides, the man was dead; actually, not dead as such, but working for County Hall which was much the same thing. He looked around at the walls of his office, as clear a microcosm of a man as you would find in a day's march.

The stars looked down. Maxwell had always had the impression that the film poster for *Lawrence of Arabia* ('best picture of the year!') was made long before the casting because the enigmatic face under the shemagh looked *nothing* like Peter O'Toole. James Dean was recognisable, however, looking, as ever, mean and moody in his short-sighted way in *Rebel Without a Cause* (rather like most of Year Nine). 'Here is a man,' another poster proclaimed. 'Here is love.' (Ahhh.) 'Here is a Motion Picture Masterpiece!' (Hmm.) Here was *Viva Zapata*, not Darryl F. Zanuck's finest hour. And here too, lest he be accused of being an old white man (which, in a way, he was) was *Boyz n the Hood*, which 'ain't no fairy tale'.

Maxwell used the poster to point out the shortcomings of Hollywood grammar — or, indeed, spelling.

Helen leaned over the back of the couch and handed him his coffee. He inhaled it gratefully. 'Mmm. First day back coffee. Nothing quite like it. Who would guess something so delicious had come out of a civet's bum?'

Helen took a step back. 'You know?'

'I know stuff,' he said, indignant. 'We even have this at home, sometimes, when Nolan has been up more chimneys than usual and we're feeling flush.' He smiled at her. 'It's kind of you to do this, though. Our little tradition. It's important, tradition.'

She flinched. Maxwell was not known for his singing, but had been known to suddenly burst forth with a quick rendition of *Don't Cry for Me, Argentina* when the mood took him. 'Tradition' in full Topol would be no means beyond him. But he didn't sing. Instead, he took another thoughtful sip of his coffee.

'Max?' she said, gently. 'Are you okay? Well, I mean. It's not like you to be so quiet on an INSET day.'

'Don't worry, Helen, strong as an ox, but there may be trouble ahead.'

She flinched again, but nothing.

'This *Fly on the Wall* thing is going to be a disaster. It's going to expose weaknesses which don't really matter, like Mavis in Textiles not being able to control her own eyelashes but turning out results year after year that the rest of us can only dream of. It's going to make people who are not fit to polish Mavis's shoes think they are Hollywood stars. I'm naming no names, but Alastair from Physics does a lot of am-dram as I understand it . . .'

'No, not any more.'

Maxwell cocked an eyebrow. 'Not?'

'Wife caught him with the props girl last pantomime season. He's had his backstage pass revoked.'

'Helen, Helen, Helen. What would I do without you? I would know nothing that goes on around here without our little chats over civet shit. He'll be even worse, probably, then. Craving the roar of the greasepaint. But the main problem will be, no matter how we cut it, is that it's a done deal. It's been thrashed out at County level and so all we can do is rail against it. The kids are going to become totally unmanageable. We're going to have to watch every word that comes out of our mouths and we can consider the next six weeks dead in the water in the sense of getting any teaching done. The powers that be are going to live to regret it, mark my words.'

* * *

One thing that had often puzzled Maxwell in his early days of teaching was why schools rang bells all day, every day, when for a good percentage of those days there was no one to hear. He had worked it out once, when he was young and fancy-free and had a nice new calculator to play with, that for more than half the days of the year, the bells rang merrily all to themselves. He equated it with the tree falling in the forest, but it made no more sense. He had been told, back in the good old analogue days, that it was easier to leave the mechanical doodahs that made it all work alone, rather than go round switching them all off six times a year and that did seem to be a good reason. But now, surely, with everything being so digital it was almost painful, they could have been adjusted . . . he wasn't sure this was possible but surely, these days . . . to only ring when they detected movement, more than a certain minimum number of bodies, or something. Because right now, without the getting on for ten thousand stone of humanity filling the void and soaking up some of the noise, the bell that was sounding right over his head as he sat in his favourite seat — not too far forward, not too far back — in the staffroom, was deafening.

The SMT sat at the front, in all their varied glory. Since the dear, dead days of Legs Diamond and Bernard Ryan, the SMT were as ephemeral as mayflies. They called themselves the SLT now, of course, Senior Leadership Team, but since any leadership was far beyond them, Maxwell refused to use the acronym — smut vs slut was a hard choice to make, but he had decided to stick with what he knew. One woman had been on it for a mere six weeks and since her tenure had coincided almost exactly with that of a very short-lived prime ministership, she was known, semi-affectionately, as Liz. Her name was Sharon, but that bothered no one; she had retreated to the depths of the Geography department and no one spoke of her again. The current headteacher was a former English teacher who had clawed her way up the ranks, always being there when another one bit the dust, bringing in cakes to meetings, always being first in, last out — eventually, that behaviour either kills a person or makes her headteacher. She hated Maxwell with a passion — nothing he wasn't used to, but she made it rather more obvious than many, almost baring her teeth when she looked at him. It had been whispered that she fancied the pants off him, but that worried him more than the thought that she couldn't stand the sight of him. Her name was Miss Preddie. It was probably true that she had others, but none of the hoi polloi knew what they were. Maxwell, inevitably, called her the Predator, then, by a natural progression, Arnold, eventually settling on Arnie.

Her first deputy, not exactly the power behind the throne, was a small and insignificant little soul named Bob Roberts. And bob he did. All the time. He bobbed up and down in his seat when ladies entered the room. He bobbed his head in mute agreement whenever Arnie spoke. There was a scurrilous rumour that he and Arnie were an item, that when they were alone after the school was empty, she sat him on her lap, shoved her arm up his jacket and he bobbed his head at her to further order. But after a while, it made people squeamish and it died the death that all rumours with more than a hint of truth eventually will.

Her second deputy was as near to a complete opposite of Bob as it was possible to be. Mandy Proctor was a big, blowsy blonde who nevertheless had a mind like a razor. She and Maxwell got on like houses afire, which made for some pretty interesting meetings in the Head's office from time to time. Mandy had been at Leighford on and off for years, having the odd child, going off on tantric retreats, opening a doomed vegan pop-up café back in the day when she was the only vegan in town — but she always came bouncing back and now found herself, to everyone's surprise but especially hers, in the upper echelons. But she did a good job, soothed feathers ruffled by Arnie and generally was like a good deed in a naughty world. That she taught craft design technology – including woodwork with all that that entailed - was just another of the surprises she kept up her sleeve, along with a hankie for all in distress and a sly fiver for the kid who had forgotten their dinner money. Maxwell often thought of her as the natural successor to Sylvia Matthews, the school nurse now elsewhere, but without smelling of Savlon.

The sundry hangers-on, the devisers of timetables, the collectors of absence notes, all the smaller fry of the SMT were banished to the ranks today. Three empty seats were at one end of the table and Maxwell got himself ready. This was going to be one humdinger of an INSET day, or his name was not Mad Max!

Arnie tapped on the table and all heads turned to her, Bob's, of course, keeping time with her raps.

'This is, of course,' she said in a voice that could go straight to the hindbrain and make the boldest lose control of their bladder just a little bit, 'an INSET day but I have obtained special dispensation from County to use it to familiarise us all with the needs of the forthcoming television—'

'Head . . . teacher?' Maxwell had taken great pains to hone the gap between the 'head' and 'teacher'. Too long and someone could butt in. Too short and the point was lost.

'Mr Maxwell.' She held up an imperious hand. 'Can we leave questions until later? Thank you. As I was saying, I have—'

'No, I don't think so.'

Heads turned at Maxwell's tone. That he had in mind the best interests of Leighford High School and its 'Highenas', past and present, no one was in any doubt. But he usually wrapped it all up in a blanket of humour and insouciance which seemed to have suddenly disappeared.

'I think that my question, when I ask it, will be one which we would all ask, given the chance. And that is — when did this become a done deal? According to the paperwork which, I might add, was snuck into our pigeonholes at the very last moment a week ago Friday, this was still at a discussion stage.' Everyone could tell how angry he was. He had used the word 'snuck'.

'Indeed.' Arnie's voice was like molten lava, seeming to creep across the desk, destroying all in its path. 'And at that point, it was. It is now, as you so colloquially put it, Mr Maxwell, a "done deal".'

The room erupted. Bob's head almost fell off and Mandy sat back in her seat, waiting for the fun to begin.

Maxwell, his job done for now, folded his arms and dropped his chin on his chest. This INSET day was one for the annals and it wasn't nine fifteen yet.

Eventually, the cacophony lessened and one voice, a voice of reason, held the floor. Polly Allington, the Head of History, newly appointed the previous September, was standing politely to one side, but she wasn't going to be ignored. Breaths had been held all over the school when she was appointed and everyone had expected Maxwell to eat her alive. But he was two things, the first being a gentleman and it was, as L.P. Hartley had already pointed out, never a lady's fault. So that was one thing. The other was that her credentials were magnificent, her teaching as good as her certificates and he always gave credit where credit was due. If she had been a bad historian or a bad teacher, she could have been his best friend for all it would have mattered — she would have been toast. But as it was, she could be a mountain gorilla, a David Icke-style lizard or even — though this was pushing it — the union rep and he would never hear a word against her. And so, for this reason, he waited, poised, to jump in if she needed him. That she clearly didn't was soon obvious.

'Miss Preddie,' she said. 'I have read your paperwork very carefully over the half-term holiday and I also showed it to my husband.'

Arnie sneered. 'How wonderful. Did you help him with the long words?'

'Thank you, no. He is a KC, so is quite good at English.' A snort from the back row element was quickly stifled. 'So, as I say, he and I had a read-through, and a little chat, and he was quite concerned on several levels.' She waited politely for Arnie to pitch in, but nothing happened so she continued. 'Firstly, he was surprised by the idea. For the avoidance of doubt,' she smiled beatifically, 'bit of legal jargon there, but it basically underlines the simple fact that I mean what I say and I have the law behind me. For the avoidance of doubt, this is not an official, paid-for legal opinion but I doubt you would find anyone to disagree with it in a long day's march. My husband is—'

Arnie had been scrolling on her phone and now looked up. 'Nobody, as far as I can tell,' she said, her lip curling as it always did when she thought she had the upper hand. She brandished her phone. 'I have a list of KCs here. None by the name of Allington that I can find.' She rapped again on the table. It was beginning to become something of a tic and Bob bobbed to acknowledge it had happened. 'So, if—'

'No, you wouldn't do,' the Head of History said, still with her tranquil smile. 'Allington is *my* name. You need to scroll again, Ar— Miss Preddie.' Maxwell gave her a small salute. A perfectly done, Maxwellian almost-insult. Nice work. 'His name is Basildon. As in Bond. Jeremy Basildon.' She looked at Maxwell and gave him the ghost of a wink. 'I'll wait.'

Miss Preddie glared for a moment and then picked up her phone, flicked it once and then slammed it down. 'So, *Ms* Allington,' she gave the hissed syllable all the menace she could muster, 'what did hubby have to say?'

'Well, he was more surprised than anything,' she said, 'that you were prepared to have the students filmed going about their day. Who is going to have final say on what appears? Do you have total veto on anything inappropriate? A child in distress, for instance.'

Arnie gave vent to a word usually spelled as 'Pfftt', then continued, 'A crying child? At their age? How often does that happen in an average day? If that's all he's worried about . . .'

'It happens a dozen times a day, if not more,' a gentle voice said from the back row.

Arnie's head snapped up like a mongoose scenting a snake. A SEN teacher. Her favourite mid-morning snack.

'As everyone knows who teaches her,' continued the SENCO, 'Lexi Morrison is apt to burst into tears at the slightest thing. I almost said provocation, but it doesn't have to be provocative at all. Before we broke up for half-term, she spent thirty minutes in her quiet space because someone had said how much they liked her shoes. And then, of course, her best friend Simon joined her, because he was worried about her. She is always tearful, but he thought she was worse than usual and he didn't want her to be sad over half-term. And so that meant—'

'Yes, yes, Tom. We get the gist. We can exclude your classes from filming, if that makes you more comfortable.'

Tom White smiled and also looked across to Maxwell. He knew that Lexi was something of a favourite of his and History was one of the few mainstream classes she engaged with.

'So thoughtful, Head . . . mmmm,' Maxwell purred. 'And that would be splendid. Except that Lexi is in my classes, too. She actually had a bit of a meltdown over the Treaty of Versailles a week or two ago . . .'

'Who doesn't?' muttered Liraz Singh, third in the History Department.

'Yes, quite. So . . . it won't be quite that simple, will it?'

'There are things to iron out, certainly,' Arnie snapped at the room in general. 'Ms Allington, do we have any more of hubby's words of wisdom to come from you or can we move on?'

'Well,' the Head of History said, raising her fingers, ready to count, 'there's data protection, identifiability . . .'

'Which is?'

'Well, put simply, it means that if someone has chosen not to be filmed, as I believe your paperwork gives us the right to do, but are in the room when something is filmed, though out of shot, if someone *in* shot is deemed to behave irresponsibly or, heaven forbid, illegally, then, if the person who *doesn't* want to be filmed is nevertheless known to work with that person . . . well, the ramifications could be quite serious.'

Arnie gave her her best thousand-yard stare.

'I suppose I mean expensive,' Polly Allington said, and sat down. Her neighbour nudged her and they both grinned. The 'e' word. Always one to get Arnie's attention.

There was a buzzing silence for a few moments. Then, the inevitable rapping before the woman spoke in what she honestly seemed to believe was a conciliatory tone. 'I can see that we have a lot of ironing out of minor details to do before we can go on. Fortunately, we have a County Hall mandarin coming this morning, along with representation from the film company. So we can make sure we have dotted and crossed the relevant letters. They will be here in . . .' She glanced up at the clock and looked viciously at Bob Roberts. 'Is that clock right?'

He nodded, which might have meant nothing, but she assumed it was assent.

'In that case, they are late.'

'I expect Thingee One is taking their inside leg measurements or something,' Maxwell offered. 'She's very stringent when it comes to security.'

'And rightly so.' Arnie was in between a rock and a hard place: She agreed with security but hated it when Maxwell pointed something good out. 'Even so . . .'

Maxwell raised a finger. 'Hark,' he said, like some biblical portent, 'voices.' He frowned. Voices he knew, which was odd. Everyone he worked with was here.

The voices grew closer and the door opened. In the doorway stood Legs Diamond. And behind him, Bernard Ryan. Maxwell closed his eyes. Either he was having some sort of psychotic episode or he was asleep or . . . James 'Legs' Diamond was now a County Hall mandarin. A stanza of 'Three Little Maids' ran swiftly through Maxwell's head but he stifled it. This might be a lot of fun. On the other hand, Bernard Ryan was here, so the chance of that was vanishingly small. To Maxwell's relief, the third man waiting in the shadows to come through the door was a stranger, and he looked fairly harmless. Then he came in and Maxwell's head dropped backwards as he gave a silent scream to the heavens. The man, with a carefully managed two-day growth of stubble and an artful curl down the side of his forehead was wearing a flat cap — on backwards. Civilisation as he knew it left the building there and then. Who knew if it would ever return.

* * *

'And so, anyway,' Maxwell continued as Jacquie came back into the room having put Nolan to bed after a more than usually splashy bath, 'Legs is apparently some kind of consultant, these days.' He handed her his handkerchief and generally indicated the parts of her that needed a bit of a mop. 'Currently, he is our liaison regarding the film company. He will be making sure that they comply with all the rules. Not that anyone seems to have written the rules, yet. Jeremy Basildon is giving them the once-over, when they are done.'

'Blimey!' Jacquie spread Maxwell's damp hankie on a radiator and sat in her favourite chair, facing her favourite husband. 'Doesn't he cost something like five hundred quid an hour?'

'I would imagine all of that,' Maxwell said. 'He's doing it as a favour. He wants to keep Polly safe, of course, and with him at the checking level, we get a bit ahead of the game when it comes to finding out what's going on.'

'Clever. Polly's idea, I assume? With a little bit of help from her friends.'

He smiled modestly. 'Possibly. But it was actually something they had already spoken of. He does a lot of work these days with people who have had images shared on social media without their consent, mostly . . . what's it called, again?'

'Revenge porn?' Jacquie suggested.

'That's the chap. It is apparently a big problem now and also a big earner for him. He's getting rather a name for it. Not for doing it, I don't mean, I mean . . . well, you get the drift. So, he is on board, for which we're all very grateful. Legs is, of course, totally useless. He doesn't have a clue how to deal with Arnie and the film bloke uses a vocabulary that appears to come from Mars. Did I tell you about the cap?' He looked with wide eyes full of pain at Jacquie as she sat there, laughing.

'You did, my love, you did. Perhaps he was just wearing it to . . .'

'Hurt my eyes? Make us all think he was a total dick?'

'Perhaps. But mainly, I expect he was doing it to stand out. Probably he is like most people, he thinks teachers all wear tweed jackets with leather elbow patches and smoke pipes. And before you say, yes, I know Maurice does both those things, but, love him, he teaches Latin on Wednesday afternoons, doesn't he? Hardly representative. So . . . what did you say his name was?'

'Zac.' It sounded more like Metternich the cat getting rid of a furball than a name, but it spoke volumes.

'Yes. So, Zac probably just wanted to look like a film director — you know, peering through a camera lens. You said he seemed very young.'

'Not as young as you'd think, once you get close. But under thirty, definitely. Which is young, I suppose. I hope he doesn't try to,' and he made ironic speech marks in the air, '"get down" with the kids. They'll eat him alive.'

'Handsome?'

'What?'

'Is he handsome?'

'Oh, sorry, I thought you were trying to get my attention.'

She threw a cushion at him. She stocked up at the start of any evening chez Maxwell with more than she needed, so she had ammunition.

'So, is he?'

'I don't know. He's not my type, I know that. About my height, I suppose, but like a beanpole. He's got curly hair, really short at the back but longer on top and he clearly trains it to trail artlessly over one eyebrow. Stubble. Tattoos. A sort of cross — or so Thingee Two assures me — between a young Keanu Reeves and someone called . . . hang on, what was it? Tom . . . could it have been Tiddleton?'

'Hiddleston?'

'Probably. I honestly don't know how you find the time to keep up. Do you have a clone? An identical twin?'

She smiled, but ruefully. 'No, but I do have a lot of girls who come in after they have been found making a few spare quid behind the cinema. And runaways. And meth addicts. And . . . well, I try not to bring it home, as you know.'

He smiled back at her. 'Who knew Leighford had so much . . . well, *sin*?'

'It hardly counts as sin these days. When Henry goes . . . when *I* go, I don't expect these girls will even see the inside of a cop car. It's just that we feel that if we bring them in, if they see we care, then perhaps some of them might get their lives changed. If only a little bit. Where there are parents, we get them involved. But there often is no one.'

Maxwell looked serious. 'If they were ours, would you tell me?'

'Ours?'

'You know, Leighford kids. My Own.'

'I couldn't, you know that. But as it happens, they haven't been. Not yet.'

'Truly?'

'Cross my heart and hope to die.' As soon as the words were out of her mouth, she regretted them. Maxwell's first wife and their little daughter had died in a car accident many years before. But she knew that on wet and windy nights, the scream of the tyres and of his girls were never far away. She stopped and he shook his head at her, smiling. Memories took second place to the here and now.

'Well, if ever . . .'

'If ever, I'll make sure they get the best care. The very best. I promise.'

'Where were we before this slightly maudlin side street?' he asked her.

She looked at the ceiling and motioned retracing steps with her fingers in the air. 'Tom Hiddleston,' she said.

'Of course, yes. He looks like a cross between the young Keanu Reeves and Tom Hiddleston.'

'Handsome, then,' Jacquie said. 'Although to be honest, I don't know what Tom Hiddleston brings to the description. He puts the "bl" in bland. Even so, I suppose that means he will go down well with the girls.'

'Not just the girls. Most of the women are a bit gooey-eyed over him as well. Arnie seems immune, but then she would be, wouldn't she?'

Jacquie didn't know Miss Preddie as well as she had come to know James Diamond, but she certainly had never taken her for soft-hearted.

'And Bernard?' she said. 'Why was he there? Not a mandarin as well, surely?'

Three little maids shuffled across the sitting-room floor again.

'Ha! No, Bernard, my darling, is an agent.'

'An agent? As in . . .' her eyebrows went up . . . 'MI5?'

He spluttered. 'Wouldn't that be wonderful? No, he is Joe Pargeter's agent.'

'Of course. His chap . . .'

'Husband.'

'Oh. Oh, right. What happened to the happily married with kids and a bit of secret stuff on the side?'

'Apparently, Bernard was irresistible when it came down to it. They got married in lockdown. All very minimalist. He had pictures.' Maxwell's smile was a little forced, remembering the very difficult conversation that he had heard Bernard having with Arnie, not the world's most liberal person.

'I thought Joe was news, wasn't he? I know he did *Strictly*, but . . .'

Maxwell and Jacquie had come to an arrangement about the dance show. Like most things in their lives, they liked to come to a compromise and so it had been here. She watched it. He didn't.

'I understand that he's branching out. He does some kind of quiz thing in the afternoons. Bernard did tell me, but honestly, he might as well have been talking in Swahili for all it meant. It involves . . .' Maxwell tried his best to muster a description, but failed. 'They can win stuff, or so it seems. Anyhoo, he is raising his profile, according to Bernard, and he, Bernard, is his agent.'

'So this means . . . ?'

'Yep, you have guessed it. You have won the giant cuddly toy. Joe is the host of FOTWL's latest extravaganza, *Lifting the Lid on Education*, or Shit Storm, for short.'

CHAPTER THREE

The day after an INSET day was always odd. To the teaching staff, it felt like it should be Friday in a minute — surely, this week had been long enough already. But to the streams of children, running, shambling and in a few extreme cases being escorted into the building by what Maxwell still called the Kid Catchers, it was first day back after ten days away, a lifetime in their eyes, and they had to tell everyone everything that had happened, right here, right now. The fact that most of them had already uploaded everything — suitably photo-shopped to hide the acne — onto every social media platform they could access, seemed to have passed everyone by. As Maxwell made his way slowly across the foyer, his mug of coffee held over his head to avoid jostling, all he could see from wall to wall was excited faces and phones being waved randomly about. He smiled quietly to himself. There was a shock coming their way and he was delighted that he would be there to see it happen.

Maxwell cleared his throat and engaged his teacher voice.

'People!'

A circle about ten deep around him stopped dead in their tracks and faced him, silent and waiting. There was something about his voice that went straight to the hindbrain and turned leg muscles to water.

He turned it up a notch.

'Oy! People! Don't make me ask twice!'

Now only one knot of girls in a corner was still talking. Even Thingee One, in her Plexiglas fastness, had stopped typing and was facing front.

'So, I said to him—'

'Oy!'

The girl who was talking as silence fell turned and looked over her shoulder. 'Oh.'

'Yes. "Oh" is right. However, I am feeling more than usually frolicsome this morning, for reasons which you will shortly discover. So if you could all quietly — and I mean *quietly* — file into the hall and sit down, Ms Preddie and the staff will join you shortly.' Maxwell waved them through with an extravagant gesture and they meekly filed through the double doors and sorted themselves into rows. Maxwell smiled as the last one went in and, closing the door after him, joined them.

Some of the staff were already in their seats, ranged along the sides of the hall. The spare ones, those who were not class tutors or year heads, arranged themselves along the back. Arnie and her minders had seats and small podia on the front of the stage and were already in place. Maxwell sat in the back seat on the right-hand side, near a handy exit for when notices became too boring for words. In front of him sat Helen Maitland, watching with eagle eyes the troublemakers — it was early yet, both in the day and in the term, but with some of them, it was never too early. Maxwell leaned forward and poked her gently in the back.

'Ready?'

'Ready.' She tapped a box on her lap.

'Excellent. On my mark, then.' He then craned up and waved a hand at his head of department, sitting on the opposite side of the hall. She caught his eye and gave him a thumbs-up.

Up on the stage, Arnie was standing at her podium. Early in her reign, she had had speakers and a mic installed but she reckoned without the passive aggression of the IT geeks. There had been an IT support at Leighford since the very first computer was merely a glint in John Blankenbaker's eye, only then they were called site caretakers. Their giant Phillips screwdrivers and paint brushes had morphed almost imperceptibly into tiny implements on the end of snake-like extensions and a weird, otherworldly look in the eye. Legs Diamond had not bothered them and they had not bothered Legs. Arnie Preddie, on the other hand, had bothered them. She had asked for time sheets. She had asked for accountability. They gave her everything that she asked for — along with a healthy dose of feedback that attracted every dog for miles. So, the mic and speakers had had to go.

She stood waiting for the absolute silence which was her criterion for starting any announcement, otherwise known to most as harangues. Eventually, the silence was so dense that the otoliths in the ears of the more attentive listeners started sparking all by themselves, out of sheer lack of anything to do. Back in the day, Hitler would have been proud of her. She cleared her throat. She didn't know why she had allowed this, but she had found herself in something of a quandary. Her own deputy — she turned to Mandy, who was smiling beatifically at her on her right hand — had made the announcement the day before as the meeting had broken up. To say it had been a difficult day was something of an understatement and, undermined and tired, she had not argued. But now, with Maxwell heading her way down the side of the hall, with his female myrmidons behind him like the tail of a rocket, she wasn't so sure. She had planned to introduce him as her spokesperson, simply someone doing her will, but in the end, she sat down, defeated for that moment. But, she vowed to herself, not for long. Mandy Proctor saw the narrowed eyes and set mouth and made a note to self to watch her back. Bob Roberts sat on the other side of Arnie, smiling and nodding benignly.

Maxwell reached the front of the hall but didn't bother with mounting the stage. He turned to face the huddled masses and looked at them for what felt like hours to those with something to hide; which was all of the students and all but a very few of the staff. Then he suddenly clapped his hands once and the spell was broken.

'Well, this is a bit of a different way to start the next part of term, isn't it?' he said brightly. 'I expect that you all are thinking that lovely Ms Preddie has given me the honour of telling you all the exciting news about the TV cameras moving in tomorrow, but I wouldn't dream of stealing her thunder on that.'

A suppressed snigger swept over the hall like a subsonic Mexican wave, along with a guffaw from the corner that housed the PE department. Arnie Preddie bridled so hard her podium shook.

'No, I'm here this morning for something much more important. Ms Maitland, Ms Allington. Your bags, if you please.'

With the air of conjurors, the two women unfurled long sacks with drawstring tops. They held them up so everyone could see their enormous size.

'Now, I expect you're all wondering what these bags are for?' He smiled expectantly at the assembled school. 'Any ideas?'

There were assorted mumblings, but no nods at all.

'Well, we can't let this go on too long,' he said. 'Ms Preddie has some important news about the TV . . . anyway, enough about that. Let's play a game. Everyone who watches the news, stand up.'

There was a lot of scuffling but in the end a disappointingly small cohort of various geeks and boffins stood scattered throughout the hall. Maxwell looked at them sadly.

'Oh dear,' he said, shaking his head. 'Well, at least this will make the rest of the process short. So, of you, which ones read a newspaper? I mean regularly, not when you're cleaning out the guinea pig.'

With some shuffling and grunting, most of the stand-ers sat down and wriggled back into a comfortable position on the floor. Seven Hyenas stood there, all, as it happened, Maxwell's Own, three Year Twelves, four Year Thirteens. He nodded — not one of them was a surprise.

'Next question, then. Can any of you cast your minds back to the Party Conferences last autumn? If you can't, sit down.'

Now he was left with two, both Politics students in their run-up to A-levels. This had been much quicker than he anticipated.

'I'll try to make this fun. What do you think will be going in these bags in just a few minutes?' He raked the whole school with a laser gaze. 'And don't blame these two when they get it right. It isn't their initiative.'

Horror began to dawn on hundreds of faces across the room, all upturned to him in mute appeal, which was getting less mute by the minute.

'Jodie. Tell them.' He always thought of Jodie as the Head Girl she would never be, not at Leighford High any-way, where such fripperies had been gone for decades. She was bright, pretty, sporty . . . a definite for being jobless in four years' time unless he missed his guess.

The girl looked around, then at her feet and swallowed hard. She said something, really quietly.

'Sorry, Jodie. Speak up.'

She raised her head, chin in the air, like Joan of Arc before they lit the first brand. If she had to go down, she'd go down fighting. 'Mobile phones, Mr Maxwell. The bags are for our mobile phones.'

And the place erupted.

* * *

In years to come, everyone who was there would agree that that assembly was probably the best one ever. It beat the one where the stage collapsed by a country mile. By sheer force of will, Maxwell had beaten the school into submission and when quiet reigned, told everyone to their relief that they wouldn't have to put their most precious possessions into a sack. They had one day's grace of keeping their mobiles with them, but the next day, there would be no quarter. And so, for that assembly at least, the fun was over. Arnie's news about the TV seemed like nothing after that.

* * *

In the Head of Sixth Form's office, Helen Maitland stowed her bag in her locker.

'Nice prop.' Tom White, being by way of no fixed abode in the school, had nipped in for a coffee. Even Helen's ordinary brew, no civet intervention needed, was streets ahead of any other in the school.

Helen smiled. 'It was my mother-in-law's. She was an avid watcher of *South Today* and kept it for her panic buying stashes.' She watched his face as he fought between laughter and disbelief. 'No, honestly, whatever the scaremonger of the week was, she was off up Londis before you could shake a stick. When she died, the entire box room was full of loo rolls.' She sighed. 'Different days. We're all hoarders now.'

'Some of my kids will still be bringing phones in,' he said. 'Who will be checking all this? Not Max, surely?'

As he spoke, the door bounced back and Maxwell bounced in. 'Of course not,' he said, automatically. 'I never do, never have, never will.' He picked up his favourite mug, waiting for him as it always was. 'Not Max what?' He thought he should check.

'Policing the phone policy,' Helen elaborated. 'Tom's right, it is going to be a nightmare. They'll be at home tonight, thinking of cunning places to hide them.'

'Of course they will,' Maxwell said. 'I'd be disappointed if they weren't.'

'So . . . how will we get them to leave them at home?'

'It won't be perfect straight away,' Maxwell said. 'And of course, what with the government and Arnie, we won't be able to do anything destructive, though one of my ideas was that every classroom should be equipped with a bucket of water to drop them in. But I think, eventually, it will cut them down to a fraction of what we have now. We've sent emails out to parents — and, ironically, text messages as well — to tell them that there are to be no mobiles from tomorrow. The fact that it was already school policy is something we have all conveniently forgotten. And of course, the right to use mobiles is embodied in the Constitution of the United States, where they're called cells because Mobile is a place in Alabama. So, some of them will comply. They'll probably be glad of it. I've never really understood it, that they are willing to let their little dears walk out of the house with twelve hundred quid's worth of tech in their pocket but forget to give them lunch money.'

'Twelve hundred quid?' Tom White's eyes nearly popped out of his head.

Helen laughed. 'Max knows where to go for bargains, Tom,' she said. 'Take no notice. There won't be many phones in this building costing less than fifteen.'

White spluttered into his coffee. 'But . . . but . . . what do they do, for that? My phone was thirty quid . . .'

'That would be off Amazon, I assume,' Helen said.

'God, no,' Tom said. 'I don't buy anything online. I don't share my card details with anyone I can't look in the eye. I bought it at the market.'

'Ah,' Maxwell sat down beside him, stirring his coffee with his pen, 'I'm glad you stick to reputable tradesmen, Tom.'

White looked at him. He was used to being laughed at, but he believed what he believed and that was that. His house was an Alexa-free zone; he watched what TV programmes he could have watched in the dear, dead days of analogue. His phone was for making calls, no more, no less. He made Maxwell look quite hip and up to date. 'I would have you know,' he said, 'that Jack and I go back years. I buy all my incandescent lightbulbs from him and the batteries for my transistor radio.' He said it with a smile, but there was something of the fanatic in there somewhere as well.

'So . . .' Helen didn't want to start him off. He had been known to go on for hours. '5G . . . ?'

'You're waiting for me to say that 5G caused Covid, aren't you?'

Helen bridled. 'Of course not, Tom. Everyone knows that it—'

'Well, it did. The science is out there if you know where to look.'

Maxwell wiped his pen on the sleeve of his jacket and popped it back into his pocket. He knew perfectly well that Covid was caused by Nine Queue Ess — that wasn't a conspiracy theory; it was a fact. He took a sip of coffee before he asked the obvious question. 'So, Tom, where do you look, old chap? As you have no internet at home . . . ?'

'IT suite, of course,' he said, surprised it needed to be asked. 'No footprint there, you see. So I can't be tracked down.'

'Ah. Right.' The questions arising from that were so many that neither Maxwell nor Helen could really begin to ask them. They were saved from having to try by the phone on the desk giving its usual discreet wurble, a tone chosen to be eminently ignorable if conditions dictated.

Helen snatched it up. After listening for a moment, she said, 'I'll tell him. Yes, right away.' She put the handset back and said to Maxwell, 'Arnie wants to see you.'

'Ooh, love to go, but . . .' he glanced at the clock, 'I've got Ten Are Vee in a minute. Roosevelt's New Deal — laff a minute.'

'Apparently, you haven't. She's arranged cover.'

'May one ask who?'

'Sally, from Textiles.'

Tom White smiled complacently. 'They'll eat her.'

'Raw,' Maxwell added, getting up. '*And* I bet she's never even seen *The Grapes of Wrath*. I'd better go, then. Did Thingee say what it was about?'

'It wasn't Thingee. It was Arnie.'

Maxwell's eyebrows shot up. 'Arnie? Arnie rang me herself? Call the court physician. Call an intermission . . .' There was always time in the day for a little Danny Kaye, misquoted or not, and having put the unrelenting tune of 'The King's New Clothes' into their heads, he went out, humming it himself.

* * *

Arnie's office, when he got there, was a little crowded. It was the biggest office in the building, as behoved the head-teacher, but even it was stretched by the number of people it was holding that Tuesday morning. Apart from Ms Preddie herself, there seemed to be, to Maxwell's untutored eye, at least a dozen totally identical men and Legs Diamond. As he went in, he accidentally rammed the door into the back of one of the identical sector, who appeared to be trying to stuff a hamster having a bad hair day into an air vent. Other than that, it all seemed to be as normal.

'You rang?' It was a perfect Lurch.

The headteacher looked up and to Maxwell's horror and surprise she had a welcoming smile on her face.

'Oh, Mr Maxwell. Thank you so much for coming so promptly.'

Maxwell met Diamond's eyes and was surprised again as he saw the left one close in a wink.

'I just wanted to introduce you to these gentlemen who you will be seeing around the school for the next six weeks.'

Six weeks until the Easter holiday? It would seem like an eternity.

'We have decided to concentrate on just a few sectors of teaching in the school.'

Maxwell looked at her closely. Had she . . . no, seriously, had she got new *teeth*? Since the day before, that was quite an achievement. They did look preternaturally white but were interfering with her sibilants like nobody's business.

'And they would be?' He desperately wanted her to say 'Sewing, Sport and Physics' and perhaps, the icing on the cake, 'Shoshone', but knew that that was unlikely. However, without such a phrase — and there was another good word for the teeth test — he would need more intel to be sure.

She skirted round it. 'On considering your comments of yesterday, Mr Diamond and I have come to the . . .' She paused and Maxwell could understand her dilemma. With her present impediment, neither decision nor conclusion was going to end well for her.

Diamond came to her rescue. 'What Ms Preddie and I decided, Max, was that there were certain sets and certain members of staff it would be easier for the team to work with. I have a list here, which will be going up on the staffroom board later, but it probably will come as no surprise to anyone that you and a selection of your sets across the abilities head it.'

Maxwell looked at Diamond with the pride and slight unease of a Frankenstein. It had been his life's work when Diamond was in what he laughingly seemed to think was charge at Leighford High to make the man's life a misery. Had anyone asked, he would have said that it was to make sure that he would eventually learn to stand on his own two feet. When he left to go to County Hall, everyone assumed he would sit there in obscurity and shuffle papers until the pension pot had grown to even more obscene proportions but no, here he was, feisty as all get-out and a mandarin, no less. Maxwell could almost see his long, tapering nails and pigtail and could almost hear the dreaded words, 'The world shall hear again of Mr James Diamond.'

'I hesitate to impose on your plans, Headteacher, and . . . do you have a title, Mr Diamond, in your current position?'

Legs smiled at him. 'James will do,' he said. 'Off camera, of course. In fact, I won't be on camera, so if you see me, you will know they are not around.'

'But . . .' Maxwell waved an eloquent arm around the room.

'We're just sound-checking,' a disembodied voice came from under Arnie's desk. 'Some of these rooms are very boomy.'

'Er . . . I see.' Maxwell bent down and saw a pair of Converse trainers sticking out from the ends of some precisely frayed jeans. 'Hello.'

'Hello. Don't mind me, really. Just checking levels.'

'Where was I?' Maxwell was rarely flummoxed but he had really lost his thread this time.

'You were hesitating to impose on our plans,' Arnie said, taking a risk.

'Yes, I was, wasn't I? I hesitate to impose on your plans, but was not the final agreement — no, not agreement, but legal opinion — that we all had to give our permission first?'

'Yes, of course,' Legs said, smoothly. 'And of course, without permission, no filming will take place.'

Maxwell's level of flummox had reached new records. 'But I haven't. I don't. So I don't see how you can have my sets at the top of the list. You can't have contacted every parent for permission and almost every student in the place is under eighteen so they can't give their own permission . . . I don't really understand what's going on.'

Arnie leaned forward. She was a vindictive woman, anyone would tell you that, including her friends, had she had any. And she was nurturing more venom than usual towards Maxwell after his little stunt that morning. She had been looking forward to the big reveal of the television company and he had stolen her thunder well and truly. So she was looking forward to this. She took a breath.

'County has made a group decision on everyone's behalf,' Diamond said, leaving her high and dry. 'Contracts are complex things, of course, but our legal team is confident that the ones signed by all teaching staff here at Leighford cover that eventuality. However,' he continued before Maxwell could interrupt, 'anyone with strong reasons for refusing — a woman who has sought shelter from abuse, or a man, of course, can refuse. Anyone in witness protection.'

Maxwell narrowed his eyes. In all the years he had known Legs Diamond, he had never been cut off at the pass like this before. 'Witness protection, James?' he said. '*Witness protection*? What is this? An episode of *Criminal Minds*? I think you're going to have difficulty getting the staff to agree to this, and there are ways of avoiding being on camera. I, for instance, have a full clown outfit in the dressing-up box at home and I'm not afraid to use it.'

Under the desk, the sound guy chortled to himself. This was going to be more fun than he had imagined when he took the gig. He had always suspected teachers were mad — who would choose to look after hundreds of other people's kids every day otherwise? — but now he was certain. A grown man with a dressing-up box. Whatever next?

'And I know for a fact that Mike Smythe — he's in the PE department, since your time — has a full Buzz Lightyear costume in a display on his landing. Imagine him refereeing the Under Fifteens in that. Because, believe me, he would be more than happy to do it.'

This time the sound guy's chortle was out loud, though quickly suppressed. 'Sorry,' he sang out. 'Frog in the throat.'

Arnie Preddie finally managed to get a word in edgewise. 'I don't really see the problem, Mr Maxwell,' she said, waspishly. 'You're personable enough, if a little unusual in some respects.'

Maxwell and Diamond exchanged glances but neither spoke.

'Your teaching is, I believe, very entertaining and has garnered us some very favourable Ofsted reports,' Maxwell gave her a small bow, 'and you have no discipline problems.' Diamond smirked at that. That was certainly true. Maxwell had managed to grow the 'Mad' epithet out of nowhere. He rarely lost his temper and had certainly never raised a hand to a child, yet the rumour of his crazed behaviour had permeated the psyche of every student in the school and most of the auxiliary staff.

'All true, Ms Preddie,' Maxwell said, adjusting his bow tie and smoothing down his recalcitrant hair. 'I agree with your precision and accuracy.'

'So,' she spread her hands in confusion, 'why don't you want to be on the television, then? There are people out there who would give their eyeteeth for fifteen minutes of fame.'

Maxwell very much wanted to believe that his esteemed headteacher knew that she had just quoted Andy Warhol, but he doubted it — though the point was well made. 'Ms Preddie,' he smiled, 'they are welcome to it. I don't mind a bit of fame, per se, but I don't like it so much when it is thrust upon me. I just like to . . . well, I like to make my own choices. I think everyone does, if truth be told. And in this particular case, when everyone seems to think that there are trolls under every bridge and stalkers behind every tree, it seems odd to me that County Hall is sticking us all up on the wall to be shot down as if we are in some fairground stall.'

'Come on, Max,' Diamond said, with his new-found mandarin chutzpah. 'Aren't you putting it on a bit thick? Who would want to stalk anyone from Leighford, just because they are on telly for a few weeks?'

One of the identical men fiddling with equipment stepped forward. 'Sorry to interrupt, Mr Diamond,' he said. 'Oh, sorry, let me introduce myself. I am Zac's assistant, Bevis. You can call me Bev, although to be honest I would prefer you not to.'

Maxwell made an immediate mental note to do nothing else.

'Mr Maxwell is quite right in what he says. We have noticed an uptick in cases of stalking but especially in trolling in recent years. The internet makes it very easy to do, of course. People have always gossiped, but once upon a time it had to be word of mouth and although that gets its own momentum eventually, at first the spread is slow — over the garden fence, kind of thing. And often, for that reason, it peters out. But with telly—' he waved his arms in a wide arc over his head '—the speed can be phenomenal. Once it is out there on one site, no matter how small and insignificant, it can go viral in moments. And, of course, once out there, it's out there forever.'

A head popped up from behind a camera in the corner. 'Whose side are you on, Bev?' the man asked.

'That's a good question, actually,' Maxwell said. He had decided not to harp on the 'Bev' business, although he had had second thoughts at 'uptick'.

'I'm not on a side,' the assistant director said. 'I just think that Mr Maxwell has a very good point. Here at FOTWL we do take steps to minimise trolling and certainly stalking. We have a fund set aside to help prosecute anyone who is found doing either.'

'And how often has that happened?' Maxwell couldn't help but ask.

'Hmm?' Bevis played for time by taking off his flat cap, turning it around and putting it back on again in just the same orientation.

'How often has a prosecution happened?'

'I'm not actually sure,' the man hedged. 'I think it must be—'

'Never,' came the voice from under the desk. It was followed by scuffling and the rest of the Converse owner appeared, somewhat flushed from his close proximity to Arnie's knees. 'I don't want to argue and make this thing more difficult than it is . . .' the sound guy said, 'but—'

'Then I suggest you shut up,' Bevis said, testily. 'You're not one of my team, are you? Agency staff?'

There were sly smiles all round. 'Agency, yes. Sackable, no. Well, you can sack me, of course, but I'd like to see you explain the stonking penalty your company will have to pay to mine . . .'

The assistant director simmered but could do no more. Maxwell and Diamond just looked on — the discussion seemed to be out of their hands and all they could do was watch where it went and try to put out any minor fires on the way.

'So,' the sound guy said, 'in a nutshell, you have no protection. But I don't think you should worry, Mr . . . Maxwell, is it?'

Maxwell nodded.

'I've seen the schedule and the plans for going forward and this is not going to be an exposé in any real sense. It's a gentle look at education after lockdown, what changes, that kind of thing.' He looked around at the faces all staring at him. 'What? I take an interest. I won't always be the guy taping microphones under desks, you know.'

'I thought you said you were checking for boom?' Arnie was on the defensive. 'I thought you said there would be no hidden microphones,' she spat at Bevis.

'Figure of speech, figure of speech,' the sound guy said. 'It's not allowed to plant hidden devices. And anyway, I expect this bloke has full sight of everything before transmission, dontcha?' He looked at Diamond, who looked flustered.

'I'm . . . I'm not sure,' he said. 'I'd have to check.'

'Blimey,' the sound guy said. 'Sorry, I thought you were the one in charge. IRL, I mean, not in this thing.'

Arnie's eyes began to swivel wildly between Bevis and Diamond. 'I think we need the room,' she said to everyone but the two men in her sights.

'Ooh,' the sound guy said. 'Someone's been watching her USTV series.'

Had he but known it, she did hardly anything else. Celebrity fly on the walls were her very favourite, then anything involving cooking unlikely and impossible-to-source ingredients against the clock. Failing that, potting as a competitive sport, or at a pinch, political dramas. So she couldn't argue with his assessment.

Maxwell took charge and ushered everyone out ahead of him He was good at clearing rooms. As he closed the door he could hear hell break loose behind him.

'IRL?' he asked the sound guy.

'In real life,' he told him.

Maxwell turned his head to the door where Arnie's voice seemed to have gained the ascendancy.

'Nothing real about life around here . . . umm . . . what's your name again?'

'Didn't use it, so it's not again,' he said. 'It's Gavin, as it happens. And you, Mr Maxwell, we all know you.'

Chuckles from the other exiles made Maxwell turn.

'Really? How?'

'Well,' Gavin said, as the unofficial spokesman, 'didn't you know? You're the star of this thing. There's even talk of calling it *Maxwell's Week*.'

'Nah,' the man who had been stuffing the hamster in the air vent said. 'Dropped it. It's gone back upstairs, for review.'

Gavin shrugged. 'Whatever. But whatever they call it, you're set for life, Mr M. You'll need to get yourself an agent, I reckon. They'll help you with that, when the time comes.'

'Don't worry,' Maxwell said, still trying to process the turn things seemed to have taken. 'I think I already know one.' And with that, he made for the stairs and the relative sanity of the sixth form block. This was going to get ugly, of that he was almost certain.

* * *

On the landing, he almost cannoned into Thingee One, who was doing her usual mid-morning postal delivery.

'Soz, Thingee, old thing. Miles away.' Maxwell doffed an invisible hat and turned towards his office.

'Mr Maxwell, can I ask you something?' Thingee had been terrified of Maxwell when she had first taken the job, but now, like so many others at Leighford High, she knew him to be a safe harbour in any storm and, more importantly, a pair of ears which took in everything and never accidentally leaked anything out of the attached mouth.

'Always,' he said, spinning back round to face her. 'Everything all right, I hope.' He knew when perhaps humour was the wrong thing.

'Yes, yes, thank you. No problems. But I . . . well, we, the girls in the office and . . . the IT department, and grounds and upkeep and . . .'

'Everyone,' he finished for her. 'Yes?'

'We were all wondering,' she giggled and covered her mouth, 'what's going on with Ms Preddie's teeth?'

Maxwell sagged with relief. So he wasn't going mad after all. 'I had noticed they were . . . very white.'

'That, yes, but whitened teeth don't get bigger,' she said. 'It doesn't make them . . . sort of, swell.'

'Could it be an optical illusion?' he wondered.

They were getting infinitesimally closer each time one of them spoke, drawn together by intrigue. Just as well there were no kids on the landing; they'd be on it like ninjas and the affair between Mr Maxwell and Whatsername in the office would be all over social media by nightfall.

'Optical illusions don't make you lisp, though, do they?' Thingee One pointed out, quite reasonably. 'They just make you wonder if it's a duck or a rabbit, that kind of thing.'

'True enough. Come on, Thingee, old chap. Surely you know more about these beauty things than I do. I mean, do I *look* as if I visit a beautician?'

Thingee had to concede that he didn't, although he wasn't that bad for someone a hundred years old. 'We were wondering . . . veneers? But they take time, you have to have them done by a dentist.' Maxwell was about to remind her that dentists didn't exist any more when the sound of a door opening made them spring apart, guilty things surprised.

'Don't mind me.' Polly Allington breezed past.

Thingee nudged Maxwell and pointed. She mimed a big smile and pointed again.

'Ms Allington, do you have a minute?' Maxwell asked.

'Not really. Apparently, Sally from Textiles has just abandoned a class for no reason I can fathom, so I am looking for its teacher. Oh, yes, that would be you.' She smiled, but there was a slightly bitter tang to it. Thingee was right. She had perfect teeth.

'I'll go and kill them all one by one shortly,' Maxwell assured her, 'but Thingee here and I were wondering where you got your teeth.'

Polly Allington had not known Maxwell all that long but even so, she wasn't really surprised. She could put two and two together as well as the next woman. 'God. And no, that's not where Arnie got hers. She got hers from a website widely advertised on social media. It's called www.perfectyourmouth.

org — you must have seen it.' Then she realised who she was talking to but Thingee suddenly clicked her fingers.

'I do know it, now you've said. They're kind of thin teeth, you heat them up and press them in your mouth.'

'You've got it,' Polly said.

'Do they work?' Maxwell ruminated.

'Well, you've been in the room with her,' his head of department said, crisply. 'You tell me.'

Maxwell and Thingee looked at each other and then shook their heads. 'I would say, on balance, no,' Maxwell said.

'They look all right at first,' Thingee chimed in, 'and then . . . they don't.'

'There you are, then,' Polly said, heading down the stairs. 'Asked and answered. And before you ask, I saw the box in her bin. She used the school address to have them sent to. Perhaps doesn't want the neighbours to know. Or the postman. Perhaps she fancies the postman.' And with another turn of the stairs, she was gone.

'Well, well, well,' Maxwell said. 'I hope they weren't too expensive.'

Thingee giggled again and shuffled the remaining post. 'I think she bought the budget ones, don't you?'

'Perhaps it was buy one, get one free,' Maxwell suggested.

'She's wearing them both at once, then,' Thingee said, heading down the landing in the direction of Business. 'I won't be able to look at her, now.'

Maxwell had never been able to look at her without serious distress, so it would be no change for him. But still, if she had gone to these lengths, he could see that she was going to be even more difficult to deal with than usual, if he was going to be the star. Not that he was going to be . . .

CHAPTER FOUR

'Mr Maxwell, could I have a word?'

It had been some years since Maxwell had heard James Diamond's dulcet tones on a daily basis, but he could still ignore them without breaking his stride.

'Mr Maxwell?' Diamond didn't have an office to lurk in any more, so he was at large in the school and therefore more difficult to avoid. 'Mr *Maxwell*!'

There was nothing for it but to turn round, and so Maxwell did. He pinned on a smile. 'Mr Diamond. How can I help you? I am on a bit of a tight schedule, I'm afraid. Going home, picking up the boy, starting the supper. Busy, busy.'

Diamond looked at him and not for the first time wondered how this crusty old git had managed to snaffle a looker like his wife. He looked ostentatiously at his watch but was disappointed to see that he had lost track of time and it was a long while since the final bell had gone. 'Sorry, Max,' he muttered. 'I won't keep you long.'

'All right,' Maxwell said, following him into the staffroom where the erstwhile Head had set up shop. 'But I genuinely can't stay.'

'Understand, yes, totally understand. I just need to make sure that things go smoothly tomorrow. Bernard is especially concerned, of course, as his . . . his . . .'

'Husband,' Maxwell said helpfully. He didn't think that Diamond was being homophobic or anything even close to it, but he knew his man and could see that he was finding it difficult to grasp that his ex-deputy head was now a showbiz mogul, even in such a minutely unimportant way.

'Yes.'

'Joe. Shall we stick with Joe? I'm assuming we don't have to call him sir or anything?' Maxwell had called very few people sir in his life, at least, not without a tongue in his cheek, and he didn't really see himself doing it now, with much conviction for the viewers at any rate.

'I think that might be best. Bernard will be here, of course, to make sure that Joe gets a proper percentage of screen time, you know, and camera angles and . . .' Diamond looked up helplessly. 'Max, I have no bloody idea what I am doing here. I was quite happy in a back office at County, following up complaints, requests for early retirement, that kind of thing. So I confess I am a bit out of my league. I think,' he looked left and right, furtively, 'I think they might be trying to force me out, give me something I can't do, that kind of thing. It's been done.'

'Indeed it has,' Maxwell agreed. What he didn't add was that on most of those occasions, it had been James Diamond and Bernard Ryan (with a few guest stars helping out from time to time) trying to get rid of *him*. He was not a man to bear a grudge, although Diamond had a master's degree in the subject. Maxwell looked up at the clock. 'So, James. What was it you wanted . . . ?'

Diamond plonked down into one of the low chairs that littered the staffroom. Some of them had springs, some hadn't — happily for him, this time he had chosen wisely. Maxwell sat opposite him, taking more care. He was pretty sure that Mrs B changed them round when cleaning the room, just for the pleasure of knowing that, in her absence, some poor soul would hit the deck and be on Voltarol for weeks.

'I know you don't want to be part of these shenanigans, Max, and I know why. But most of the rest of the staff have been to see me, separately, and none of them want to be filmed. I thought, *County* thought, that everyone would be keen to participate, to show teaching in a different light. Most people just think that teachers have stonking salaries and long holidays and that's where it ends. I wanted to . . . share what it's like to teach young minds. I was a proper teacher once, Max, you know, in the classroom.'

Maxwell nodded, though he, along with the rest of the staff, had never quite believed it.

'And I thought that was what we were going to be making, a kind of . . .' He lifted his hands and clapped them down on his knees, defeated. 'And Joe, when I knew Bernard, was a news reporter. Bernard did mention him from time to time and I think I always assumed they had been to school together, something like that. I didn't know . . .' Again, Diamond's voice fell away. He sighed. 'But now, it turns out, he is a media tart, like all the rest. Some dancing thing, apparently, he was on. Do you watch?'

Maxwell shook his head.

'Nor do I. But apparently, he did very well. Limber, Bernard said. And . . . some thing where they go to Australia?'

'Yes,' Maxwell said, 'I know it, but I don't watch that either. I didn't know he had done that, though.'

'Next season, Bernard says, if first outing goes well. So, there's a lot riding. And now the staff don't want to be in it. I can't name names but . . . Max, they all have such good reasons. One — and I can't name him — has apparently left his wife after she knocked him about. He was very embarrassed, but he seemed very sincere. One is on the run, would you believe, from a foreclosed mortgage and an ex-husband.' The ex-Head looked at Maxwell in despair. 'Is any of it true, Max, do you think?'

Maxwell didn't know what to tell the man. He thought he knew who both of the examples were, but didn't like to say that both cases were common scuttlebutt in the staffroom. He thought that it was probably because no one wanted to be involved in something that looked as though it might end up as some kind of game show, with a lot of teeth and hair and knowing looks to the camera. He knew that he had been chosen as the Face of Leighford High School because his lessons were always fun but disciplined and Joe could bask in his one-liners and look cleverer than he was. It was all going to end in tears, but this was perhaps not the moment to tell that to Legs.

'It might have some kernels of truth, Hea— James. The thing that has surprised me is that the parents have given permission. Surely some of them must have declined.'

'A few. We've told the camerapersons — Bernard said I have to make my speech less gender-specific — that any child in the back two rows mustn't be filmed.'

'Well, you've sorted that, at least.'

'Some of the parents, of course, have asked that little thingummy is made a lot of because they are hoping for modelling contracts and so on. We've had to tell them that that won't be possible, that we are not doing auditions or anything. For that reason, we're not filming music lessons or drama. No "Annies" or "Olivers", thank you very much.'

'I notice you are saying "we", James.'

The man sighed again. 'In the end, it's just easier. I can't wait for all this to be over, actually.'

'Speaking of which, when *will* it be over?'

'Easter holidays, although they tell me they may need to do what they call continuity shots after that. And they're coming back on results day, to film.'

'Now, there I do draw the line. Filming results is never acceptable. I know they do it on the news, to make a point usually, but . . . no. I won't have that.'

'Miss Preddie . . .'

'Mzzz.'

'Sorry?' Diamond looked confused.

'Mzzz. Mzzz Preddie. She doesn't like "Miss".'

'Oh. I . . . think I may have . . .'

'No, you haven't. I can tell, because you still have all your teeth. She can be very forceful.'

'I'd noticed. I told them at County when she was appointed, but they wouldn't have it. She came with excellent references.'

'Of course she did. Haven't you ever written a golden reference for someone you wanted rid of?'

'Certainly not!' Diamond was outraged and then gave Maxwell the benefit of one of his rare smiles. 'Yes, of course I have. But . . . you think so? In Ms Preddie's case?'

'I don't see how anyone could have given her an excellent reference while telling the truth, do you? The woman is a nightmare. Vindictive. Rather stupid . . .'

'And with very odd teeth,' Diamond mused. 'I don't remember those from her appointment interview.'

'No, well, you wouldn't. No one remembers them from before this morning. I think she thinks they make her look rather fetching.'

Diamond laughed, not something he often indulged in. 'Perhaps she will see sense once she realises she isn't going to be in close-up. The camera isn't kind to her, I'm afraid.'

Maxwell sketched an outline of himself in the air. The mad hair. The pork-pie hat. The cycle clips. 'And I am?'

Diamond raised an eyebrow. 'Apparently, yes. To quote Zac, "the camera loves that man". So, there you have it.'

Maxwell stood up. It seemed that this conversation had gone as far as it was going to go. If he really was some sort of combination of Cary Grant, Johnny Depp, George Clooney and Brad Pitt, well, he'd just have to live with that. 'If you're done, James . . . ?'

'What? Oh, right. Picking up son. Getting supper. How are the family, Max?'

'Very well, thank you. Nolan will be fine; he pops in next door if he gets home before we do. I don't like the thought of it, but his friend's mother always waits to see he is safely in before she drives away.'

Diamond looked surprised. 'Isn't your neighbour about a hundred years old?' he asked.

'No, no, Mrs Troubridge has sadly left the building. Gone to that great retirement home in the sky. No, Mrs B lives next door now. She looks after Nolan for us on a kind of ad hoc, almost-granny sort of way. And the cats. And the house . . .'

'And the school? You're talking about Mrs B the cleaner?'

'The very same. Sometimes, I wonder if she has a couple of clones tucked away somewhere. You know she's a computer whizz? If anyone has cracked the technology, Mrs B has.'

'Mrs B? Computers? I had no idea.'

'And for all I know, lots more. Mrs B has hidden depths and I'm not sure I want to plumb them all. But she is reliable and Nolan loves her. So that's fine.'

'You said cats, emphasis on more than one.' Diamond had only met the gargantuan Metternich once but he had left an impression.

'Oh, yes. The Count now has a partner in crime: Bismarck. Not my idea — the cat, that is, although the name was mine — but I confess I rather like the little chap. Not so little, now, but all cats are small compared with Metternich. Most dogs as well, to be honest. He downed an XL Bully the other day.'

'Things move on; you lose track.' Diamond looked bereft.

'Well, life, you know, Headmaster. Oh, sorry . . . I forget . . .'

Diamond's smile was bleak. 'Not to worry, Max, not to worry. I'm sure we'll get to the Easter holidays and no bones broken.'

'Yes, very possibly.' It was faint comfort, but it was something.

* * *

As Maxwell pedalled home in the gloomy grey of a February afternoon, Surrey's tyres hissing on the wet of the tarmac, he mulled over Mrs B. She wasn't often at the forefront of his thoughts, but when she was, he always ended his inner monologue by wondering why she had settled for being a school cleaner. Her computer skills, wholly self-taught, were legendary. She had shown intelligence and compassion when coping with an increasingly confused Mrs Troubridge in her last days. Nolan and the cats adored her; the Maxwell lads had tapped a hidden stream of humour in her that often had them all rolling in the aisles. Maxwell senior regretted that he didn't seem to have the right funny bone, because they really did seem to be having a blast. When Arnie had started her reign of terror at Leighford — soon after the storming of the Bastille, it seemed to Maxwell — she had had a go at shaking up the cleaning team. Gwen Harris, the site manager, had told her it wouldn't work, but she was adamant and the site manager had learned in the short time of Arnie's rule, that it wasn't worth arguing. As far as Gwen Harris was concerned, she had a nice simple job and a nice warm office to do it in. On the days she could stomach it, she even had free school lunches, as long as she ate them in the dining hall with all the little dears — she never really gelled with the students. To her, they were just an unfortunate side effect of working in a school. Her job, as she saw it, was to make sure the place didn't fall down and that any surface you could stand on wasn't slippery. And if it was temporarily slippery it had a sign on it. Simple.

And indeed, it hadn't really worked, although Arnie thought it had — the cleaning team were now in attendance throughout the day, rather than coming en masse after the school day was over. In principle, it was a good idea. The school never became overwhelmed by piles of paper and other detritus and, in general, it was never as dirty at any one time as had been the case. It was never as clean either, but that, Maxwell knew, was an argument for another day, probably when an Ofsted inspection was looming. For now, he was just grateful, as it meant that Mrs B, who had opted for a morning shift, was at home these days for when Nolan got home. He hoped Arnie never found out how useful she had been — she would undoubtedly re-tweak so that no one benefitted, especially not Peter Maxwell.

* * *

In deference to the weather, Nolan and Mrs B were chez Maxwell when his father got home. They were playing Scrabble at the kitchen table and neither really did more than give a brief acknowledgement to the master of the house when he walked in. A pile of chocolate fingers on the table bore testament to the fact that this was a needle match. Usually, they played for points alone; the addition of chocolate to the mix meant that they were playing for keeps. Maxwell made a cup of coffee, leaning on the worktop while his machine did its thing, watching his son. The sight of his bent head and his knuckles white around his tiles brought a lump to his throat. He really wanted to scoop him up and give him a kiss, but Nolan had reached the age when such behaviour was not welcome except behind closed doors. Even his beloved Mrs B wasn't allowed to see PPDA — parental public displays of affection. Maxwell leaned nearer. A 'Q' and a 'W' — the lad was toast.

Taking his cup, he wandered into the sitting room to find that Metternich and Bismarck had taken possession of the couch. When stretched out, the two of them filled the whole seat without unduly taxing a whisker. Their nominal master was reminded once again of that excellent film about two man-eating lions, *The Ghost and the Darkness*. The only question was, which was which. Maxwell sighed, turned on the lamp in the corner over his favourite chair and picked up the book he had put down the night before. He had read *The Pursuit of the Millennium* a dozen times and had found it enormously satisfying. He had only got a few pages in when there was a shout from the kitchen and he leaped to his feet as if stung. Surely Scrabble was a safe enough game. Although the tiles could be a bit sharp, he supposed. The Remington painting flashed into his mind. Called *A Misdeal*, it showed gamblers in a dark, smoky saloon, chairs scattered: one, standing, leaning down to take the winnings; the others dead or dying from gunshot wounds.

'Dads, Dads, come and look at this!'

Not death and destruction, then. Probably a spelling altercation.

In the kitchen, Mrs B was scooping the pile of chocolate fingers into her handbag. Nolan was sitting back in his chair, eyes wide with disbelief. Maxwell bent over the board and whistled in amazement.

'Two triples and an "X" in the mix. Blimey, Mrs B, that comes to . . .' He counted on his fingers.

'*And* she's used all her letters, Dads!' Nolan was both disappointed to lose and proud that he knew a straight-up genius.

Mrs B pointed at the scorecard, to save Maxwell any more brainpower.

'One hundred and eighty-seven.' Maxwell was impressed. He turned to his son. 'I don't think you can come back from this one, matey,' he said. 'Why not go and watch a bit of telly? I won't tell if you don't.'

Nolan showed a clean pair of heels and soon distant cartoon music filled the air.

'Quietly!' Maxwell and Mrs B shouted in unison.

'Sorry, Mr M,' the woman said. 'I sometimes forget . . .'

'No problem,' Maxwell said. 'Too loud is too loud. Doesn't matter who puts it right. Did you want a word?'

She looked at him. With a score like that, words were the last thing she needed, but this was something else. He might look a bit simple, but he had a head on his shoulders, no doubt about that. 'How did you know?'

'You don't usually beat Nolan that comprehensively. I've never known there be more than twenty points in it.'

'Oh. I didn't think you would have noticed. He hasn't noticed, has he? I do want a word, as it happens. It's about them Up at the School. Her Up at the School, mainly. None of us wants to be in this film. We've all seen that kind of thing on telly, they take the p— mickey out of people. Doreen . . .

you might not know her, got a bit of a cast in one eye and dyes her hair green . . . does the Biology labs and floors . . . she don't want to be on the telly.'

'I had, but thank you for doing it. He hasn't. Let's do it. I thought it would be, and I thought it would be. I don't blame you. Of course you have. They do. I know Doreen, of course, and where she does. Umm . . . why not?' Maxwell had honed the skill of replying to Mrs B's omnibus questions over the years and rarely fumbled, but the Doreen remark had him stumped.

'Because of her limp. Her knee is giving her gyp and she doesn't want her other jobs to know.'

'I didn't know she had another job. Isn't dinner lady and cleaner enough for someone of her years?'

'Forty-seven? What's that got to do with anything?'

As Maxwell had had the numbers reversed as a general guesstimate, he said nothing.

'Everyone has another job. Who can live on a cleaner's wage? And some of them don't want the other lot to know they work Up at the School. Taxman. Husbands. That kind of thing.'

Maxwell smiled. Mrs B had had some husbands over the years; only she knew exactly how many. She had ditched the latest to look after Mrs Troubridge and had never looked back. As far as Maxwell knew, she hadn't given her rather disreputable family another thought since she walked out of the door last. And he was pretty sure that that was at least some of the reason that she didn't want to be on the telly.

'So, you'll have to tell them telly people we don't want to be on it.' She stepped back and folded her arms. When Mrs B folded her arms, you knew you were in trouble. Maxwell responded accordingly.

'I'll do my best, Mrs B. I don't expect you would have any need to worry, though. You're gone before anyone arrives in the morning, aren't you?'

'I stay around to just report to Dilys, she comes on until the mid-morning break. We all just overlap, so there's continuity, like. Her Up at the School, she don't like it, but she has to lump it. We can't just guess what's going on. The things you find . . .' Her eyes unfocused as she thought back to some of the horrors she had found, mostly behind the sofa in the staffroom. She gave herself a little shake. 'Anyway, we'll leave it to you. I told them all you'd fix it for us.' She reached for her coat, thrown over the back of a chair. 'I best be on my way. See you tomorrow.'

And with that, she was gone, pausing only long enough to say goodbye to the three men in her life who had never let her down. In reply, she got one lick, one nuzzle and one kiss, in no particular order. So that was it; Peter Maxwell was now the official spokesperson of the Leighford Ladies Cleaning Circle. He could picture them now, sitting at the base of the guillotine from where Arnie Preddie's head was about to tumble.

* * *

Wednesday is always a weird day at school. It's not the beginning of the week, to be dreaded, nor yet the end, to be welcomed with cries and sighs of relief. It's just the bump in the road, that everyone has to negotiate to reach the other side. In Maxwell's long-ago schooldays, it was also the day when all afternoon was devoted to games, regardless of the weather. He still lay in bed for an extra few minutes on a Wednesday morning, eyes tight shut, making sure that he no longer had to climb into shorts still slightly damp and muddy from the week before, smelling of the bottom of a kitbag, and boots which pinched the toes of one foot but slipped loosely around at the heel of the other. He would discover as regular as the sun that he had been wearing one of his own boots and one of his classmate's since the first week of term. Eight years of such Wednesdays left a mark on a man. And he never did get the call from Twickenham HQ.

So it was nice today to pedal happily up the drive to Leighford High School with no blisters and no festering kitbag over his shoulder. What wasn't quite so nice was the sight of almost every student in the school ranged across the entrance, some of them with placards, some even spelled correctly. Maxwell came to an elegant stop and dismounted. A single cameraman lurked to one side of the mob. He knew it was unlikely this footage would be used, but if it were, there would be a bonus in it for him, for sure. He hefted his camera into a more comfortable position on his shoulder and zoomed in on Maxwell as he approached the front-line protestors.

The Head of Sixth Form stood there silently, reading the placards with care. Above the heads of the protestors, through the first-floor windows, he could see the faces of most of his colleagues. A window opened and Helen Maitland hung precariously out.

'Ms Preddie has asked us not to engage, Mr Maxwell,' she called. 'She's in touch with County and the governors for advice.'

Maxwell rolled his eyes. As far as he knew, neither august body had ever been able to organise a piss-up in a brewery. 'So,' he said to the pair of ringleaders who had stepped bravely forward to meet him. 'This is about mobiles, I assume.'

'Human rights,' a bolshie girl from Year Eleven said, pushing further forward still. 'Our human rights have been violated.'

Maxwell reached for her placard and plucked it gently from her hand. He turned it to face her. 'Human *rites*, Charlotte,' he said. 'Your human *rites* have been violated.'

She looked puzzled. 'Yeah. That's what I said.'

'No,' Maxwell said patiently. 'You *think* you have said human rights, but what you have written here is human *rites*. Which, as I am sure he is about to do, Spencer here will explain.'

The boy standing next to her leaned over and whispered in her ear.

Charlotte tossed her head. 'So I can't spell. So what? You don't need spelling these days. You've got spell check and that. On your *phone*.' She leaned forward, emphasising the word.

'True enough,' Maxwell said. 'So, harlot . . .'

'What?' The girl bristled.

'Sorry,' Maxwell said. 'Autocorrect.'

A few sniggers rippled along the front row and Maxwell could hear his name spreading through the crowd as the bon mot was passed on.

Maxwell took a step back and addressed the mob. 'Listen up, people. I know that you are all attached to your phones, some of you almost literally. But you really can do without them for . . . what are we talking, here? Six hours? What do you use them for during the day? Ummm . . .' He scanned the faces in front of him. 'You. Marlie. What do you use yours for?'

The girl shuffled her feet. She tried as best she could to keep a low profile in all of Maxwell's lessons. She hadn't even caught his eye. And yet, here she was in the spotlight. 'I . . . er . . . keep it for emergencies.' She knew this was the party line and she was sticking to it.

'Oh?' Maxwell was solicitous. 'Problem at home? No one ill, I hope.' He knew that Marlie was the only child of high-achieving, sparklingly healthy and efficient parents. He couldn't envisage any emergency, which was precisely why he had chosen her.

'No,' she muttered. 'It's all good. I . . .' Her voice died away.

'Pardon?' Maxwell leaned closer. The crowd held its breath — everyone present knew this technique and some began unzipping their coats and picking up their bags, ready to go in to school. For them, the war was over.

She lifted her chin. 'I play games.'

'Oh.' Maxwell rocked back on his heels. 'You can play *games* on these things? And there's me thinking you were all perusing your personal *Encyclopaedia Britannica* subscriptions. Or perhaps "talking" to your "friends" who are sitting right next to you "IRL".' He made ironic rabbit ears as he spoke. 'But *games*? Personally, I am ROFLMAO.'

The crowd erupted into applause and whoops of laughter.

'Now, bugger off to your lessons. One-day moratorium on phones, but tomorrow, people, to bring one in is to have it taken off you and accidentally dropped in a bucket of water. Shoo!'

And still laughing, the whole school went about its business.

In reception, Arnie Preddie stood behind Thingee One, watching events unfold. Thingee turned to her boss with a big smile on her face. 'Isn't Mr Maxwell marvellous?' she breathed. 'If you don't mind my saying so, Ms Preddie, you did the right thing there getting him to talk to the students. They really relate to him, they really do.'

Arnie Preddie gripped the back of the Thingees' shared chair so hard she left permanent dents in the foam padding. 'Indeed they do,' she said, through her gritted new teeth. Then she gave herself a shake. This wasn't going to get a film filmed. She patted her hair and made her way into the foyer, where Peter Maxwell was sharing a joke with a colleague. She hated that. She hated laughing. She hated camaraderie. But most of all, she hated Peter Maxwell.

After she had swept past, lips clamped tightly over her improbable incisors, Don from Maths leaned in closer.

'"Ready for my close-up, Mr DeMille,"' he muttered.

The two men looked at each other, too kind to laugh out loud but too amused not to smile.

'Very nice,' Maxwell nodded. 'Very nice. Keep 'em coming — I've a feeling we'll all need a laugh or two before this term is out. By the way, that's the best Bill Holden I've heard in years.'

* * *

'Do I need a haircut?' Maxwell asked, turning this way and that and assessing his profile in the dark window as he closed the curtains.

'Of course you do, Dads.' Nolan was in like a ninja. 'You always need a haircut.'

Jacquie raised an eyebrow. She didn't need to add anything to the conversation except to ask, 'Why do you want to know? As the boy says, you always need a haircut.'

'And perhaps a different hat?' Nolan suggested, quickly pointing to Metternich, as the great beast lay prone in front of the fire. 'Asking for a friend.'

'And new trousers,' Jacquie chimed in. 'The cycle clips have made a permanent groove in those.'

Maxwell sat down and faced his little family. 'Everyone's a critic,' he observed, without rancour. 'All I asked was whether I wanted a little trim, perhaps, and you have ripped my fashion style to shreds.'

'You have a fashion style?' Jacquie and Nolan looked at him in mock amazement. 'I don't think we were under the impression that you dressed like that on purpose, were we, Nole?'

'Oh, har. But . . . about the hair . . .'

'Max,' said Jacquie, serious now, 'I don't think that the film company has chosen you for your appearance. I think they have chosen you because you are an inspirational teacher whose lessons are always a blast. With no misbehaviour — or if there is, it's short-lived. So, really, don't get a haircut. We wouldn't recognise you if you did.'

'Actually,' Maxwell preened ostentatiously, 'Zac says the camera loves me.'

'Well, good for Zac,' Jacquie said. 'He is clearly a man of taste and discernment. When do you start filming? Tomorrow?'

'Supposedly. They seem to be all over the place, though. The whole school seems full of people with cameras and miles of cable and weird little things they keep holding up to the ceiling. Soundchecks. Light checks. Whatever happened to pointing a camera and turning a handle?'

'Technology,' Jacquie said to her favourite dinosaur. 'And don't pretend that you remember all that handle-turning nonsense. You're not that old.'

Nolan sat up and put his book aside. 'That's a good question. How old are you, Dads?'

'As old as my tongue and a bit older than my teeth,' Maxwell said. He played the 'how old am I?' game every September with Year Seven and their wild guesses were getting closer to his age of 150 with every passing year.

'No, Dads, really. How old are you? Plocker says his grandpa is ninety-nine and that you are older than his grandpa. But I told him that can't be right.'

Maxwell flicked a glance at Jacquie. The age may be wrong, the glance said, but the fact that he was almost certainly older than Grandpa Plocker was probably not. 'Well, Plocker knows best about his grandpa,' he said, 'but I'm not ninety-nine or anywhere near it. So, let's drop the age conversation and get the Scrabble out. Did you tell Mums about Mrs B yesterday?'

'She beat me fair and square,' Nolan said solemnly. 'But you won't; I'm learning all her tricks. I'll beat her one day, I know I will. It just takes practice.'

'Mrs B is a helluva Scrabble player,' Maxwell acknowledged. He ferreted in the bag and held up his tile. '"Q"! I go first.' He rubbed his hands together. 'You're toast, Nolan Maxwell. What are we playing for?'

The boy narrowed his eyes. 'Half an hour on bedtime.' He knew he couldn't lose. The old man was stuck with a 'Q' already — the game was as good as won.

CHAPTER FIVE

When Mrs B had heard the news of Arnie Preddie's new plans for the cleaning rota, she had considered hanging up her mop. She didn't really need the job any more. Mrs Troubridge had left her nicely settled in her house and without having to pay for the current Mr B's drinking habits or the even less salubrious goings-on of her sundry children, she was doing nicely, thank you. She had not missed the family, not a single one of them, since the day she had moved out during lockdown to live with Mrs Troubridge for the duration. Sadly for Mrs Troubridge, of course, she had not seen the end of lockdown; she had died, as had so many, scarcely knowing what had happened to her. Mrs B missed the old lady more than she had expected to, but every morning when she woke up in her own room in her nice quiet, clean house, she had given up a little prayer to say thank you to the often cantankerous old bat.

But a week or two into the new regime, Mrs B acknowledged to herself — but not to anyone else, it didn't do to let them know that you weren't still annoyed — that mornings suited her. True, a seven o'clock start was a bit of a challenge on a dark cold morning in late February, but already she could sense spring in the air and after ten o'clock, the day was her own. She would be able to garden, take a turn round the shops, go out for the day, perhaps even hit the one-armed bandits in the Amusement Arcade. There was something about the whole hands-on experience that knocked online into a cocked hat. She smiled, something she rarely did, but, in her own way, Mrs B found she was happy.

She trudged up the drive to the school but only because trudging was her usual mode of travel. There had been an early primrose poking out from under the hedge where she got off the bus and a blackbird was singing somewhere off in the dark. The low lights on in the school building made her tut — she had told them time and again that that Brenda what did the final shift had a memory like a sieve and needed watching, but no one checked to see if she had turned the lights off. She shook her head. Some people!

She shook her head even more when her putting in her pass key just pushed the big double doors open. Usually, she had to jiggle the key about a bit and then push quite hard, so this was not right. She looked behind her then told herself not to be stupid. The risk was not behind her — if it was anywhere, it was right ahead. Mrs B was a cleaner of the old school. Not for her the namby-pamby water wipes and microfibre. She carried her cleaning equipment with her in a substantial bag and she reached into it now and pulled out a pump spray of Mr Muscle All Purpose. She wasn't sure what was in it, but she guessed by the smell that a face full of it would probably stop even the most determined miscreant in his tracks. Or her tracks, indeed — some of the girls Up at the School were far more scary than any of the lads.

She stepped carefully around the door and checked behind it. She had watched enough crime series to know that that was almost always where the perp was lurking. No one. She checked the floor ahead of her for footprints — that Brenda wielded a good mop, she'd say that much for her — and there was nothing to be seen. She looked around and all the doors leading off to other parts of the school were closed and the corridors behind them were dark. The faint glow she had seen from outside was coming from reception. She crept forward, pump spray at the ready. She cleared her throat, ready to call out a warning before she let whoever it was have it right between the eyes.

She wished now she had put her glasses on. She told everyone she only needed them for close work and to an extent that was true. But she was increasingly aware that if she wanted detail rather than a rough outline, she really did need her specs. And she knew they were at the bottom of her bag, well out of reach by this stage of the game. However, she could do almost as well by slitting her eyes and so she did that and stepped carefully and quietly across the office. She looked behind every desk. After behind the door, that was where people tended to lurk the most. But there was nothing. The only other door from this room led into the Head's office and although that was on her rota for cleaning, she didn't like going in there. She always had the feeling that there were eyes on her and she had complained more than once to her union rep that Her Up at the School had hidden cameras in place. Everyone had nodded; they were pretty sure she had, too. But where they were and what they could do about it remained mysteries.

She pushed the door open and the soft light was revealed as the desk lamp, turned at a strange angle, facing the door. There was an odd smell in there as well, metallic almost. Perhaps it came from all the equipment in there, on stands, stacked in corners, taped to walls. Mrs B began to breathe more easily. All this fuss; she put a hand to her chest to feel her madly beating heart begin to slow. It was just one of those daffy telly people working late and not realising they had to lock up behind them. Only kids, anyway, most of them. She'd give them kids, though, if one of them pointed a camera at her. She'd told them, she . . .

Her heart sped up again. Laid out behind Her Up at the School's desk was one of those daffy telly people. And the metallic smell was coming from the pool of blood which had spread out from the stab wound in his chest when it was first made, many hours before. Mrs B did something she had thought she had forgotten how to do. She screamed. And she was still screaming when she got to the bottom of the drive and grabbed the first jogger who she could catch. And inside her head, she was still screaming when the police arrived.

* * *

Breakfast chez Maxwell was going well. With a dippy egg each and the toast soldiers in infantry square formation, Maxwell and Nolan were playing magnetic chess, Nolan using his dominant hand, Maxwell his less-used one, with three fingers taped together. The handicapping system was getting to be quite complex and Maxwell knew it was only a matter of time before he would be blindfolded as well. But still, it was better than a screen and the quiet clack of the stones was a nice background to breakfast. Maxwell knew perfectly well there would come a time when it would be Nolan playing with the handicap. Jacquie was also playing a game, hers with Metternich and Bismarck. It was called 'Give Us a Second Breakfast and We Won't Claw Your Legs to Ribbons'. She was currently winning but only by a whisker. Just as she scraped the last bits of piscine goodness out of the sachet and tapped it onto the dish, her phone rang. She wasn't due in until midday so she answered it in her cold-call-answering voice.

'Yup?' She listened to the voice at the other end, which sounded rather more urgent than the usual person trying to sell her solar panels. 'She . . . sorry. Can you slow down . . . okay. Okay. Where is she now? Have you called 999?'

Maxwell's head came up. This wasn't right. If Jacquie got a work call, that essentially meant that this was 999; what was going on that she had a call and also there was a need for 999?

'I'm on my way.' She rang off and turned to the table, where the two Maxwell men were looking at her big-eyed.

'I've got to . . . go out,' she said, distracted. 'Can you ring Mrs Plocker . . . or, no, hang on . . .'

63

Maxwell had rarely seen his wife this distracted and was concerned. He quickly riffled through his mental filing system to see if he could work out who was causing it. He knew it wasn't him or Nolan, so that was a comfort. She wouldn't have asked the 999 question if it were Henry. Since Mrs Troubridge had left them, it couldn't be her . . . The light dawned and he mouthed over Nolan's head, 'Mrs B?'

She nodded imperceptibly and went out to get her coat. She slipped her feet into her work boots, elegant but serviceable and with no heel to speak of. She had often laughed at women policemen in cop shows on the telly who gave chase down cobbled alleys while wearing stiletto heels and somehow not only managed to not break an ankle but to rugger-tackle the perp to the ground as well, 'so, perhaps, in view of the time, it's a taxi day today. I'll see you later.' She paused, not knowing whether to add the next bit, but did anyway. 'Up at the School.'

Nolan looked at her. 'Are you going to watch Dads being filmed?' he asked her, excited. 'Will you be filmed, Mums?'

'Hopefully not,' she said. 'But yes, that's it, I'm watching Dads being filmed. Should be fun.'

Nolan chuckled. 'All my friends at school are jealous. Jamie's mum was on the news once. She was stood outside Morrisons when that lady had run in some muck with a gun.'

Maxwell blinked, then remembered. 'Standing, mate, standing, not stood. And yes, I do remember that.' The woman in question had been a Highena parent and it had been the talk of the school. 'Well, I don't expect I will be very interesting, so they might not even show it. But still . . . say bye to Mums while I ring for a taxi.'

Not for Maxwell the conveniences of Uber. He had a little man he knew who had a car almost as old as he was, but who still did simple short-haul jobs for people he reckoned. He kept booster seats in the back for children, tissues in the front for women leaving home with just the clothes on their back, and a back seat covered in plastic for late-night revellers. He had clearly once been a Boy Scout and he was Maxwell's sort of taxi driver.

'Bye, sweetie,' Jacquie said, kissing the top of her boy's head. He smelled of shampoo, toast and little boy and she hoped that it would never change, that he would always dip his head for her kisses. 'Do you fancy a sleepover at Plocker's tonight? I can ring his mum if you like.'

'Yes, please!' Sleepovers at Plocker's never palled and he had a drawer there, with jamas, toothbrush and a change of school uniform. Jacquie offered up a little prayer of thanks for the ever-accommodating Mrs Plocker; Mrs B would be in no condition to babysit today. Even Mrs B had to have a little bit of downtime after what she had been through. Leaving Nolan to his egg and Maxwell to his phone call, she slipped out of the house and was soon turning in to the drive at Leighford High.

* * *

Someone had indeed called 999 and the emergency services had responded quickly. There were four police cars on the forecourt and an unmarked one she recognised as DCI Henry Hall's parked in a spare place in the car park. A stocky police constable, whose winter overcoat didn't really do much to cover his stab vest, stepped aside to let her into the school. Inside, it was oddly quiet, with none of the barely contained hysteria Jacquie usually associated with a murder in what was essentially a public place. She glanced at the clock above the reception window; it was coming up to quarter to eight and already there were sounds of the breakfast club coming from the dining room. Henry Hall had had to decide whether to close the whole school off or let people in and on balance he had decided to let the early comers in; he had little choice in most cases, as the children arriving for their banana and cereal were by and large not able to be sent home without many hoops being jumped through. However, the stocky policeman would be turning away all other arrivals and school buses had been alerted.

A plain-clothes man in the foyer pointed Jacquie in the direction of reception and she opened the door and went in, unsure of what she would find. Mrs B was sitting in the furthest corner, tucked away behind the photocopier. Beside her sat Thingee One, an arm around the woman's shoulder. The cleaner held a mug between her hands, clutching it as if only its warmth could keep her grounded. This was not a view of her friend and neighbour that Jacquie was familiar with. Mrs B seemed as invincible as the white cliffs of Dover, down the coast. But she wasn't invincible now, with a pile of sodden tissues at her feet and a trembling lip.

Thingee One looked up and sagged with relief when she saw Jacquie. 'Oh, Mrs Maxwell, thank goodness you're here. I didn't know what else to do.'

'You did the right thing, Caroline,' Jacquie said. Thingee One would have been staggered to discover that Mr Maxwell knew her name and was indeed the one who had informed his wife of what it was. She would also have been a little disappointed; she was quite fond of being called Thingee, Thingee Old Chap when she had performed a task particularly well. She hoped that this was a Thingee Old Chap moment. 'Shall I . . . ?' Jacquie gestured to the chair and Thingee vacated it, going back to her desk. The phones would start ringing soon and Thingee had jotted herself a little message down on the notepad. This wasn't a day to inadvertently say the wrong thing.

Mrs B still hadn't spoken, but leaned briefly against Jacquie's shoulder, before giving a gargantuan sniff and starting to talk. Her voice was low, but gained strength as she went on. 'It was horrible, Mrs M,' she said. 'I come in and the door was open and there was a light in there.' She pointed to the back office but didn't look in its direction. 'I went in . . . I knew there was something wrong. I could smell this smell . . .' She waved a hand in front of her face, as though to waft it away. 'It was . . . like rust, like old, wet iron. That's the worst part.' Her voice trembled again. 'I could smell his blood, Mrs M. That's not right, is it? To leave someone there, in all their blood.' She looked up and a wobbly smile appeared for a moment. 'She's going to have to get herself a new carpet, ain't she? She brung it from home, you know, that one. Says it's valuable. Serves her right, bringing it in. No place in a office, a valuable carpet. Like her, though. Stupid woman, really. Very stupid to be a teacher.'

Maxwell had often been heard to say that you had to be pretty stupid to be a teacher at all, but Jacquie got the gist of the message. But it was hardly Arnie's fault that someone had been killed on her carpet, and she moved the conversation on.

'Had you seen the man before?'

'Yeah, he's one of them film blokes. Not with a camera, though. Microphones, loads of wire. He's been sticking things up on walls; just before I went home yesterday, I saw him with a big roll of tape. "Oh, yes," I said to him, "oh, yes. Stick things up all right, but where will you be when we're trying to get that sticky stuff off these walls?"' She suddenly realised what she had said and looked at Jacquie, stricken.

Jacquie patted her arm. 'We all say things we would like to take back,' she said. 'You weren't to know.'

'He was a bit of a pain in the you-know-where,' Mrs B told her, 'but not enough for anybody to kill him, I wouldn't have thought. Although . . .' She screwed up her nose, thinking. 'From what I saw, he didn't really seem to fit in. He was older than the others, for a start. Not by much, eight, ten years, but that's enough in their kind of business, probably. And he was bolshie, you know what I mean? Didn't take no rubbish.' Her throaty chuckle was almost back to normal. 'A bit like Mr M, in some ways.'

'I'll find out all about him,' Jacquie said, 'if I'm assigned to this case.'

'Surely, though,' Mrs B said, all practicality again, 'be stupid not to be, wouldn't it? You know everybody here, dontcha?'

'Not the film people, though,' Jacquie pointed out.

'No, but everybody *else*, though. And those you don't, Mr M will, won't he?'

There was a sigh from the doorway. 'Of course he will,' Henry Hall said to the universe in general. 'Jacquie, when you've a minute, can you pop in here?'

'I'm just looking after . . . I wasn't called to this,' Jacquie said. She had been at home happily having her legs clawed when this had all kicked off.

'You would have been, though,' Hall pointed out. 'This lady is quite right. You don't know everyone, but knowing half of them is more than the rest of us do. So consider yourself officially assigned. We'll go into the nuts and bolts of who does what later.'

Jacquie put an arm around Mrs B's shoulders. 'I really need to take her home first,' she said. 'She's in shock.'

Mrs B was feeling quite recovered, and said so. She stood up, hefted her bag into the crook of her elbow and stepped out of the corner. 'I need to get on with me cleaning,' she said. 'You can't afford to lose a minute in this place. Filthy, it'll be, given half a chance.'

'Ah, now, that's something that can't happen,' Hall told her. 'No cleaning for the foreseeable future, I'm afraid. We're not allowing anyone in; the children in the dining room are only there temporarily and as soon as we find out how to send them home and where, that's exactly what's going to happen. The blue-and-white tape is going up outside as we speak.'

Mrs B's hand went to her bag. 'But . . . I have to clean. Otherwise . . .'

'Otherwise, we might be able to find some DNA, fingerprints, something that can find a killer,' Hall said reasonably. 'Now, would you like to give your statement to DI Carpenter-Maxwell, or would you like to come down to the station at some point in the next twenty-four hours? Your choice.'

Mrs B drew herself up. 'Aren't I a suspect, then?' She sounded almost annoyed.

'Not . . . as such,' Hall said, sliding his eyes sideways at Jacquie. Why was nothing to do with Leighford High School ever easy?

'Well, I call that bad police work,' Mrs B said, affronted. 'On the telly, it's almost always the person what finds the body. Classic plot structure, that.'

Hall had to concede that, as on TV, so in life. But that was really for domestics. Not a random body found somewhere it had no rights to be.

'We know where to find you, Mrs . . . er . . .'

'B!' Mrs B said, closing her mouth with a snap. No need to go spreading her personal details all over the shop. There were laws against that, she was almost certain.

'Right. So . . . now with Jacquie, or later at the station?'

Mrs B looked at Jacquie who tried to look neutral. She would much prefer for Mrs B to give her statement to a stranger. Jacquie was afraid that she would use her knowledge to second-guess what the woman might mean and would possibly get it wrong. Only Maxwell really had the knack for deciphering Mrs B-speak.

'I'll come down the station,' she said. 'To be honest, I could do with a bit of a sit-down at home.'

'I should think so too,' Jacquie said. 'I'll get a car organised for you.'

'No need,' Mrs B said. 'The bus goes past the door. And what would the neighbours think if I came home in a cop car?' She started to chuckle, a noise deep inside like a volcano thinking of erupting.

Jacquie patted her arm. 'Even so,' she said, 'a car it is, followed by a nice cuppa and a lie-down. Promise?'

Mrs B looked at her and eventually nodded. 'Okay. Umm . . . is Nolan . . . ?'

'He'll be with Plocker,' Jacquie said. 'I rang his mum. So, if you fancy coming round this evening, or even this afternoon, with Mr M being at home . . .'

'Will he?' Mrs B was puzzled.

'Of course,' Henry Hall said, although without much conviction. 'Nobody will be coming in here today.'

Mrs B looked the Chief Inspector up and down. She didn't have him down as a stupid person, but really — as if!

* * *

After Jacquie had seen Mrs B off in the back of a police car, not all smiles, exactly, but certainly more chipper than she had been earlier, she made her way to the back office off reception. Typically for Arnie, she had two offices, one alongside the staffroom, where she held meetings and scared the living daylights out of newly qualified teachers and one-off reception — now otherwise known as the crime scene — where she could lurk and annoy the pants off the admin staff. The SOCOs held sway in there currently; what seemed like a football team of white-swathed figures moving silently around, with small brushes, tweezers and pocketsful of evidence bags.

Cameras clicked, as if mocking the dead man who lay there. Who needs you, sound guy? they seemed to say. A picture paints a thousand words. And a picture taken with a camera, even more. As Peter Maxwell could have reminded them, they used to make movies without sound at all.

Gavin Masters didn't fit too well behind Arnie Preddie's desk. To be fair, the space had not been created for a corpse. His elbows nudged the chair and the wall; one leg jutted out at an awkward angle. His head was turned to the left, as if he had done what countless old people did when it had all become too much and turned their faces to the wall.

* * *

Alan Hargreaves had once had all kinds of plans. Once his houseman years were over, he'd discover something astonishing in the lofty world of medicine, make a fortune out of it and then saunter down Harley Street and choose his premises. An emeritus consultancy, the inevitable K from a grateful king — the whole world before him . . . But somehow, it hadn't quite gone that way and here he was, at thirty-something, with a wife and three kids, up to his armpits in dead bodies. 'Pathologist to the stars' still beckoned, but somebody else was already that and Leighford was a *long* way from Hollywood. He loved his wife dearly, but she always told him what to do and was always right. Which would have been fine, if only Donald in the lab had not been identical. Not in a physical way, of course, but certainly in terms of who ruled the roost. And so, as he looked at the crime scene that was Leighford High, he heard his inner demon asking him, 'What would Donald do?'

But Donald was miles away, tucking into a full English at his favourite eatery in Tottingleigh, and had no idea how busy he was about to be.

'What have we got?' he asked the nearest alien in white gear crouching over the body. It never hurt to get a second opinion. Patients in the private sector paid a fortune for that; but because of the nature of this particular beast, Hargreaves got it for nothing.

'Stab wound to the chest, doctor,' the alien said, muffled behind the mask. It had not been so long since *everybody* wore one of those; now SOCO had them all to themselves again.

Hargreaves knelt at the dead man's feet, fumbling in his kitbag for a thermometer. 'Who was he?' he asked absent-mindedly.

'Name of Gavin Masters,' the SOCO told him. 'Got a pass thing in his back pocket. Sound engineer with the telly crew, apparently.'

Sound engineer? Telly? Hargreaves wondered briefly if he had stumbled into some parallel universe. The phone call had said a body at Leighford High. He naturally assumed teacher, some poor bastard who had crossed a zombie-knife-carrying delinquent. Or, failing that, a robbery gone wrong. But then, high schools didn't have nightwatchmen, did they?

'Telly crew?' he repeated.

'They're making some documentary, apparently. Looks like it'll be a true crime thing now. The DCI can tell you more.'

* * *

Jacquie had left the SOCOs to it and gone out front to help the police on duty there to turn people away. Although she didn't know all the names, she knew most of the staff by sight and — often — by reputation. She knew, for example, that Sally from Textiles would turn around and leave without question, that Don from Mathematics would make what he thought was a funny quip. She knew that her husband would try to wheedle his way in — and probably succeed. The unknown quantity was the TV team and unless she was much mistaken, their van had just turned into the drive, followed by a minibus for the woofer and tweeter brigade. She tried to remember some names from her chats with Maxwell. She didn't intend to greet them like old friends, but a bit of a heads-up on who was who was always going be a help. She could see heads rubbernecking from side to side when they saw the police cars. She wondered if it was just her imagination when she thought she could see a gleam in their eyes. She stepped forward to fend them off before they got too near the building. The uniform on duty stepped back, just happy not to have to deal with them. He would tell his missus a small lie when he got home, though, that he and he alone had stopped that Joe geezer from *Strictly* and he was a lot shorter than on the telly, with less hair.

Maxwell's description of the team had not been detailed, but Jacquie could weed out who was who from what she knew. Joe Pargeter was recognisable, of course, within the strictures of height and hair. However, whether she had ever seen him on the box before or not, she would know him now as he was arm in arm with Bernard Ryan, erstwhile deputy head at Leighford High.

Bevis and Zac appeared at a distance to be more or less interchangeable, but she took a guess that the more intelligent-looking of the two was the assistant, as was the usual run of things IRL. She stepped forward. 'Good morning,' she said, looking down at the list that the constable had had clipped to his board. 'You are,' she smiled at Bevis, 'Bevis Woodford and . . .' She looked down the list again. This should have been simple, but there was no one called Zac there. 'Umm . . . sorry, I seem to have inaccurate information. I was expecting the director, Zac, to be here but . . .'

The clone who wasn't Bevis stepped forward. 'Yes, that's me.' He gave her a quick flash of his smile which he had once based on Phillip Schofield but was now trying to morph into Cillian Murphy.

'Oh.' Jacquie rummaged in her pocket for a pen. 'Let me add you.' As she was only going to let them through the door and then herd them into the staffroom to await her and Henry's ministrations, it wasn't as if she was committing a mortal sin to add a name in pen. 'So . . .' She wrote 'Zac' and looked up hopefully but he just stood there, the smile drooping slightly on his face. Bevis, on the other hand, looked as happy as a clam. 'So, your surname is . . . ?'

'Littleton,' he muttered.

'Little . . .' She started to write and then stopped. 'Ah, so I suppose I would be right in assuming that you are on this list, but your actual name is Ernest?'

Bevis's smile almost cut his head in two and even Joe Pargeter allowed a chuckle to escape.

'It's a family name,' the director flounced. 'Everyone calls me Zac, always have.'

'Until today,' Bevis muttered to himself. He had been waiting forever — in other words, six weeks, forever in TV terms — for this to become common knowledge and now his moment had come. And from the lips of a very nice bit of totty as well — bit old for him, perhaps, but nicely put together.

Jacquie smiled coldly at him. 'I'll just put "prefers to be known as Zac" alongside, shall I? Right, now who else do we have? Bernard, of course, hello. How have you been keeping? And this is . . .' She looked down at her paper. 'Joe, yes, of course. I'll have to ask you to stand over there a moment, gentlemen, while I check in the rest of the staff.'

She went over to the minibus and took the roll call through the driver's window. When that was done, the agency staff jumped down from the rear door and stood in a huddle at the top of the drive. A couple of them took out vaping gadgets of various sizes and one — almost instantly ostracised — a cigarette. Jacquie asked the constable on duty to move down the drive a little, to fend off staff and pupils who would be arriving any minute. It would be easier if they didn't even reach the step. Then she took his place and raised her voice a notch.

'If you could just gather round, everyone . . . thanks. I'm afraid I have some bad news for you. This morning at just gone seven, one of the staff here at the school found a body which was identified from personal belongings as being a colleague of yours, Gavin Masters.'

Usually, when that kind of news was shared, especially in a public setting, there was at least one person who would set up an ululation which would spread through the crowd like tear-stained wildfire. This time, there was nothing, just a few mutters and shaken heads. Eventually, Bevis spoke for everyone.

'Who?'

'It's that sound guy,' someone said from the back.

'I thought his name was Gary,' one of the women said. 'I'm sure he said his name was Gary.'

'He was agency,' Bevis told Jacquie. 'We only have a very small team with us permanently, and we fill up on numbers from the agency. We do usually have the same people, if possible, but one of our usuals . . . umm . . .'

'Tyler,' someone filled in for him.

'Yes, Tyler got a gig in Dubai, so we had to get Barry—'

'Gavin,' Jacquie corrected him. She felt somehow as if she had to keep Gavin in everyone's mind as a real person.

'No, Gary, I think,' the woman at the back said.

'Yes, we got Ga . . . vin from an agency. It was handy, because he lived fairly locally, so we didn't have to arrange hotels and things.'

One of the technicians snorted. 'Hotels? We're in the Travhotel off the A3.'

Bevis shot him a vicious look. 'Sometimes, of course, rooms are limited. But the Travhotel does wonderful breakfasts, doesn't it, Zac? We often join the team there, just for the coffee, don't we?' He beamed around and got little in the way of response. 'But the long and the short of it, Miss . . . er . . . is that we scarcely knew the guy and while it's very sad and all that, we're already two days behind schedule and we need to get a wiggle on. So . . .' He made as if to push past Jacquie into the building. She might be easy on the eye, but no jumped-up little secretary was going to make him miss a deadline.

'That's Detective Inspector,' Jacquie said, coldly. 'DI Carpenter-Maxwell, as a matter of fact.'

Bernard smiled. He hadn't smiled much when he was deputy head of Leighford High School, for obvious reasons, but he did it more these days and seeing Jacquie in action was a joy. It was like watching Mad Max himself, but without the pork-pie hat and cycle clips. He waited for the penny to drop.

'Maxwell as in . . . ?' Zac asked, almost afraid to hear the answer.

'Maxwell as in, that's right,' she said. 'Not that that comes into it. And I'm afraid that there will be no filming today. We have closed the school down for now, pending scene-of-crime investigations. When they are over, it may be able to reopen partially by Monday.'

'Monday?' Joe Pargeter nearly burst a blood vessel. 'Bernie, Bernie, check out the schedule. Can we do that? Do we have any spare time? We can't overrun beyond . . . what, third week of March?'

Bernard — Jacquie just couldn't really picture him answering to Bernie, and yet here he was, doing it — pulled out a phone from his inside pocket, tapped it and peered at the screen. 'We might just squeeze to Easter, I suppose. But we wouldn't be able to do any post-production then until . . .' he flicked the screen upwards with a perfectly manicured forefinger, then grimaced at Zac, 'fifteenth of April. Sorry,' he added. 'We can't really change it, we're doing an ad in Tenerife.'

'Poor you,' Zac spat. 'We'll manage, I daresay. As long as Detective Inspector Carpenter-Maxwell here lets us back in by Monday.'

'It might even be Friday,' Jacquie said. 'If all goes well.'

There was a silence and then the woman who was so sure the deceased was called Gary piped up. 'You mean if you find who did it, don't you?'

Jacquie heard the slight hysteria in the last two words and took a step back against the sudden onset of shouting.

'Don't you? *Don't you?* Oh, my God! Gary's dead, people! Whatever will we do without him?'

And Jacquie knew that, as night follows day, there would be a row of dying bunches of flowers and a rain-doused candle outside the doors of Leighford High School before the end of the day. Teddy bears would feature too. But for now, she ushered them into the building and turned them sharp right inside the doors and around the corner into the staffroom. The floor had been footprinted and the woodwork fingerprinted and so it was safe to pass across, but even so, they walked as if on eggshells. Death had suddenly come calling and although everyone there was already having problems remembering Gavin's face, the mass hysteria of mortality was in the room with them.

CHAPTER SIX

The DCI had taken over the deputy heads' office. It wasn't much as incident rooms went, but it would do for now. After all, the largest office in the school was now a crime scene. Gwen Harris, the site manager, had been allowed through the cordon and had unlocked all the rooms that the police might need. She hoped that they wouldn't need hers. She did like her personal space to be kept personal and that was nothing to do with the small baggie of purely medicinal weed she kept at the back of the bottom drawer of her desk. This was definitely not in her job specs and she would be on to County to tell them so, as soon as the lazy so-and-sos got to their desks. As most of them worked from home these days, that should be any time now, though she somehow doubted it. She had given DCI Hall a printed list of who had keys, who was usually first in and last out and now, as far as she was concerned, that was that. She finally made her way out of the building and was in the car park before you could say Jack Robinson. She hadn't been gone two minutes when there was a tap on the door.

'DCI Hall.' The pathologist stood there.

'Dr Hargreaves.' Hall stood up. 'Come in. Come in.'

Neither was in the mood for shaking hands. Hargreaves had taken off his gloves, cap and boots, but he was still in his pale blue scrubs and Hall preferred a certain length of time to have passed before there was anything resembling physical contact.

'What have you got for me, Alan?' Hall gestured to a chair and Hargreaves sat down.

'Single blow to the chest,' he said, 'to the left of the midline, severing the aorta and slicing the left ventricle.'

'Knife, I take it?'

'Most probably,' Hargreaves said. 'Single-edged blade, about five inches, possibly six. SOCO found nothing on that score, I understand.'

'That's right. How long has he been dead? I know it can only be a guess, but tell me anyway.'

'I'd say about eight or nine hours. I'll know more when I get him on the slab, as they habitually say in *Midsomer Murders*.' The doctor was grinning. The policeman wasn't.

'Watch that sort of stuff, do you?' Hall asked.

'No, no.' Hargreaves was a little too quick to reassure him. 'Paula does, though. It's on in the background, you know.'

'Well,' Hall stood up. 'I look forward to your report, Alan. But before that, I suppose I'd better make my way into the staffroom. Jacquie's rounding up the telly crew and taking them in there for a chat. I'd rather keep them apart from each other, but having them all milling around contradicting each other has also been known to bring results.' He threw his arms in the air and brought his hands down on his thighs with a slap. He pushed himself off the chair. 'Well, let's let the dog see the rabbit, eh, Alan?' He held the door open. 'After you.'

* * *

Henry Hall was standing at the staffroom window looking out at the wet and cold of the football pitches, the nets hanging disconsolately from too few nails in the crossbar. He turned as Jacquie led the TV crew in and fixed his blank gaze on them. He couldn't help but notice that some wag — and he suspected Peter Maxwell — had written 'Who *is* the Secretary of State for Education this week?' on a piece of paper on the noticeboard.

'Good morning, everyone. Thank you for coming. Mr Ryan . . .' He nodded at Bernard and everyone wondered how he knew the man; but then, they all decided separately, there is nothing as dodgy as an agent, so he must have done something.

'I know that DI Carpenter-Maxwell will have shared the bad news with you. If anyone wants to take some time to process it, we can arrange a quiet place, but I understand that you and Mr Masters had not been colleagues for long. Is that the case?'

Heads nodded and wobbled uncertainly. It was a bit of a grey area. Their speciality was a fairly small one along the South Coast and so most of them had bumped into each other from time to time. The rather more cosmopolitan ones who worked in London bumped into each other constantly. The ones who wanted to work no more than twenty miles from home, not so much.

Bevis Woodford seemed to have become the group's mouthpiece. 'We didn't really know Gavin all that well. He was living at home while we were in a hotel.' He ignored the snort from the woman to his left 'Well, several hotels.'

'At home?' Hall raised his eyebrows. 'He's from Leighford?'

'Not as such, I don't think,' Zac Littleton said. 'Nearby, though. Near enough not to need accommodation.'

'Go, Ernie,' someone muttered at the back and there were a few answering sniggers.

Jacquie felt for the man. He was never going to live it down. She did give him full marks, though, for having kept his real name hidden for such a long time in an industry where everyone was picked over on social media constantly.

Hall made a note. 'Thank you.' He looked up again and asked another question. 'Does anyone know if he has family? It would be handy if we had the name of anyone we need to inform. Although he had his pass in his pocket, we need a person to identify him.' He scanned the faces and every one was a blank. 'In that case, we will need to have one of you help us out, if you would. Mr . . . Littleton, is it? I understand you are the director . . .'

Zac Littleton shrugged. 'I am. But that means out of everyone I am least likely to know anyone on the team. I have . . . people.' He hated people who had people, but there seemed no better way to describe it.

Hall looked stern. He had people as well. One of his people was standing right by him. But he would never ask any of them to do something he wasn't prepared to do himself. And he had a feeling that Mr Zac Littleton was doing just that. He decided not to make an issue of it, though. This surely was a nice simple murder within a finite group of people and why make it difficult? 'All right, then. Is there anyone here who could be said to know Mr Masters better than anyone else? A closer colleague, perhaps? No? Had he made any particular friends, then? A romantic encounter?'

Jacquie felt sorry for Henry. He so much preferred being behind the scenes and yet here he was, standing up in front of perhaps the most cynical lot of people she had seen gathered in one place for a long time. She remembered the brief hysteria from the woman who had thought the dead man was called Gary and scanned the faces to see where she was. She was, perhaps inevitably, standing at the back, the arm of a clearly unwilling technician around her shoulders as she wept silently into his hankie.

'Excuse me,' she said, raising her voice a little. 'I'm afraid I don't know names as yet . . . you, at the back.' She nodded to the man who was being wept on, who jumped at the chance to get rid of his burden. He shrugged her off and she blew her nose vociferously.

'Mel,' he said, 'I think the DI is talking to you.'

'Me?' The woman's eyes were wide and red-rimmed. 'Me? Why me?'

'You seemed to be the most upset,' Jacquie pointed out.

'Oh, take no notice of me,' she said, with an enormous sniff. 'I cry at anything. Ask anyone.'

No one spoke.

'Let's go into another room, shall we?' Jacquie suggested. 'Where we can chat.'

'I don't see as how I'd have much to tell you,' the woman protested, hanging on to her erstwhile comforter, who prised her fingers off his sleeve. 'I hardly knew the man. Only met him at the weekend. We had a little meet and greet, you know the kind of thing. Sound in one room, cameras in the other.' She smiled and sniffed. 'Stick together, we do, in this business.'

There was an evil chuckle from the back of the room and Jacquie knew that her instincts were right. Something rather more than a quick gin and tonic had happened between Mel and Gavin, for sure. But whether there had been any pillow talk afterwards remained to be seen.

Jacquie turned to Henry Hall. 'Are we using the deputies' office?' she checked.

'Yes,' Hall said. 'I'll just have a few more words with this lot and then get them down to the nick to take statements. Easier there, with the equipment.'

'Absolutely. I'll follow along behind with Mel. But we might be popping in on Alan first.'

Hall understood. No point in using the M word yet. People had such strange expectations of the morgue, either imagining a spider-strewn blackness peopled with ghouls in hoods and humps or a bright space where white-clad masked creatures crept about holding clipboards and dodgy pseudo-science of the American variety held sway. Leighford Morgue was neither, being a brick extension at the back of the hospital which tended to smell more of the day's special in the canteen than antiseptic or decay. The waiting room had old copies of *Hello!* and *Good Housekeeping* on a scratched table and a coffee machine which only dispensed soup. And then, of course, there was also Donald to contend with, a sunny soul but perhaps a little intense for most people's liking. He had recently been on an empathy course along the lines of equality, diversity and inclusion, although Maxwell could have told him that EDI actually stood for education-ally dinosauric idiocy. Donald had taken it very seriously. But people dreaded the morgue all the same and so Henry appreciated Jacquie's thoughtfulness.

Jacquie ushered Mel out into the foyer and immediately was aware of a voice that she knew, coming from outside.

'If you could just wait in here,' she said to the woman, opening the door to the deputies' office, 'I'll be back in just a minute.'

* * *

She pulled open the big front door and was immediately presented with the blue serge back of a constable's winter coat. Peering over his shoulder she saw what she had expected to, the face of her husband, beaming from beneath his pork-pie hat, worn on the back of his head as it was when he meant business.

'Hello!' Maxwell said, catching sight of his wife. 'I saw the car, I wasn't sure you were still here.'

'Is this gentleman bothering you?' Jacquie asked the policeman on duty.

He chuckled. Everyone at the nick knew Maxwell. 'Not unduly, ma'am,' he said. 'No more than usual, perhaps I should say.'

'So, a lot, then,' Jacquie said, sliding out from behind the man. She hugged herself in the cold morning air. 'I'm busy, Max. Really, couldn't you have just done what everyone else has and stayed at home? There quite literally is nothing to see here.'

'Clichés, clichés, always clichés,' Maxwell muttered. 'Jim here has been filling me in.' Jacquie shot the constable a look. The constable looked ostentatiously at the far horizon. 'I understand one of the sound guys has been found dead in Arnie's back office. It's the last of a long line of murders in there, but the first one to literally end up with someone dead. Mostly it's just death of the soul that happens where the sun don't shine.'

'It's not funny, Max. A man is dead.'

'I'm sorry,' he said, meaning it. 'It's just hard to believe, though, isn't it? These people have only been here for one day, and one of them is dead. I know there was a lot of ill feeling and everyone got a bit aerated — including me, I admit — but killing a sound engineer seems a bit . . . well, unrelated, surely. No one knows him here.'

Jacquie gave a short, sharp laugh. 'And that's the truth. Even the people he worked with won't ID him.'

'Well, that's because they just don't want to ID him, surely,' Maxwell pointed out, reasonably. 'Not because they don't know who he is.'

'Almost certainly. But that isn't making it any easier for us. I do have one woman stashed away, who . . .' She stopped and looked at him. 'You're doing it again. Go away. Go home. You'll see me when you see me.'

He pulled a rueful face. 'I came in a taxi, though. It's gone now.'

The constable tried and failed to stifle a laugh.

'Don't encourage him,' Jacquie snapped. 'Find another taxi. Catch a bus. I'll see you at home later. Actually, there is one thing you could do for me.'

He smiled in what he hoped looked like an eager fashion.

'You could look in on Mrs B. She had a shock and she was trying to not acknowledge it. Finding a bloodstained body—'

'So, there was blood, then . . . ?'

' —isn't very nice at the best of times but she was on her own and in the dark. So, pop in and make sure she's resting. Make her a cup of tea. Let her make you a cup of tea. That would probably suit her better; she likes to keep busy. You'll find out more from her than from me, anyway. So, off you go. Taxi. Bus. Home. Mrs B.'

Maxwell knew when he was beaten and set off at a sprightly rate down the drive.

'He's a one, your old man,' Jim the constable remarked.

'Oh, he's a one, all right,' she said, slipping back into the welcome warmth of the foyer. What she didn't say was what she was thinking; that with any luck, he would find out more from Mrs B over a cup of tea than anyone else would in a twenty-four-hour grilling.

* * *

Mel the sound engineer sat slumped in the one comfy chair in the office that the two Leighford High deputies shared. Although it was a space for both of them, only Mandy Proctor had made the slightest impact on the place. There were plants everywhere, some of them wearing small reindeer antlers left over from Christmas, others sitting in macramé pots. The office chairs behind the two facing desks had fluffy throws over their backs and on one desk there was a mug with 'World's Best Bob' on it, clearly made at a paint-your-own pottery, with which the esplanade in town was littered. There was a faint smell of Marc Jacobs in the air.

Jacquie closed the door and the click made Mel start. 'Sorry to make you jump,' Jacquie said. 'Are you comfy there, or shall we sit at the desk? I'll use my phone to record us, if that's okay, then you can come and sign the typed-up statement later, or tomorrow even, if you need some time.'

Mel nodded and picked up a pink fluffy cushion and hugged it to her stomach.

Jacquie pulled up one of the office chairs and let it down to its lowest setting so that she was more or less eye to eye with the woman who, now she came to look more closely, was a little older than she had first thought. She was trying her best to look young, with spiky hair with deliberate dark roots and a short skirt and heavy boots on the end of almost impossibly thin legs. But she wouldn't be seeing thirty again, Jacquie guessed, possibly even thirty-five.

'First thing,' she said, putting her phone down on the low table between them, 'is your name, date of birth and address.'

'Melanie Bright,' she said. 'Why do you need the rest?'

'Just for our records. Nothing will be shared. Is there a reason why you don't want to give that information?'

The woman looked down and dug her fingers into the fluff of the cushion. 'I . . . lied about my age. Zac doesn't like working with people older than him, that's well known. So I shaved a few years off.'

Jacquie gave herself a private high five. It was nice being right, even if only in the privacy of her own head. 'Well, we'll just have it here on the record, no one else will know. And your address?'

'Don't have one.'

'What, not at all?' She knew about the boomerang generation, ending up back with mum and dad, but someone with a career and good money being homeless seemed strange.

'I did have. Still have, I suppose. My name's on the mortgage and everything. But . . . well, everything went a bit pear-shaped and . . .' She shrugged. 'I'm doing a bit of sofa-surfing right now. That's why this gig was so welcome. A month or so in a hotel, it'll give me time to get myself together. I think that's why . . .' her voice dropped almost to a whisper, 'why I am a bit fragile at the moment. Sorry.' She wiped her eyes with the back of her hand, leaving an inadvertent piece of pink fluff from the cushion in her hair. Jacquie wanted to pluck it out, but didn't want to invade the woman's space.

'Let's get on, then. You can fill any gaps in when you go to the station to sign your statement. Now, I couldn't help but notice that you thought Gavin's name was Gary but also you were very much more upset than anyone else by his death. Those two things don't seem to go together.'

'Yes, I can see what that would look like.' Mel seemed to be calming down, although her eyes were still red and her nose was stuffy with tears.

'I have my own ideas on what might have happened. Would you like me to tell you, or do you want to explain to me yourself?'

'I'll explain. Although I don't think your idea will be very wide of the mark. We all went out for drinks and a planning session on the Saturday of last weekend.' She blew out a breath and then breathed back in deeply, which seemed to calm her. 'Zac and Bevis have been planning this for ages, of course, they've been having meetings with that nice Mr Diamond from the education authority and with Joe, of course.' She lowered her voice. 'Is he gay, do you know, Joe? Because if not, that agent is very touchy-feely with him. You don't see much of that.'

'They're married,' Jacquie told her. 'Bernard used to work here as deputy head.'

Mel's red eyes opened wide. '*Really?* Well . . . Anyway, we didn't know each other that well, the rest of us, although we'd worked together before in one combination or another. But Gary . . . sorry, Gavin . . . was new and so I thought I would try to help him . . . fit in, I suppose. And he took me wrong, thought I was coming on to him. And in a way, I was. He wasn't as young as the others, nor as fit, but he was . . . nice to me, you know. He didn't know about me moving out, or anything like that. He didn't judge me. He was just . . . nice.'

Jacquie nodded encouragingly.

'So . . . well, I'm not proud of this. We went to the toilets at the back of the pub and . . . I'm not going into detail, but we . . .'

'But you still thought his name was Gary.'

'I *know*! Isn't that *dreadful?* But we didn't exactly talk much after and since then . . . well, he lives round here somewhere, so he's not at the Travhotel so we didn't really bump into each other again until yesterday. And to be honest, he didn't seem to recognise me. Perhaps he'd been as wasted as I was at the pub.' Another fat tear rolled down her cheek. 'That's a nice thing to remember about a dead person, isn't it? That they didn't even remember you exist.'

The tears were coming in earnest now and Jacquie handed her a box of tissues, hidden in a crocheted box which was clearly meant to look like a frog. Mel took a handful and blew her nose.

'Perhaps he was embarrassed,' Jacquie suggested. 'Didn't want to draw attention to what had happened.'

The woman tossed her head. 'I didn't know him well, granted, but I knew him well enough to know that he wouldn't give a toss about being embarrassed. He just spoke his mind. You ask that bloke who they're gonna film. He was talking to Gary . . . Gavin, yesterday. He heard how he was going on.'

'Mr Maxwell?' Jacquie was intrigued and yet not surprised. Max had beaten her to the punch yet again.

'No, not Maxwell. Marlowe. Madison. One of those. Anyway, yes, ask him. Even though I doubt he's had a knee-trembler in the gents' with him, I reckon he knows the bloke as well as any of us. He looks the sort who can judge a person pretty well.' She sighed. 'I don't expect they'll be filming now. Shame. It could have won awards, it could. That Mr . . .'

'Maxwell.'

'Morrison, he has star quality, let me tell you. I've seen a few of these things made now and — star quality, no question.'

Jacquie thought that over quietly for a few moments, trying not to smile too broadly. This would be one description of Max that she would not be sharing when she got home. 'So, is that all you can tell me?'

'Yeah. Sorry it's not much. And I would rather you didn't let the others know. Well, they *know*, they saw us go out and that, but they don't *know*, as in being told straight out.'

'I understand,' Jacquie said, reaching for her phone and saving the file. 'You can rest assured it will go no further.' She offered the woman another handful of tissues then stood up. 'Let's get back to town. I can drop you off at the Travhotel if you'd rather, or you can wait at the police station for this to be typed up and ready for your signature.'

'Where are the others?'

'At the station. Or at least, most of them will still be there. It's a slow process, interviewing.'

'There, then. I don't fancy being on my own in a motel room, really.'

'Let's go, then. And please try to cheer up. If for no other reason than by the time we get there, we may have found the man's actual family. It's not really something I would recommend, playing the grieving one-night stand in front of a bereaved wife.'

Mel gathered her coat and wound her scarf around her neck several times. 'Point taken. I'm better now I've told someone. I'll be all right now.'

Jacquie hoped so, but her money was still on a row of dying flowers outside the school the next morning.

* * *

Maxwell hadn't expected to get in to the school, so had been quite chuffed with himself to even get as far as the door. One silver lining in the cloud had to be that there would now be no filming. Although it was not his habit to jump to conclusions, practically speaking it had to be one of the team and surely, they would have to be unusually thick-skinned to go on after this. He got home eventually after a rather circuitous trip on more buses than seemed to make any sense for such a short journey and let himself in, grateful to get out of the cold. It would be March any minute, with the Easter bunny and all sorts of exciting things involving chocolate at the end of it, but he was finding it hard to actually sense any kind of spring in the air. He mulled over asking Mrs B in or popping round, but he decided to go round. He would just change his coat, ditch the hat and rustle up some biscuits first. The great thing about nipping round to Mrs B's was that the place was always spotless, she always had milk and was always ready for a cup of tea.

Before he had a chance to do anything, his phone rang. The timing was fortuitous for the caller, seeing as how the phone was actually on the table in the hall. It didn't normally get so near to going out with him, but in the excitement of the taxi and everything, he'd had it in his hand when he and Nolan were putting their coats on. He looked at it askance. Answering the phone rarely ended well, in his experience, but his wife was dealing with a potential murderer and his son was at school where who knew what dangers lurked, so he picked it up gingerly.

'Hello?'

For once, the voice on the other end was not an unconvincing AI telling him his Amazon Prime account had been compromised.

'Mr Maxwell?' a semi-familiar voice asked.

'Speaking.'

'Excellent. It's Bevis here, from FOTWL. We spoke briefly . . .'

'Yes, I do remember, Bev.' He might have imagined the in-drawn breath, but it was fun anyway.

'As you probably know, there has been an . . . incident at Leighford High School.'

'I do know, yes. You probably met my wife. She's a DI.'

'Yes.' Bevis gave a nervous laugh. 'We have all met her. And a DCI Hall. In fact, we're all here waiting to be interviewed by the team at the station. We're all a bit nervous, to be honest, though . . .' the nervous laugh came again, 'none of us has actually done anything wrong. Not *murder*, at any rate.'

'Hopefully not,' Maxwell said drily. 'How can I help you, though, Bev?'

'We've been chatting and coordinating schedules while we are waiting and it does seem obvious that we are looking at an overrun. So, we — that is, Zac and I — were wondering if you would like to do a bit of post-production tomorrow, while the school is still closed.'

'Post? Doesn't that mean after?' Maxwell knew exactly what it meant, but there were times when it was fun *not* to let it be known that he was a celluloid genius.

'In a perfect world, yes, of course, although we do do it throughout, to save on location costs, etc. What we had planned was that you and Joe would do some chats — walking on the beach, that sort of thing, perhaps having a coffee in one of the nicer shops on the front, even a beer, perhaps — and then we could just pop them in when we edit.'

'Can I ask a question, Bev?'

'Of course.'

'What does this kind of thing have to do with *Fly on the Wall*? I had assumed that we would be just filming and, apart from a bit of editing for when a child farts or someone slams a distant door, it would be shown as is. I'm not sure I really want to go for a walk on the beach with Joe, who I am sure is delightful but who doesn't know anything about teaching or history, his being married to an ex-teacher notwithstanding.'

'I didn't know that,' Bevis said and it was obvious from the change in his voice that he was looking around the nick waiting room to eyeball the man in question.

'The married bit or the teacher bit?'

'Either. Both.'

'Well, judging by my admittedly small experience, if you look either to his left or his right about six inches, you will see both his husband and an ex-teacher. I'll leave you to pick the bones out of that. But as far as walks on the beach go . . . I really am not at all sure. Especially with your "incident", as you so elegantly call it. Who knows who you will have on your team by tomorrow, without wishing to be too much of a Job's comforter there.'

Bevis gave an enormous sigh that almost ruffled Maxwell's eyebrows over the phone. 'I know, I know, but please, Mr Maxwell, can't you just do this?'

The refrain from a long-ago song, 'Sylvia's Mother', ran through Maxwell's head.

'If we use it, we use it? If we don't, no biggie, surely? You get to walk on the beach with a mi— a celebrity and also have a nice cup of coffee. What could possibly be wrong with that?'

Maxwell thought things over. It was indeed unlikely that school would be open the next day and he had nothing else planned. The weather forecast said cold but sunny, so the beach might be bracing. He couldn't recommend a coffee shop — they came and went seemingly on a weekly basis — but there would be plenty to choose from, he knew. So he put Bevis out of his misery.

'I'll do it, Bev,' he said, 'but with reservations, I will admit. And I want to be able to look it over before you finalise anything. And I want Bernard to promise to give Joe a few pointers about what it means to be a teacher, if he can remember back that far. Also, I will need picking up; Surrey is a bit chilly in this weather.'

'Surrey?' Bevis was confused. 'But . . . we're in Sussex, aren't we?'

'Sorry. Surrey — White Surrey — is my bicycle. And Richard III's horse, of course. Look, just ask Bernard. If you're still confused by tomorrow morning, then all bets are off. Bye.'

Maxwell stood there for a moment with the phone still in his hand. He had forgotten how to ring off but assumed that Bevis had done that bit. He looked at his watch and was horrified at the time. Where does the morning go when all you have done is harass young policemen and arrange for a day's filming with a Z-list celebrity? He chuckled to himself as he went upstairs to change his shirt for something a bit more casual; no need to wear out the bow tie when there was no one to intimidate with it, after all.

* * *

If this was Hercule Poirot — which it wasn't, not by a long chalk — the diminutive Belgian would have corralled them all in the country house/hotel miles from anywhere because of the snow/sea/general inescapability. Henry Hall didn't often think of the procedural shortcomings of Agatha Christie. He had long ago stopped watching television cop shows, ever since Margaret had suddenly screamed at him for criticising their lack of accuracy. By virtue of the length of his tooth, he *was* a copper of the old school, but in his case, that post-dated PACE, so here he was, in his office at Leighford nick, with an eager young DS beside him, pressing buttons and checking recording levels to further order.

'Mr Littleton.' Hall leaned forward, hands clasped. Behind his glasses, his eyes were not merely inscrutable, they were virtually invisible. The strip lighting saw to that and the effect on interviewees, especially those of the 'no comment' tendency, could be electrifying. 'Ernest Littleton,' he added, for the benefit of the tape.

'Zac,' the director corrected him.

Hall checked Jacquie's notes. 'It definitely says here Ernest Littleton.'

The director chuckled. He didn't mind his dirty laundry being washed when there were only two policemen to see. It was when it was done in front of his whole production team that he tended to get testy. 'No, no. Littleton is right, of course, but I prefer to be known as Zac. Ernest went out with Oscar Wilde.'

Henry Hall had not known that; no doubt Peter Maxwell would have.

'I understand that you are the director of the high school documentary.'

'For my sins,' Zac said, all teeth and PR.

Henry Hall had long ago stopped reading too much into casual remarks. No doubt Zac Littleton was guilty of many sins; wearing his cap on backwards was only the tip of the iceberg.

'How well did you know the deceased?'

'Scarcely at all,' Zac said. 'Masters was agency. We get techies assigned to us on a rotational basis. We *had* met, now I come to think of it. You remember the *Now It Can Be Told* series?'

Hall didn't.

'Well, he was the sound guy on that. We never finished it, of course, because of Covid. Got three episodes of the last series in the can and then . . . whammo. Lockdown.'

The DCI nodded. Everyone had their own memories of that. 'Was it usual for him to be working so late — and on his own?'

'Well, he wasn't on his own.'

Hall and his DS both looked up. 'No?'

'No. Sound can be a bitch.' Littleton pointed to the tape recorder. 'You've almost certainly got too much reverb on that. Fine for your purposes of recording interviews, but it wouldn't do for TV. And the day they make an acoustically friendly school, I'll hang up my clipboard.'

'So, who was with him?'

'Mel, I assume; his Number Two, Melanie Bright. Now, her I do know. We go way back. Didn't she tell you?'

CHAPTER SEVEN

Mrs B had surprised herself when she got home. She discovered that all she wanted to do was to have a quiet sit-down with a cup of tea after all. She had spent her entire life — since she was about twelve — looking after people in one way or another; her feckless mother and the resulting long line of siblings; husbands various, both lawful and common; children and children's significant others and *their* children; whole generations of school children who without her would have disappeared into a pile of discarded rubbish; and, ultimately, and most lovingly, Mrs Troubridge. The Maxwell family were outside her list of the looked-after — she was all too aware of what a two-way street it was, although both sides tried their best to make little of that. The first cup of tea had gone cold and she was putting the kettle on for another when the doorbell went. She toyed for a moment with not answering, but it might be important — what with the events of the morning — so she stumped off down the stairs and flung open the door.

Maxwell stood there, wrapped up against the weather and with a plate of Hobnobs in his hand.

'Mr M,' she said, holding the door open. 'I was expecting you to be Up at the School.'

'I was, Mrs B, briefly,' Maxwell said, stepping in and slipping off his shoes in the expected way. Mrs B was a bit of a stickler. 'But Mrs M sent me home with a flea in my ear. I thought we could have a cuppa and a Hobnob, catch up a bit.'

'I don't know nothing, really,' the woman said, climbing the stairs and talking over her shoulder. 'I found him, I know, but I didn't hang around. I'm not ashamed to say I had a bit of a scream. Mrs T and me, we used to have a laugh over that when they did it on the telly, but when it happens to you . . .' she looked rather stricken as she ushered Maxwell into the sitting room, 'well, it's different. But I didn't *notice* anything. That's what made me so wild, after. That I didn't have anything to tell Mrs M, not really. Just about the door being open and the light on the desk being on.'

That didn't really leave very much for Maxwell to get his teeth into, but he had promised Jacquie he would check on Mrs B and so check he would.

'It must have been terrifying,' he said, 'all by yourself, in the dark. Has the sun even come up that early?' He would be the first to admit that he was a bit of a stranger to setting out at six as Mrs B had had to, to get to work on time.

'Just about, this time of year,' she told him. 'But it's still dark inside, really. I was really scared, and that isn't like me,' she said. 'I even forgot I had a phone and went running outside like something demented. I *never* forget my phone, Mr M, but I did. Shows how shocked I was, doesn't it? And I've been racking my brain ever since in case I heard somebody else in the building. I know that building like the back of my hand, Mr M. I'd know if a door went or something.'

A shriek from the kitchen nearly made Maxwell jump out of his skin.

'Oh, kettle. Mrs T always liked an old-fashioned kettle, on the gas. She said it made the tea taste better. I used to curse her up in a heap sometimes, under me breath, but I haven't had the heart to change it, somehow. Tea or coffee?'

Maxwell knew that Mrs Troubridge had been an adherent to Camp coffee, bought for her in her last years by Mrs

B off Amazon. He suspected that Mrs B now had something rather arcane of the Nespresso variety, but didn't want to risk it. 'Tea, please,' he said. Mrs B knew how he took it and pottered off to make it, warming the pot and all the usual shenanigans.

He sat back and looked around the room. Little had changed to the naked eye since Mrs Troubridge had died but there were fewer ornaments with crusty, dusty flowers adorning shepherdesses' heads and the curtains were now hung with the right side in. It was a comfortable room and Maxwell felt at home in it, as well he should as at least half of his son's Hot Wheels collection was in a box to one side of the hearth.

Mrs B batted the door open with a practised hip and put the tray down on the coffee table. She poured the tea out and then settled back with a sigh.

'I'm asking that Gwen Up at the School if I can change my shift, at least for the rest of term. I can't really fancy letting myself in first thing again. I know that there isn't likely to be another body anywhere, but . . .' Her hand shook momentarily and she put down her cup.

'I can quite understand,' Maxwell said. 'She'll change it for you, won't she?'

Mrs B shrugged. 'Dunno. Never sure with her. She's got her favourites and I'm not one, that I do know. The shift's not a popular one, y'see. I like it because I get the rest of the day free. I didn't want to let Her Up at the School know, but she done me a favour when she split all those shifts. I couldn't really get on with things in the afternoon, knowing that I had to be at work at three.'

'Would it help if I had a word?' Maxwell said. He had never had much to do with Gwen Harris, the site manager, beyond knowing where her office was, but it was worth giving it a whirl.

Mrs B screwed up her face, doubtfully. 'I s'pose it's worth a try. I'll send her an email now and see what she says.' She whipped out a phone from her apron pocket and even

Maxwell the dinosaur could see that it was a model so new that any of his Own would give their eyeteeth just to hold it for a moment. He nodded at it.

'Nice.'

'What?' Mrs B looked at the phone in her hand. 'Oh, this? Yes, it's coming out next year. I'm one of the panel, I get to test all the new stuff, iron out the glitches.' She tapped at the screen while she was talking, not even looking down. 'They offered me full time but, well, there was Mr B and then Mrs T of course . . . This suits me, a bit of pocket money and a new phone every few months.'

Maxwell knew she was a tech wizard, completely self-taught, a kind of natural savant, a computer whisperer of some repute, so he wasn't surprised. She put the phone away still without looking at the screen.

'See what she says. She's usually pretty quick to answer, she's always on her computer, that one.' She rolled her eyes. 'Candy Crush, probably, bless her.'

From what he had overheard from his Own, Maxwell knew that this was something of a serious insult.

'So . . . would you like to tell me about finding the body?' he said. 'Get it off your chest?'

Mrs B smiled and shook a finger at him. 'Don't think you can get me to tell you all the gory details,' she said. 'I know your game and also, there *are* no gory details. A bloke from the telly lot was lying in a pool of blood and that's it. I didn't notice no footprints, no handprints, no feathers laid across his lips. No dead flowers, no . . .' Mrs B had exhausted her store of weird things found on bodies.

Maxwell smiled and put down his cup. 'I understand,' he said. 'Sorry, Mrs B. It's just that . . . so near and yet so far, if you see what I mean. I'm never in as early as you, but sometimes I am almost the first through the door, so . . . it could have been me, couldn't it?'

'As the body?' his neighbour said with an ironic grin. 'I don't know how they would manage the list of suspects if it was you. As it is, it's easy, innit? It's one of them telly people.'

'Do you think so?' Maxwell said. 'Surely, though, they're all friends, aren't they?'

'That's who kills you, though, ain't it? Friends? Family? Who would bother, otherwise? The random loony is another risk, I know that, but they're rare compared to your son, your brother, the kid you sat next to in school for fifteen years? They're the ones you've got the dirt on. They're the ones who hate you for that thing you did at their wedding. You mark my words, Mr M. It's one of them telly lot.'

Maxwell couldn't really argue. He had rather hoped it would turn out to be Arnie, but surely even she wouldn't be so dense as to kill someone and leave him bleeding to death all over her favourite carpet? 'I have to agree with you, I'm afraid,' he said. 'This is going to be a bit of an open-and-shut case. As it happens . . .' He leaned forward and she did the same. She loved it when Mr M gossiped — no one else she knew was quite as good at it as he was. 'As it happens, I am spending the morning with them tomorrow. Walking on the beach with Joe Pargeter.'

She laughed. Although her smoking days were long behind her, her laugh still sounded as if she were on sixty Woodbine a day. 'That'll be fun,' she said. 'I hope he's got his wig well stuck down.'

'Wig?' Maxwell fell back in his seat in amazement. 'Joe Pargeter wears a *wig*?'

'It's a good 'un,' Mrs B conceded, 'but it's a wig. Tell you how you can find out. Look at that bit just above the ears. The glue tends to gather there and you'll see it, for sure. One of my, well, let's say *a* Mr B used to wear a wig when he called Bingo on the front, back in the day. Proper idiot he used to look, but apparently the OAP coach tours liked it.' She folded her hands in her lap and looked stern. 'But we don't need details, do we?'

Maxwell decided that, on balance, he probably didn't, so he scooped up his random Hobnob crumbs into his palm, dropped them into his empty cup and stood up to go. 'I promise I'll look for you.'

A ping came from Mrs B's pocket. She looked at her phone and rolled her eyes. 'There you are,' she said. 'That Gwen Up at the School has said no.'

'Not to worry, Mrs B,' he said. 'I'll have a word with her. Umm . . . have you got a piece of paper? Jot it down so I don't forget.'

'Not to worry, Mr M,' she said, brightly. 'I'll send a reminder to your Alexa. She'll not let you forget.'

'Super,' Maxwell said, trying to sound grateful. 'Very . . . helpful. Thank you.' It was either helpful or creepy, but in the interests of domestic harmony, he decided to go with helpful. 'I'll let myself out. Oh, before I go, though, can you send me Gwen's email address, so I can arrange a visit.'

Mrs B humphed. 'With her, best thing is to take her by surprise. I tell you where and when you'll find her. Any break time, in her storeroom. Mind you, there'll be a load of kids in there as well. She lets them go in there, the nerdy ones, to play on their phones, do whatever they do. Funny, because I never had her down for somebody with any feelings for kids, but she seems to have a soft spot for them.'

'That is strange,' Maxwell said. 'I think I need to look into that. It's . . . well, it's not really recommended, that kind of thing.'

'They're only playing on their phones,' his neighbour said, the voice of reason. 'They can get bullied, these kids, if you don't watch out for them.'

'Hmm. Even so . . . any break, you say?'

'Yeah. Breakfast club an' all. You know where her store-room is?'

Maxwell knew every last inch of Leighford High and could find his way with his eyes closed. 'Yes, I know it. Thanks, Mrs B. Now I really am going. Make sure you have a rest, now.'

Mrs B heard him clatter down the stairs and then the distant slam of the door. She leaned back in her chair with a sigh. He was right. She did need a bit of a rest . . .

* * *

A stickler for hierarchy, was Henry Hall. He'd begun at the top — which didn't turn out to be very high after all — with the director. Now he went for his Number Two.

'So, Mr Woodford . . . Bevis?' Hall was a little chary after the whole Ernest confusion.

'Yes, afraid so. My father is a bit of an astronomy nut and named me after John Bevis, an eighteenth-century astronomer.'

Hall nodded. That was one for Maxwell, probably.

'I'm luckier than my brother. He was named after Tycho Brahe.'

There was no arguing with that, so Hall got everything back on track. 'You've been working on the *Fly on the Wall* series for a while now?' he asked.

'It seems like forever,' Woodford told him. 'One of those things that looks great in boardrooms and on storyboards. Not so great in reality.'

Hall was confused. 'But it is a reality show?' he checked.

'Ah, Chief Inspector,' Woodford chuckled. 'There's reality and there's our reality. Have you ever considered what kind of person makes up the average TV audience?'

'Pretty much the same as the average jury, I would think,' Hall said.

'Bingo!' Woodford clapped his hands and the needle on the recorder bounced into the red. 'Sorry. GSCE grade 4, or so the tabloids tell us. That's one up from the studio cat. Oh, audiences love nothing better than a good bit of smut and, begging your pardon, crime. So, if we can find a school where knifings are common, everyone from the Head down snorts cocaine and things go on behind the bike sheds which makes *Love Island* look like *Songs of Praise* . . .'

Hall raised an eyebrow. 'So you naturally thought of Leighford High, a sleepy school in a sleepy town on the South Coast?'

'Well, I grant you the death of poor old Gavin is a shame, but the rest of it promises to be about as exciting as footage of the Forth Bridge. The selection is done by our researchers, based on algorithms, of course.'

'Of course,' Hall said. 'Was it usual for a sound engineer to be working so late at night?'

'I didn't know he was.' Woodford shrugged. 'In my experience, techies do the bare minimum — like teachers, really; my old man included. Bell goes at four o'clock, they're out of there like rats up a pipe. Unless . . .'

'Unless?' That was a word that Henry Hall liked in investigations; it opened up a world of possibilities.

'Unless he was so woefully inept that he'd got behind setting himself up. That school is so bloody boomy. I know he was talking about baffles or something. Or perhaps . . .'

'Perhaps?' There was another good word.

'Perhaps he had other things on his mind.'

* * *

Bevis Woodford had little else that was helpful to tell Hall. His alibi was rock solid — having dinner with Zac Littleton, and he had the receipt to prove it. So he was released back into the wild and Hall had a moment to stretch his legs and nip to the canteen for a quick coffee and a bun.

'Is Jacquie back yet?' Hall asked the desk sergeant, who was having a similar break, the difference in his case being that it was his fourth that day so far.

'Just come in,' he said, round a mouthful of doughnut. 'I wasn't expecting her till this afternoon, according to the roster, but I suppose . . .' he waved the doughnut and a glob of jam missed Hall by a whisker, 'what with her old man working there and all.'

'It wasn't that,' Hall said. 'It was the old dear who found the body. Jacquie's neighbour. It was a kind gesture and I'm afraid I took advantage of her. It's handy, though, her knowing the territory as well as most of the staff. Plus, of course, one of the telly people.'

The desk sergeant looked askance. 'She gets about,' he commented.

'Oh, no, he used to work there. And we've felt his collar in the past as well. This promises to be interesting.' Hall looked over his shoulder. His timing was impeccable. His trusty sergeant had just got to the table with two coffees and a couple of buns. 'Well, I must just grab a quick bite. Let me know at once if anyone comes in with anything.'

The desk sergeant sketched a salute. 'Will do.' Hall decided not to tell him about the sugar he had just applied to his own eyebrow.

* * *

As Henry Hall had hoped, DI Carpenter-Maxwell was waiting for him in his office and the DS gratefully scuttled off to his desk down the corridor. He had better things to do than interview these stuck-up telly lot, although it was a disappointment not to see that Joe Pargeter, who his wife had rather fancied on the telly for years.

'Anything interesting from . . . ?' Hall shuffled his papers.

'Mel,' Jacquie said. 'It was the typical thing. She and Masters had had a one-night stand . . . no, not even that, just a quickie in the gents' the other night, and so she was embarrassed more than anything, I think. She hadn't told anyone, but these people aren't stupid. They make a living by watching out for human behaviour and there's no one looks more guilty than two people who have been having nookie on the sly. Especially when it's all over bar the shouting during the ad break on any of the cheaper TV channels.'

'Well, that's odd, then, because she was supposed to be helping Gavin that evening, sorting out boom or something. Baffles were mentioned but is that just how I am beginning to feel?'

'She didn't mention that to me, but there again,' Jacquie said, 'it's probably all down to embarrassment. Working late in an empty school with someone you have had ill-advised sex with . . . that's not going to be easy on any level. Unless they carried on where they left off — I don't see it, myself.'

'You're thinking she had some kind of revenge thing going, then? Felt he had used her, perhaps.'

'She isn't as young and innocent as she looks. She lied about her age and dresses young on purpose, because she says the directors and that level staff don't like working with people older than they are. I think she has probably overemphasised that, but then again, I suppose she should know. It was just a drunken thing, a mistake on both their parts which they would rather forget.'

'We won't mention it in the rest of the interviews. See if anyone noticed, feels it's worth commenting on,' Hall said. 'Shall we have the next one in? Have you managed to grab a drink?'

Jacquie pointed to a bottle on the table.

Hall had never really come to love bottled water, especially carried around all day like a pet, but just nodded and pressed a buzzer on his phone. The door opened and a constable ushered the next member of the team in. Hall had decided to reverse his hierarchy rule and was saving the star turn until last.

'Danny, is it?' He sensed that the young man sitting in front of him needed a bit of TLC. Somebody had told the lad that the only way to become Director General of the BBC was to start at the bottom. So here he was, the youngest and greenest of the runners, those put-upon dogsbodies who kept the cogs of television running smoothly.

'That's right,' the lad said. Hall had shirts older than this boy, but he didn't let that detract from the job in hand.

'How long have you been with Fly On The Wall?'

'FOTWL.'

'I'm sorry. Fotwool?'

'No, I'm sorry,' Danny grinned. 'In television, we use initials all the time and eventually, we stop spelling things out and say it like a word. It's eff oh tee double-you, ell for limited. FOTWL.'

Hall sensed that the boy was a piece of toilet paper away from the gibberish that teenagers used in their online and actual casual conversation. 'Did you answer the question?'

'Er . . . no, sorry. Eighteen months,' Danny said. To be brutally honest, Danny Erskine wasn't cut out for television. People with panache, fake tans and attitude bothered him and television was full of people like that. The cougars who manned the front desks, whether they were presenters or telephonists, scared the bejesus out of him. And he wasn't at all happy about this interview either. Henry Hall looked like a battleship out of one of those grainy black-and-white faux documentaries Danny had once made tea for. Little children, which included Danny that morning, were afraid of him. Even the nice DI looked threatening. Then, there was the tape recorder, its innards whirring silently, condemning Danny to God-knew-what should any of this come to court.

'How well did you know the deceased?' Hall asked.

'Er . . . I didn't,' Danny said. 'I just got his coffee.'

'Once or on a regular basis?' Hall pursued it.

'I wasn't really supposed to take coffee to anyone but Zac and Bevis and Mr Pargeter. And that chap that is usually with Mr Pargeter — I don't know quite who he is, but they seem close.'

Jacquie smothered a smile. Henry Hall rarely smiled so he had nothing to smother, but even so he did find it amusing. Poor Bernard Ryan would be mortified to be demoted to 'that chap usually with Joe Pargeter'.

'So, how often?'

'Um . . . twice, I think.'

'You think?' Henry Hall wasn't a vindictive person, but he was thorough. Vague answers bothered him and he knew that defence counsel drove horses and coaches through such waffle. 'I know you think that this is just so much box-ticking, but we mustn't forget a man is dead.'

'I'm certain,' Danny said, proving that he had inner steel after all. 'Twice. Because the third time . . .'

'Yes?' Hall and Jacquie looked up in unison, a foretaste of the future if the CID ever became AI.

'He bawled me out.' Danny looked worried, but whether because of the bawling out or the revenge killing it might have led to was difficult to say.

'Why?' Jacquie asked. It was true that instant coffee made on the fly was unlikely to be delicious, but having seen the team dynamic up close, she couldn't imagine that Gavin Masters had been in a position to bawl out anyone.

'It was cold, he said. He lost his rag and shouted at me.'

'When was this?' Hall wanted to know.

'Um . . . yesterday afternoon.'

'Where were you?' Jacquie asked, knowing she would be able to place the scene in her head.

'Well, I made coffee in the staffroom.'

'That must have been popular,' Jacquie said, 'with the teachers, I mean.'

Danny looked bewildered. He had been so busy that he hadn't really taken any notice of anyone else being there. So, those muttering people who kept trying to elbow him out of the way were teachers, were they? That explained it.

'In the middle of making it, Mr Pargeter wanted something and I had to break off. By the time I got back and handed the coffees round, yeah, it was probably cold. But he didn't have to be quite so unpleasant.'

'How unpleasant, exactly?' A details man, was Henry Hall, through and through.

'He said — can I say this on tape?'

'You can say anything you like,' Jacquie said kindly, 'as long as it's the truth.'

Danny took a deep breath. Another reason he would get nowhere in television was his innate dislike of bad language. 'He said, "This is fucking cold, you useless shit. Go and make me another one."'

'Where were you at the time?'

'In the corridor outside the headteacher's office. He was wiring up, checking his levels. To be fair, that place is a pig to mic. All kinds of odd corners, the levels are all over the place, they say. But also to be fair to me, the man was an arse.'

'And did you?' Hall asked. 'Make him a new one, I mean.'

'I wanted to *rip* him a new one!' Danny blurted out, then he saw the expressions on his interrogators' faces and

105

wished he hadn't said that. And all the time, that damned tape recorder was humming away.

* * *

As takeover bids went, it was subtle and cunning. There had been a time when only Count Metternich, black, white and homicidal, had padded silently up the stairs to Maxwell's secret lair under the eaves at 38 Columbine. Now, Bismarck, the iron predator, had joined him. They lay curled up on the sofa, cheek by jowl, comparing notes of former rodent and bird kills like two old serial killers doing time; Henry Lee Lucas meets Jeffrey Dahmer.

For more years than he cared to remember, this had been Maxwell's bolthole. Nolan was allowed there, under strict supervision, and Jacquie had long ago given up visiting rights because of the risk of an ill-judged movement causing unimaginable chaos. On the long table in the centre of the room, under the skylight, Lord Cardigan's Light Brigade, in all their 54 mm plastic glory, sat patiently, waiting for the off. Maxwell had all but bankrupted himself many times over buying these figures that came in tiny pieces and plastic packs. Technically, they were Napoleonic cavalrymen, but the master adapter, with a hint of gravura and gallons of Humbrol, could easily leap forward a few decades to the October of 1854.

The soldier in question today, to add to the 549 he had already assembled, was Troop Sergeant Charles Wooden of the 17th Lancers. The man was actually German, which would have confused the hell out of anybody but Maxwell, and his English wasn't very good. His favourite exclamation, especially when he'd had a few, was 'Tish Me — the Devil'. It had started back in England when the sergeant, then a mere corporal, had staggered back to barracks one night and been challenged by a sentry. 'Tish me — the Devil' was the answer he gave and it sort of stuck. Once Maxwell had fixed the man's lance cap in place and painted the stripes on his sleeve, Wooden would go on to help save the life of Captain

Morris of his regiment and win the VC. Whenever Maxwell was working on his diorama, he wore the soft cloth forage cap he'd bought in a junk shop years ago, before militaria collecting became the playground of the super-rich. His Lear jet and stretch limo, of course, he kept elsewhere.

Then, the phone rang.

'War Office,' he murmured, with a tube of modeller's glue open and glistening in front of him.

* * *

Thingee Two was in the office from lunchtime in solitary splendour. Most of the staff turned away that morning had assumed that the crime-scene status would last over the weekend and after all, Thingee Two told herself, grumpily, as well as all her 'friends' on Facebook and her followers on X, Insta, TikTok and all the other rather niche platforms she lived on and for, they are blooming teachers, after all. They're supposed to be clever, IRL as well as at work. She had lots of laughing emojis at that as well as a rather acerbic message for her to call HR at her earliest convenience. Whatevah. But that blooming Ms Preddie had made her come in and ring everyone over the course of the afternoon — 'Put in your usual hours, please,' the woman had said rather snappily on the phone — and make sure they knew not to come back until Monday. She was to ring Mr Roberts and Mrs Proctor and tell *them* to be there first thing on Friday, to turn away stragglers and watch out for press trying to weasel their way in. Mrs Proctor, she knew, would be up for that. Mr Roberts, not so much. She had a horrible feeling sometimes, when talking to Mr Roberts that one of these days his head was going to come right off. She hoped the rumour about him and Ms Preddie wasn't true, poor little chap. He was annoying, but no one deserved that.

She had rung them first and got that over, now she was going through the staff in alphabetical order. She had rung the Head of History, Miss Allington, and *ever* such a nice man answered the phone, with a lovely voice. He said she was out but he would pass on the message. She wasn't sure whether to tick the box to show *she* had passed on the message, but he sounded very reliable. Most of the rest answered their phones themselves, pleased to be at home in the warm when they should have been at school. Lucky them, she moaned to herself. The school was a scary place when you were there by yourself.

She had saved one name for last, out of alphabetical order. It was a funny number, it didn't start with 07 like everyone else, it started 01273. She dialled it and found it was right, it was ringing. After a couple of chirps, it was picked up.

'War Office.'

'Oh, pardon me,' Thingee Two said, blushing all by herself in reception. She *knew* there was something wrong with that number. 'I must have dialled . . .'

'No, no, Thingee Old Chap. As long as you were ringing Mr Maxwell, you've done it perfectly. Sorry for the greeting — thought it was my wife. How can I help you?'

'I have to ring everyone and tell them not to come in tomorrow, because this is still a crime scene.' She went quiet. 'I asked Ms Preddie if I could do this from home, Mr Maxwell, because that room is right behind me and . . . I expect there's blood and everything, is there? Do you think?'

Maxwell heaped a silent imprecation on Arnie's head. 'I doubt it, Thingee, dear old thing. There's a rug in there, isn't there? So I expect they've taken it away. So, no blood.'

'But even so . . .'

'I know.' Maxwell's voice could calm a volcano. 'Have you finished now? Am I the last?'

'Yes. I . . . I saved you till last.'

'May I ask why?'

'Because . . . well, you never answer your phone. And I didn't know what the funny number was. It's a landline, though, isn't it? Silly, I should have known, but I'm a bit stressed out, Mr Maxwell.'

'Of course, you are. If I'm the last, go home now.'

'But Ms Preddie . . .'

'I'll deal with Ms Preddie,' Maxwell added the woman to the list headed by Gwen Harris. 'if it comes to that, and I'm sure it won't. But as it happens, I've had a text from the film company that we're meeting at the school tomorrow morning, so I might see her then.'

'Mrs Proctor and Mr Roberts are going to be there,' Thingee told him, 'to make sure no one tries to get in.' She tried to deal with the idea of Maxwell receiving a text and actually couldn't do it. She and everyone else knew he was a total dinosaur.

Like the receptionist, Maxwell struggled to imagine Bob Roberts stopping anyone even slightly enthusiastic from going anywhere, but if Mandy was there, no one stood a chance. She was Horatius, Herminius and the other guy whose name nobody could remember, standing on the bridge into Rome in the brave days of old.

'Well, even so, I have to be there, so that's all fine. Go home, now, there's a good Thingee, and I'll see you on Monday.'

'Thank you, Mr Maxwell,' the girl said, taking off her headphones as the phone went dead at the War Office. Without looking behind her, she groped for her coat and skedaddled out of the door, not forgetting to reset the alarm by randomising the numbers. She shuddered and not just because of the cold. You really couldn't be too careful.

* * *

Jacquie and Henry had worked all over lunch and had polished off the tech team in between bites of sandwich. No one had known Gavin Masters very well, but what they had known about him, they didn't like very much. It was the story as before in many respects; hardly anyone loved by all gets killed with a single stab wound to the chest. Work was still ongoing to find out his home address and it was proving to be unusually difficult. The address he had given on his application to the agency was years out of date. Checking with the DVLA had come up with a different address but also one where no one knew him. But he wasn't staying with the others in the Travhotel so he had to be living somewhere. Henry had made a preliminary call to the local TV and radio stations, pending a small segment in the local news that evening. They had the picture from his ID, he assured them, it wouldn't be anything gory.

And now it was time for Joe Pargeter.

CHAPTER EIGHT

'Should I have my lawyer present?' Joe Pargeter wanted to know. 'God knows, he doesn't do much for the amount I pay him as a retainer, so perhaps it's time he earned his crust.'

'Do you feel you need a lawyer, Mr Pargeter?' Hall asked. Television presenters like the man in front of him got right up Henry Hall's nose. He was fake from head to toe, the carefully groomed hair swept back with just the right amount of grey at the temples, probably to hide the glue. He wasn't conventionally good-looking but the teeth alone could have won all sorts of awards and he made great play of the dimple in his left cheek. The Chief Inspector was secretly delighted to see so much dandruff on the man's collar and shoulders and was mildly surprised that he hadn't brought his make-up team in with him.

'In my business,' Pargeter smiled, giving the law the full celebrity schtick, 'you've no idea how bitchy — and litigious — people can be. It's all come over from the West Coast, of course. When I started out, there was still a modicum of civility.'

Hall smiled in turn, only Jacquie knowing just how rare that was. 'I didn't have you down for a traditionalist, Mr Pargeter,' he said.

'Joe, please. Don't let Bernie hear you say that; part of his puff when he goes out as my agent is that I am down wid da kids. Although I have yet to hear him say that phrase, it's what he aims for. I started a bit later than many at the celebrity thing so we have some time to make up. Before I'm too old. Bernie says—'

'Bernie?' Hall knew perfectly well who he meant, but it amused him, as much as anything did, to make him explain.

'My husband,' Pargeter said, 'who is, of course, also my agent. Keep the 15 per cent plus VAT in the family, I say.'

'That would be Bernard Ryan,' Hall checked, 'formerly of this parish?'

'That's another traditional phrase I like. Yes, Bernie used to work here as a teacher — I suspect that was the link that gave us the location in the first place. He reached out to Jim Diamond at County Hall, apparently.' He beamed at Jacquie. 'And your husband as well, as I understand it.'

Jacquie smiled and wondered what James Diamond would think of being called Jim. Somehow, it just wasn't him. Legs, yes. Jim, definitely not.

Hall got Pargeter away from his trip down Memory Lane. 'Had you worked with Gavin Masters before?'

'Probably.' Pargeter crossed one leg over the other, tweaking his perfectly pressed and tailored jeans as he did so. He leaned back in the chair and gave Jacquie the benefit of his best side. 'To be honest, one techie is very much like another. I judge them by their efficiency. If I don't know they're there, they're doing a good job.'

'And you didn't know Masters was there?'

'Well, you have to realise, Chief Inspector, that we haven't actually started filming yet. I believe Masters was the sound man in that airport series I did. *Fly Me to the Moon*, it was called. You saw that, I'm sure. It was highly acclaimed. All sorts of awards.'

'Er . . . no,' Hall said. 'Had you spoken to him on this particular set?'

'No. The presenter usually arrives when everything else is in place. I'd had preliminary meetings with Zac and Bevis, of course, courtesy of Bernie. But the nuts and bolts . . . well, I have people for that.'

'Yes, of course,' Hall said. 'And Gavin Masters was just one such nut and bolt, was he? One of your people?'

Pargeter's smile faded and he leaned forward. 'If you're trying to make me feel somehow guilty about all this, Chief Inspector, I'm afraid you're wasting your time. With all due respect to my hubby — whose lair this hellhole used to be — I suspect that the solution to your murder will be found squarely in Leighford High School. My people had nothing to do with it.'

After that, there seemed little to do but ask the man to pop back later to sign the transcript of his statement. He left without a backward glance and as the door swung to, Hall turned to Jacquie.

'Well, he wasn't very nice, was he?' Jacquie said. 'I feel a bit sorry for Bernard, although he wasn't exactly a teddy bear when he was at Leighford High. It was more or less his life's work to get rid of Max, at any rate.'

Although Hall had become grudgingly fond of Maxwell, he could see Bernard Ryan's point. He stretched and yawned. 'He was the last, wasn't he, please God?'

Jacquie consulted her list. 'Strictly speaking, no. There's Bernard still to go and I suppose we really ought to speak to James Diamond, as he is liaison with the team and the school.'

Hall shook his head and got up. 'Nope. I'm done. I don't think that Bernard Ryan or James Diamond has the remotest idea who Gavin Masters was, any more than most of his colleagues. Just give them the usual warning — don't leave town without letting us know and let them go about their business. We'll keep the school shut tomorrow, just to put a spoke in their wheels, really. They are an objectionable crowd, possibly the worst I have seen, en masse. If you could just give . . . Mel, is it?'

Jacquie nodded.

'Give Mel a ring and check on exactly what the plans for last night were and why they changed, if they changed, and then I think we can go and get on with whatever we had planned before all this hit the fan, don't you?'

Jacquie nodded. She was in the middle of collating evidence from several other cases and although it wasn't riveting work, it beat having to deal with FOTWL by a country mile.

* * *

'But was he wearing a wig, though?' Maxwell asked. He had heard all the rest, now he needed to know about the important stuff.

'A wig?' Jacquie almost choked on her gin and tonic. 'Why do you ask?'

'Mrs B thinks that he wears a wig.'

'Do wigs have dandruff?'

'I don't have much experience, but I'm guessing not.'

'In that case, he doesn't wear a wig.'

'Hmm. Right.' Maxwell sipped his Southern Comfort. These evening mulls were something that the Maxwells had down to a fine art. A drink each. A bowl of crisps for her, nuts for him, a few triangles of Toblerone if the day had been particularly dire. And a nice unburden and a laugh. Always a laugh.

'I'll just text Mrs B,' Jacquie said, reaching for her phone.

'Why?'

'Well . . . so she knows.'

'This is it, though, isn't it? It's what we're trying to teach the kids. You don't have to communicate all the time. You can communicate when you see the person next. You can write them a note and stick it through the door or — for what it would be worth — into the post. You don't have to text and email as soon as it occurs to you. She won't lose any sleep not knowing whether Joe Pargeter wears a wig or not.'

Jacquie looked at him for a long minute and then put the phone down. 'You're right. But you can be sure she'll be on the doorstep as soon as you get home tomorrow, wanting to know.'

'And that would be lovely. We can have a cuppa, a chin-wag. She can get me up to speed on Gwen Harris and her strange ways — come to think of it, isn't that a prison somewhere?'

'Gwenharris Prison? Possibly somewhere in Scotland.'

Maxwell just raised an eyebrow and continued, 'She lets some of the geek squad lurk in the storeroom in breaks, apparently. I can't think why she would do that, it goes against almost every rule in the book, written or unwritten.'

'Perhaps she likes children,' Jacquie said.

'I'm assuming you've never met Gwen,' Maxwell said and Jacquie shook her head. 'She doesn't like anyone. If you have fingers to leave marks, feet to wear shoes which by defi-nition are muddy, you need to pee once in a while — these and a million other sins will have you on Gwen's naughty list. Anyway, I'm going to check it all out on Monday — without phones to be glued to in there, perhaps they won't bother. But . . . Anyhoo. How was the rest of your day?'

'Dull. But at least it didn't have Joe Pargeter in it. I had always had the impression that he and Bernard were a sort of couple made in heaven, two lost souls finding each other in a naughty world, that kind of thing. But in fact — well, to coin a phrase, the man's a dick.'

'A murderous dick?' Maxwell asked.

Jacquie sighed. 'Sadly, no, I don't think so. We just can't get a handle on the dead man at all, although I know Henry was putting out media feelers tonight to see if we can track him down. And until we do, we can't work out why anyone would want to kill him. It seemed quite premeditated. No one stabs someone as cleanly and accurately as that without having brought a weapon with them. Arnie has checked her office and nothing is missing, no letter opener, that kind of thing, so . . .'

'I don't expect even Arnie has a set of stilettos in her desk drawer,' Maxwell conceded, a little unwillingly. 'A Glock 9 mil, probably, but not knives. I'm sure this will get wrapped up soon, though. It seems such a *simple* crime, no frills.'

'No,' Jacquie agreed. 'No frills at all. Not even a home address. But we'll get there, I'm sure. Now, then, what will you be chatting about with Joe tomorrow?'

'I'd like to discuss something that would show up his dickishness, but I doubt that will be in the script. Which reminds me, do you know where my wellies are? Apparently, we are starting with a walk on the beach.'

Jacquie put down her empty glass and got up. 'In that case, I'll fish out your warm undies. It'll be a bit chilly round the headland.'

'Nothing too thick,' Maxwell said to her retreating back, then added to the cat stretched out at his feet, 'they say the camera adds ten pounds.'

* * *

That Friday morning, the curtains of 38 Columbine twitched as Maxwell made his way out to the waiting car. It wasn't a stretch limo as such, but it was enormous and the driver deserved a round of applause when he made the three-point turn at the end of the close with consummate style. The car already held Zac, Bevis and Joe; Bernard was apparently still held up back at their hotel, finalising an advert filming in Bangkok for after Easter. He sent his apologies and a threat to catch up with Maxwell later. James Diamond was meeting them at the school. Maxwell was distracted through all the detail but as they drove through a patch of weak winter sunshine, he had his answer. Dandruff and a wig; a good wig, to be sure, covering only the very top of Pargeter's head, but in the brighter light the difference in texture was unmistakeable. Maxwell smiled to himself; Mrs B would be so pleased.

Zac passed Maxwell his iPad and asked him to have a look at the questions that Joe would be asking. The trick, he said, was to mention the question in the reply, because this was meant to be a chat and not a question-and-answer session. Maxwell took the tablet gingerly — the last time he had used anything similar, he had brushed his sleeve on the screen and everything had disappeared. He'd probably also started World War Three. This time, however, the technology behaved but the questions were so stultifyingly dull that he suspected that the scene would end with one or the other of them dashing his brains out on a rock, just to make things a bit more interesting.

Maxwell speed-read to the bottom and then looked up. 'I don't think this is going to work, Zac,' he said. 'No offence, but how can we possibly take these questions seriously? For instance, "What made you become a teacher?"'

'Fair enough, surely?' Bevis — who had actually written the questions — said huffily.

'It's a fair question, yes,' Maxwell agreed. 'But it's no good when the answer is, "Because I had a History degree and no one told me when I began that it would mean I could become a member of the civil service or a teacher. If they had, then perhaps I would have opted for something more useful. Like plumbing."'

'I don't see you as a plumber, somehow, Mr Maxwell,' Zac put in, smiling. He knew the questions were rubbish but Bevis had whined so much he had let him write them.

'You don't see plumbers at all,' Maxwell said, 'which is why I chose it. They must all be millionaires if they are as busy as they claim.' He scrolled down and kept shaking his head. 'Look, here's an idea. Why don't Joe and I just walk along the beach and I will tell him a bit about the history of this bit of coast? About shipwrecks and mutinies. Smuggling. That's what I do in my lessons, after all. Who can teach the economics of the Weimar Republic without adding in a bit of *Cabaret*-style ooh-la-la to keep the little dears on side?'

Joe Pargeter had also seen the questions and had had the same reservations. But he had to remind this upstart who was the star around here. 'That sounds like a good idea . . . umm, Bernie says that you like to be called Max. Is that okay?'

Maxwell had been warned about the 'Bernie' thing, so didn't flinch. The 'okay' didn't surprise him either. 'Fine, yes, fire away.'

'So, Zac, Max has a good idea, there. But I do need to . . . how shall I put it? I do need to come across as the *intelligent* one here. I don't want it to sound as though I am having to be told everything because I don't know it.'

Maxwell raised an eyebrow. '*Do* you know it?' he said.

Pargeter bridled. 'I know much of it, I'm sure,' he said. 'I was very interested in smuggling, when I was a boy. "Watch the wall, my darling," that kind of thing. I love poetry too. Can't beat G.K. Chesterton.'

Bevis chewed his lip and looked out of the window.

'Indeed not. Nor Kipling, of course,' Maxwell said. 'I didn't mean to make it sound as if I would be *teaching* you anything, Joe,' he said, taking the temperature down a notch. 'If you follow my lead, I think you will find you can carry your weight. So, what do you think, gents? Shall we wing it?'

Zac and Bevis looked at each other, then at Maxwell. They nodded in unison. 'Why not?' Zac said. 'We can always go to the script if it isn't working. Joe?'

Pargeter looked peeved. 'I spent hours last night learning those questions,' he said, sniffily.

'Well,' Zac leaned forward and patted his knee. 'Come in handy, later, perhaps. Oh, look. We're here. A few placing shots, I think, then off to the beach.'

A fragment of the whole team was waiting for them, stamping their feet in the cold. Mel, recovered from her hysteria, was in charge of sound, and the cameraman this morning was Reg. Like everyone else, or so it seemed, that wasn't his actual name but he was a fan of Elton John with a rather unusual and quirky sense of humour. He hefted his camera on his shoulder and Mel gave her hamster-on-a-stick a final comb-out with her fingers.

'Hi, guys,' Bevis said, with scant regard for gender. 'Just a few shots here; we might not need sound, Mel, but perhaps if you just do it anyway, in case . . . we . . .' He faltered and stopped. 'Who are they?'

The three of them spread across Leighford High's drive like something out of Bruce Springsteen meets the Earps.

Or was that just Peter Maxwell's take on it all? Duster coats to the ground looked great in Arizona or Wyoming — not so much on the South Coast of England as winter grudgingly gave way to spring. Each of them carried a brass-headed cane which Darcy in particular was quite good at handling. George's bandana streamed out on the nasty little northerly that was whipping round the corner of the building. Only William looked slightly awkward; he didn't really have the shoulders for a duster coat. In fact, in certain lights, an actual duster would have been a stretch.

Unfortunately for them, Peter Maxwell was ready for them. 'Let me stop you there, amigos,' he said. It was an impeccable Clint Eastwood but the three sixth formers in front of him didn't know who Clint Eastwood was, still less what he sounded like. 'School's closed, I'm afraid.'

'What, *still?*' George's bandana streamed no more, but hung limply from his neck, in lieu of the school tie of yesteryear.

What is it about Year Twelve? Maxwell asked himself in his head. It was a question that crossed his mind several times a day, along with, *Why am I still in this job?* 'It has only been twenty-four hours, George,' he said, 'Didn't you get the memo?' He quoted, 'The school will be closed until further notice.'

'We thought that was for the hoi polloi,' Darcy said. If Maxwell had had the time, he would have made an in-depth study of Darcy Quincy. Not only did he have the most ridiculous name since James Fenimore Cooper's Natty Bumppo — or was it the other way around? — but the boy was also such a public-school stereotype that Maxwell could not believe that he was toiling at what used to be the chalkface at a humble comprehensive like Leighford High. True to form, he always played aristo parts in school shows. He was pharaoh in *Joseph*, Herod in *Superstar* and Richard the Lionheart in *Blondel*; and he could never understand why he'd never got the email of congratulation from Sir Tim Rice. It must have got lost somewhere along the internet highway.

'I thought they'd have sorted it out,' Darcy said. 'Whatever it is that Ms Preddie couldn't talk about.'

There was a lot that Ms Preddie couldn't talk about, like anything historical or literature-based, but Maxwell wasn't about to discuss the headmistress's shortcomings with an entitled layabout of seventeen. 'And I can't either,' Maxwell smiled, knowing exactly where Darcy hoped the conversations would go. 'For the record, we will be open on Monday, so stand by your phones, iPads, tablets, carrier pigeons, whatever you young people use that passes for communication, and we can go from there. Although, having mentioned all that, don't forget they are all banned from the premises as of now — except your pigeons, of course, assuming they are emotional support pigeons.'

'Aw, can't you tell us, sir?' William was at his most wheedling.

'My lips are sealed, Will,' the Head of Sixth Form said, 'but I have to tell you, gentlemen, that what is due to happen is a documentary, showing the school as it really is on an everyday basis. It's not your moment in the sun and, with respect, William,' he hauled the Driza-Bone onto his shoulder, 'I don't fancy your chances on the casting couch. When school *is* resumed, I trust you'll have left the costumes at home and appear — shudder, scream — as you really are.'

And, deflated, the three amigos wandered away, almost certainly to make a grand entrance in the Starbucks down the road.

* * *

The trip to the beach was less palatial as it seemed easier to all pile into the minibus than take both vehicles. The cameraman was muttering to Mel and she gave a chuckle.

'What?' Joe Pargeter snapped. 'Don't whisper. It's rude.'

'Not when it's just tech stuff,' Reg said. 'But of course, if you know the answer to how we're going to get the sound in this wind walking along a beach and how you're going to manage your . . . appearance . . . in self-same wind, then we're all ears.' Reg had worked with the greats, Reg had.

This tuppenny-ha'penny upstart from a digital news channel meant nothing to him. Besides, Reg already had his next gig booked, so he didn't really care.

'Of course I don't know anything *technical*,' Pargeter said, as if technical was a synonym for cleaning sewers. 'I was merely pointing out that with a guest present, it would be polite to not whisper.'

'Oh, don't you worry about me,' Maxwell said. 'There's no such thing as a whisper to a teacher. We can hear pins drop in another building — another town — if it is likely to disrupt a class.' He smiled at Reg and Mel who paled significantly. 'And technical stuff is always so dull to everyone else, isn't it?'

They nodded, their heads seeming to be on strings.

'Do you have any particular part of the beach in mind?' Maxwell asked Zac.

'We thought we'd concentrate on the eastern arm of the bay, starting where the shops end on the esplanade. Then we can just walk back not filming and go and have some coffee. I've had a chat with a couple of independents who won't mind all of us crowding in. It will be good publicity down the road, but they'll lose trade today.'

'Which independents, do you mind my asking? Only the Chocolate Teapot . . . not a good idea.'

'Any particular reason?' Zac might have known; his favourite choice about to go up in flames.

'You know how some people say that currants remind them of dead flies?'

'Yes.'

'I'm sure I don't have to draw you a picture.' Maxwell looked at Zac from under lowered brows.

'Oh, no, then,' Joe Pargeter quickly jumped in. 'No, no, no. I have to take *extreme* care of my digestion. *Extreme* care.'

'Yes, we get it,' Zac muttered. 'Okay, then. We'll be eating at the Merrie Muffin.' He looked startled. 'Does that sound rude to you?'

Everyone shook their heads but Zac wasn't sure.

'I think we'll avoid the name over the door, Reg, if that works. And, Max, anything about the beach we should know?'

Maxwell knew he was being ironic, but answered seriously all the same.

'There's quite a bit of gault. They call it "blue slipper" in some places. It's kind of a gummy blue rock that looks solid until you step on it and then it is just like putty.' He glanced down to Pargeter's immaculate shoes. 'You'll need something else on your feet, Joe, or say goodbye to a couple of hundred pounds worth of bespoke bootery.'

Pargeter looked big-eyed at Bevis, who sighed. 'I've got something in the wardrobe trunk, I expect. What size are you, Joe?'

'I'm a ten and a half. *Extremely* narrow.'

'You'll have to wear some socks, I expect but . . . anything else, Max?'

'No. I suppose you checked the tide?'

'Oh, bugger.' Bevis fell back in his seat, eyes closed. 'I hate the bloody seaside.'

* * *

The minibus driver pulled into a coach space, which was not forbidden in the off season, and everyone tumbled out. The place was mercifully free of the Gauleiters who called themselves Traffic Wardens and everybody breathed easier. Bevis tried not to look at the sea. Finally, he bit the bullet and turned around.

'Oh, thank the Lord! The bloody water's out.'

Maxwell looked with a practised eye. 'It's on the turn,' he said, 'but that's a good thing. It means we will have a nice wide band of dryish sand near the top of the beach and with good luck we'll have plenty of time to film this little bit. Not too many rocks in that band either, so hopefully, not too much gault . . .' Joe Pargeter had already forgotten what that was and looked blank. 'Blue sticky stuff,' Maxwell continued, 'so we should have a nice walk and a chat.' He jammed his hat down further on his head and turned up the collar of his winter coat.

'No, no, no.' Zac came round the back of the minibus. 'Lose the hat.'

'But . . . it's my signature look,' Maxwell complained.

'I was going to talk to you about that,' Zac said. 'We need to lose the hat, the jacket, the cycle clips. We're getting someone in to see about the hair . . . there was something else as well, but I can't remember. Never mind . . .'

'So, is Joe Pargeter getting rid of his wig?' Maxwell hissed. 'And the dandruff?'

'Sssshhhh,' Zac said, shaking his head. 'He's sensitive. Look, Max, if you just lose the hat, we'll manage without changing the rest.'

Maxwell set his lips and very reluctantly removed the hat. He agreed, actually; in this wind it would almost certainly have blown away.

Zac talked them through the walk. He wouldn't be joining them, he said. He had calls to make. He'd see them in the Merrie Muffin later. Maxwell was unconvinced. He thought, correctly, that Zac Littleton and the Great Outdoors had as little as humanly possible to do with each other. The tan came out of a bottle, not from the sun, that was obvious. The rest of them gathered at the top of the steps leading to the beach, all now in wellingtons, which Joe managed to convey were almost painful to a sensitive soul like him; They made him walk like a penguin doing a take-off of a camel, but hopefully with clever camera angles from Reg, no one would ever know.

They lined up carefully, Reg letting Bevis look through the viewfinder to make sure that there was nothing unwholesome or overtly advertisery in the background, and they were off. It was far from ideal weather for filming. The wind wasn't blowing evenly but came in gusts, which when they were in full flow played merry Hamlet with the mics. Maxwell had always prided himself on his diction, but he had no faith at all in that giant grey hamster that hovered over his head. And, of course, the cameraman was walking backwards, Ginger Rogers-style, which didn't inspire confidence either. Not for the first or last time did the Head of Sixth Form realise why he had not chosen the career path of Tinseltown.

'So, Max,' Joe Pargeter had his professional presenter face on, his collar turned up just so, his hair glued particularly carefully to his head. 'Here we are on Leighford Beach. What am I looking at? What happened here in our nation's past?'

Maxwell wanted to say 'Bugger all' but he knew perfectly well that that would engender a 'Cut!' from Bevis, who was walking sideways just a threat ahead of them, in a kind of crouched crab-like gait to be out of the line of the camera. He had almost cannoned into Mel once already, but she had cat-like reflexes and managed to avoid him while keeping the hamster at exactly the right place overhead. Maxwell could sense that Pargeter, although like him walking forward on firm ground, was rather on edge as it was, increasingly out of his comfort zone. So 'Bugger all' was definitely out.

'Not a lot here, I'm afraid. But out there,' he swung his right arm out to sea and slightly behind him, 'on a clear day, you can see Palmerston's follies.'

Pargeter hoped that wasn't the punchline to a filthy joke and he seized the moment. 'Ah, yes, Lord Palmerston. Can you fill us in?'

Maxwell had no idea what the front man's hourly rate was, but he knew it was considerably higher than his, viz and to wit, zero, nada, but then he'd been teaching history to herberts for next to nothing for years now, so there was nothing new in that.

'The French were threatening,' Maxwell said. He felt he could tell it like it was now that they'd left the EU, 'in the 1850s and Lord Palmerston — as you rightly call him, Joe — was Foreign Secretary. He pushed the idea of state-of-the-art forts out at sea to deter an invasion. They extend all the way along to the Solent.'

'So, this is a pretty dangerous part of the coast? Shipwrecks, smugglers, that sort of thing.'

'Undoubtedly, yes. With navigation a pretty hit-and-miss affair, ships ran aground from time to time. Wind, fog, all part of the "sailor beware" sort of life. As for smuggling, that was a way of life too. Everybody was in on it, from the squire and the parson to the poorest fisherman. And nobody, except the government, saw it as a crime, a bit like parking on double yellow lines today . . .'

'Cut!'

Maxwell smiled. He thought Bevis had been quiet for a while.

Eventually, when it was obvious that the cold was starting to turn odd bits of the presenters a delicate shade of blue, Bevis called it a day. It was a relief to walk in the opposite direction, so the little lazy wind cut through them from the opposite side.

Maxwell fell into step with Mel, who bridled slightly when he said hello. As a sound engineer, she was so used to being invisible that it always came as a bit of a shock when someone noticed her.

'I'm sorry about your friend,' Maxwell said, driving his hands deep into his pockets for warmth.

'Who?' Mel looked at him sidelong.

'The victim. Um, Gavin, was it?'

'I suppose your missus told you all about us,' Mel said shortly, reining in her hamster which threatened to blow away.

'Good heavens, no,' Maxwell said, feigning shock. 'She can't discuss things with me. I am just a civilian, after all.'

Mel wasn't the brightest apple in the barrel when it came to judging men, as her chequered love life could attest, but she knew that this geezer was lying through his teeth. Still, he seemed pleasant enough and she liked his wife, so she gave him a bit of extraneous information, just to make his morning less boring. Because could there be anything more boring than being pompoused at by Joe Pargeter. 'I should have been there, you know. The night he died.'

'Really?' Maxwell was genuinely surprised.

'Yeah. He said we had to finish the job, make some last-minute adjustments. I knew he just wanted another . . . well, you know . . . and I wasn't keen, but he was my boss as far as hierarchy went in this crowd, so I said I'd go.'

'But you didn't,' Maxwell said. 'Good for you.'

'That's kind of you, thanks, but I wasn't being all feminist and MeToo. I would've gone, but he called it at the last minute. So I stayed in the hotel.' She blushed and Maxwell knew that somewhere there was a waiter telling his friends how he shagged that skinny bird out the telly lot. But that was a story that never needed to be told.

'Well, good for you anyway,' he said. 'You could be alive today because of that.'

'Or he might be alive if I had gone,' she said. 'Have you thought of that?'

* * *

In the Merrie Muffin, they found Zac sitting at a corner table next to the fire, ensconced in the shelter of a monk's bench, with his phone in his hand.

'Ah, there you are!' he cried, as if they were his dearest friends. 'Let's get you warmed up.' Everyone noticed he didn't give up his prime seat, though. He waved his hand in the air and the owner of the shop sashayed over, her brand-new hairdo for the occasion still giving off the fumes of the hairspray. 'Coffees . . . no, hot chocolates all round. Marshmallows, all the trimmings.' She smiled inanely and went into the kitchen. Later she would always claim that they had had *ever* such a nice chat, but that blooming director had cut it.

'I don't really do hot chocolate, Zac,' Pargeter complained. 'Chocolate moustache.' He mimed the problem.

'Good grief, no one is expecting you to *drink* the stuff,' Zac said, 'although you do look very cold, all of you. We just need about three minutes in here, I think. Nice pally long shots and short on the cocoa. Just for atmosphere. Mel, we won't really need close-up sound. Just get some ambient and wait for us in the bus, eh?'

'She's chilled to the bone,' Maxwell said. 'Surely she can at least have a hot drink.'

'Just get the driver to put the heat on, there's a love,' Zac said, as the sound engineer made her way to the door, collecting ambient as she went. 'Now then,' Zac rubbed his hands together. 'How did that go? Splendid, splendid.' Zac never waited for an answer when he wasn't certain that it would be something he wanted to hear. 'All ready for Monday, are we? I just got a text from that rather . . .' he caught Maxwell's eye, 'friendly and super-efficient Detective Inspector to say that they will have finished with the school over the weekend and it's all systems go for Monday. So, that's good, isn't it?'

The four men gathered round the table would have nodded, but it's hard to nod when your teeth are chattering so hard they sound like castanets. But Zac got the general sense of the meeting and leaned back in his seat to wait for the drinks. Even Maxwell couldn't help noticing that the screen of his phone, though dim, still showed that he was halfway through a game of Solitaire.

CHAPTER NINE

With Monday looming, as it always did, on the horizon, the Maxwells' weekend was as uneventful as they wanted it to be, bar one rather hilarious lunch with Mrs B on the Saturday when they amused her with descriptions of Joe Pargeter's interesting combination of wig and dandruff.

'I knew it,' she said, 'I knew it. I had it for a full syrup, though, not just a toop. Still, all that dandruff, eh?'

'He carries a little roller,' Maxwell said, 'like you use for cat hair. Someone has to do the back of his collar for him, though.'

'Ooooh, they couldn't pay me enough to do that,' Mrs B said. 'What a horrible job!'

'Oddly, I don't think the kids who end up doing it get paid much at all. They see it as a leg-up in telly.'

'Poor little bleeders. They wanna get proper jobs, something with a future. Like teaching. Or the police.'

'Or an astronaut,' Nolan chipped in. He was rewatching the *Toy Story* franchise from the beginning for what Jacquie had calculated was the seventieth time, and was rather struck on the idea of 'to infinity and beyond'.

'You're right, mate,' Maxwell said. 'I reckon they have more chance of being an astronaut than making it in telly, any day.'

When Nolan had moved into the sitting room to do his homework — 'A Walk in Winter'; his teacher had loads of imagination, just not when thinking of essay titles — Mrs B turned a solemn face to Jacquie. She didn't usually get involved in her work, but she thought of the dead man as hers, as if he wouldn't be dead if she hadn't walked in at that moment. A sort of Schrodinger's corpse train of thought.

'Did you find out any more about that dead bloke, Mrs M?' she said, trying to sound casual.

'Yes and no,' Jacquie said. 'We had the small bit on the news, I don't know if you caught it? We had some calls — we always do, of course, largely just people wanting their taste of fame. According to one woman, he was her husband who had just popped out for milk that morning in Aberdeen. Not all of them were that easy to weed out, but we got it down to three likely contacts in the end. One was too old to be useful, a neighbour from about five years back. But one was a recent ex and the other a flatmate. Henry and I are going to interview them this afternoon. They both work and weren't keen to come on a work day. I don't think that Mr Masters was a very popular person, one way and another. And having said that,' she drank the rest of her water and pushed back from the table, 'I have to love and leave you guys. They're travelling together, these two, and they should be arriving in about an hour.' She kissed Maxwell on the top of his head and then, after a pause, did the same to Mrs B, who blushed with pleasure. She had had family making demands on her since she was hardly more than a child, but for the first time she felt she had a proper one, who gave as well as took.

They heard Jacquie call goodbye to Nolan and then she was gone.

Mrs B got up to go as well. 'I tried that Gwen Up at the School again,' she said, as a parting shot. 'She still won't let me change me slot, so I've called in sick for Monday. I don't do that, Mr M, as you know, but I just can't do it. Not yet.'

'Don't worry, Mrs B. I'll have a word with her. We'll sort it out.'

And she knew that they would.

* * *

At the nick, things were marginally quieter that Saturday morning than they would have been on a weekday, but it took an expert eye to tell the difference. Henry was, of course, already there when Jacquie arrived. She could count on the fingers of one hand the times that she had managed to beat him in to work. The ex-girlfriend, Kirsty Daniels, and the current flatmate who had so far preferred not to give his name, were due in half an hour, so they had a catch-up in Henry's office until they arrived.

'How's Mrs B?' Hall hadn't met the woman that often, but Jacquie had a fund of stories and although Henry was not known for his well-developed sense of humour, he had often smiled on the inside when she told them and he felt he knew her. It had bothered him to see the unflappable so flapped.

'She's not too bad. She just had lunch with us and she was fine, but she has asked Max to talk to her boss about changing her shift. She doesn't fancy being the first one in for a while.'

'The boss a bit difficult? It's Ms Preddie, I assume.'

'Ultimately, I suppose, but no, it's the site manager. She seems a bit of a mystery, keeps herself to herself but Max was a bit concerned that she lets kids congregate in her storeroom.'

Hall's head came up with a snap. 'Anything we should know?'

'I don't think so, but Max is on it, so we'll soon know if it's otherwise. I think he just found it a bit weird. Teachers don't want to go near kids in breaks, but I suppose if you don't spend all day with them, it's different.'

'Hmm. Let me know, anyway.' He looked at his watch. 'Where are those two? Do you think they've changed their minds?'

'Can they?' It was a bit of a grey area. 'They aren't material witnesses as such, but we do need them for background.'

'So it's optional, still, I hope . . .'

He was interrupted by a secretary putting her head around the door. 'I've got two people down in reception,' she said. 'A Miss Daniels and a Mr L'Augère. I think that's his name, we went there once on holiday, but that's what it sounded like.' Her head disappeared again, like a cuckoo into a clock.

'Lohgere? What kind of name is that?' Henry said, getting up. 'And where is it? Who is that woman? No wonder he wanted to keep his name to himself.'

Unconsciously channelling Maxwell and Mrs B, Jacquie said, 'That's right. It sounds French. It's in the South of France, I think. She only comes in at the weekend, I think her name is Marie. He's probably fed up with spelling it to everyone.' She grabbed her notebook. 'Anyway, let's go and do this. Are we having one each or shall we double up? Nice cop, nasty cop sort of thing.'

'How are you for time?' Henry was always aware that Jacquie put in far more than her allotted hours.

'Nothing pending. I expect there will be mild chaos when I get home, but it shows they've had a good time. That's the cats. As for Max and Nolan, they will have made their own amusement.'

'Together, then,' Henry said. 'Saves having to catch each other up after.' He opened the door and stood back. 'After you. And I suppose we should do the ladies first thing in the interview as well.'

'You're such a gent,' she chuckled, and headed for the stairs to Interview Room 1.

* * *

Kirsty Daniels looked rather out of Gavin Masters' league at first glance, as well as being a fair few years younger. It was only when the two police persons were sitting opposite her

131

across a table's width that it became obvious that most of the effect was make-up and hair. She was immaculate, though, which didn't really go with the somewhat slovenly clothes they had found her ex wearing. Jacquie had been particularly struck by his trainers, which were worn down on the heels and scuffed along the toes. His jeans were frayed along the bottoms, though everything seemed clean enough. Kirsty's clothes weren't expensive, there was something a bit cheap as to the fabric, but they fitted like a glove and were the very latest colour and style. Her hair was fitted to her head like a cap and was either the most amazing shade of auburn or she had an incredibly talented hairdresser. What there was no sign of, however, was any distress at all.

Henry pressed the button on the tape recorder and trotted out the usual rubric, asking his interviewee to state her name, date of birth and address for the record. This she did in a rather nasal voice which both of her listeners decided would get right on your wick after an hour or so of it. Her date of birth surprised Henry, who had not looked beyond the make-up, but Jacquie gave herself a private tick in the 'got that right' box.

'So, Miss Daniels . . . may we call you Kirsty?' Henry began.

''F'ya want.' Suddenly, she was chewing gum.

'Right, so, Kirsty. Could you tell us how long you and Gavin Masters were . . . close? Did you cohabit during that time?'

She snorted. 'Nobody was never close to Gavin. And if you mean did he move in lock, stock and barrel after our second date, yes, we did *cohabit*.' She looked at them as if she was the interviewer and they had applied for jobs way above their capabilities. 'He was a charmer, was Gav. At first, that is. Didn't do the flowers and chocolates thing, but he had this kind of way of looking at you. As if he'd been waiting for you all his life. And, o' course, in a way he had. He needed a roof over his head, you'd got one. If you had all the right bits in the right places, that was just a bonus to Gav. And I must say, when it comes to the right bits . . .'

Jacquie looked at Henry, who nodded — he had seen the autopsy results and he had the proof in black-and-white.

'Kirsty,' Jacquie said, 'could you tell us something about Gavin, from when you knew him. We're just trying to build up a picture, so we can perhaps weed people out from the suspect list.' She made it sound as if they had one and was almost convinced for a moment.

'Well, I first knew Gav years back. We were friends with benefits, I suppose you could say. That was when he was with his missus, I suppose . . . his first missus. She went abroad with some bloke she met at work. Don't know her name. Then . . . ooh, four years ago, would it be? He'd left his second wife — I call her his second wife, I don't think he's got another one since, so call her his last wife, I suppose. We met up in a pub, the usual happened like always happens with Gav and next thing I know, he's moved in. She'd claim she kicked him out, I suppose. Women do.'

'I'm getting the picture of . . .' Henry paused. A total tosser didn't seem very professional, and yet it was ideal in so many ways.

'He was an arse, a user, a loser. I didn't know his flat-mate, only really met him properly on the drive here this afternoon, but for all he pretends they shared a flat like normal people, I'm guessing Gavin never so much as bought a pint of milk. It wasn't his way.' She looked down at her hands, which were clenched together on the table top.

Jacquie noticed it. 'Would you like a break, Kirsty? A drink of water, perhaps? Coffee?'

The woman looked into her eyes and there was no sign of distress, just anger. 'I don't need none of that. I'm not upset. I'm bloody furious that I let him use me for so long, over and over again. The only good bits were in bed. Although they *were* good, I'll give him that. He had no conversation, all he did was whinge about how he was better than this, how he wouldn't be running after directors and the rest all the time, he would be the boss. He was just . . . not really a very nice person, sorry, but I need to tell the truth. I'm glad he's dead. Because he won't be coming round to me with a sob story again.' She looked up and gave them a crooked smile. 'Because I know I would have fallen for it, again. And it makes me so bloody *wild*.'

And then she did cry, for her foolishness, for all the wasted time, but not even a little for dead Gavin Masters.

They let her cry herself out and then got details for checking her alibi — she had been at a friend's baby gender reveal. Apparently, despite the cold, they had let off lanterns, one of which had set fire to the neighbour's shed. That was eminently checkable and Jacquie delivered her back to reception before joining Henry in Interview Room 2 and the secretive L'Augère.

* * *

'Could you state your name for the record?' Henry was saying as she went into the room.

'Loojer. Aristide, to be formal, but my friends call me Harry. My dad was French.'

Well, that explained that, but Jacquie thought it was a shame that Mr L'Augère senior hadn't taught his little boy how to pronounce his own name.

Jacquie sat and got out her notebook while Henry asked for the rest of the man's details. He was young, probably ten years younger than Masters, and he looked it. He also looked like someone who didn't have to worry about money overmuch, his clothes were stylish, but unlike Kirsty's were expensive and well-made and not in the absolute top of fashion; Jacquie suspected they were bought by his mother.

'You're not under caution, of course,' Hall told him. 'We have asked you to come in as one of the very few people who knew Gavin Masters. Can you tell us how long you have known him, and how you came to be sharing a flat?'

'I did mislead you a little there,' he said. 'He wasn't my flatmate in the usual sense of paying rent and utilities and things like that. I'm a student and my parents bought me a flat in Brighton for while I'm at college.'

'What are you studying?' Jacquie asked.

'Media. That's where meeting Gavin was *so* amazing. He's worked with everyone, you know. All the greats. Tom Cruise . . . people like that.'

'Ah.' Henry could see how this interview was going to go almost before it had begun. They weren't going to find out much that was accurate about Gavin Masters from this rich little twerp.

'We met about six months ago, in a pub. Some of my college friends and I had a project to complete; we had to make a short film and we were having real trouble with the sound. We could only use iPads, phones etc., that was the brief, and we couldn't get any resolution. Gavin heard us and asked if he could help. He was a sound engineer, you see.'

'Yes, we knew that much,' Henry said.

'He helped us with some software which we could use for editing and then he came back to mine to help us out. Not to *do* it, of course, just mentor us, sort of. And, it got a bit late and so he crashed on the sofa.' He laughed nervously. 'Actually, he crashed in my bed and I had the sofa. He was that much older, you see, and it seemed a bit rude, after he had been so useful.'

'And when did you see him after that?' Henry was beginning to feel he had sprouted psychic powers, because he knew all the answers in advance.

'That's just it.' Another nervous laugh. 'He never really left. Because, to be honest, I'm not finding this course very easy. I've already changed to media from creative writing. And I'd already changed to that from law. My parents are lovely, but I think they are wondering when I will ever graduate. So, I really need to succeed this time. And Gavin was a huge help, you see.'

'Let's get this straight,' Jacquie said, keeping her voice low. She could see the little confused boy behind the sophisticated, well-dressed front and wanted to hug him rather than interview him. 'You met a man in a pub, you took him home, he helped you with your homework and never left.'

Harry Loojer looked at her and seemed to be ticking off the points in his head. 'Yes, that's it, more or less.'

'And you've been sleeping on the sofa ever since?' Hall confirmed.

'Er, not really. After a night or two it was getting to my back a bit, so Gavin suggested we share my bed.' He blushed. 'It wasn't how it sounds. We didn't . . .' He cradled his forehead between his interlocked fingers, resting his elbows on the table. 'We didn't *do* anything. It was just mates, just bunking up, that sort of thing. And . . . you don't have to tell my parents, do you? They wouldn't understand. There wasn't . . . anything in it.'

Jacquie reached out and touched his arm. 'But you wish there had been?'

He looked up, his eyes brimming. 'Oh, God, yes. And now he's *dead*. He's dead. Gavin's dead.'

And although the dead man was clearly, as described by everyone but Harry, a total dick, Hall and Jacquie were somehow glad that, against all the odds, there was someone who could cry for him.

* * *

That Monday morning, the teachers stood like Gog and Magog on either side of Leighford High's main doors as the reason for their being there herded into the building, a basket next to Mr Maxwell, Head of Sixth Form, and another next to Mrs Allington, Head of History, in her heels almost half a head taller than Maxwell. Between them was an ostentatious bucket of water, the death knell of any electronic device, the repository of the damned. Why was it, Maxwell wondered to himself, that it was always the History Department that upheld standards?

'I daresay you have all remembered the ruling,' Maxwell bellowed above the hubbub, 'that mobile devices are now banned from the school premises. However, if you have forgotten, you have a choice. Your phone can go in one of these baskets. Anybody who doesn't hand their phone over and who we later find to have one on them, will find it easily enough at the end of the day. It will be in here.' He pointed to the bucket.

'Are you allowed to do that?' Zac Littleton sauntered past, trying to mingle with the sixth formers and almost carrying it off.

'They're trying to outlaw phones in schools,' Maxwell said. 'That's why, a lifelong Marxist, I now vote Monster Raving Loony. If they outlaw nose jewellery as well, I'll vote Fascist.'

Littleton's scowl was one of contempt, but he didn't want to mix it with the man they called Mad Max, especially on the first full day of filming.

'Roll up, roll up,' Maxwell went on. 'Drop your cells in here or here, as our American cousins would say. And I'm not talking DNA here.' His cigar-waggling Groucho Marx was pitch-perfect but of course it was lost on everybody. Maxwell put the 'die' in dinosaur.

'Even I am amazed,' Polly said. 'How many thousands of quid have we got here, Max?'

Maxwell chuckled. 'A lot,' he said. 'It used to be Barbies and trainers; before that flares and big shoulders. Now it's mobiles, iPads . . . oh, and of course Barbies. Some things never change.'

Polly waited until Zac Littleton was out of earshot. 'I hear they're filming you this morning.'

'Wanna take my place?' he asked. 'Who've you got?'

'Eight Bee Zed.'

'Christ,' he murmured. 'Bad luck. I can't see you getting any Baftas with that lot.'

'You got that right,' she laughed. 'Even so, you won't—'

'—say anything un-PC? Anti-woke? Vaguely illiberal? Trust me, lady, I'm a teacher. I leave indoctrination to the under thirties.' He did a quick — and rather belated — bit of Maths in his head. No, it was all right — Polly Allington was over the threshold. Phew!

'Just checking,' she winked, with that sternness in her voice that she would soon be using with Eight Bee Zed.

'Roll up! Roll up!'

* * *

Maxwell's time-honoured rejoinder to his classes in Room 8 was not to look out of the window, to the view across the playing fields where all kinds of distractions lay. He told Years Seven to Nine that if they did, a great hairy monster, half Gruffalo, half Mary Berry, would eat them alive. He told Years Ten and Eleven that they wouldn't pass any GCSEs at all if they did. He didn't have to tell Years Twelve and Thirteen anything at all, because a) they'd heard it all before and b) he taught them in the sixth form block, not in Room 8.

This morning, however, was different. That funny man in the backwards cap was telling Nine Aitch Queue not to look at the camera, pretend it wasn't there. Bearing in mind it was huge and black, with legs, wheels and flashing red lights, that was a difficult ask.

'Normal, people,' Zac grinned. 'Just be yourselves. This is a normal lesson, okay?'

Considering that any child using those two letters in combination was routinely keelhauled by Mr Maxwell, 'normal' hardly cut it. One or two of Aitch Queue, who saw themselves as the next Rupert Grint or Emma Watson, couldn't look away because they were staring at their future. Others, like serial shoplifter Cynthia Gregory, couldn't look at it for fear of being recognised on some future CCTV. It must have been just like that, Maxwell mused, when they started filming in the Commons for the first time — a handful of stars, loving the limelight, and hundreds of time-serving nobodies, wishing the ground would swallow them up.

'So, Mr Maxwell,' Littleton said. 'Over to you.'

Nobody expected anything other than perfection from Mad Max. He wouldn't put a foot wrong. So it came as rather a surprise to the director when the old dinosaur calmly opened his laptop and started reading out a list of names.

'Cut!' Littleton shouted and the camera stopped whirring.

'Problem, Zac?' Maxwell asked. It was an unwritten rule at Leighford High School and probably every school in the land, that when speaking to colleagues, it would be surnames all the time, every time. But somehow, Maxwell couldn't see in which universe that rule applied to the Telly Lot, as they were already known throughout the school.

'Um.' The director crossed to the teacher. 'It's just that it's a bit . . . well, dull. I was hoping for a few fireworks, in the educational sense, that is.'

Maxwell looked at him grimly. 'I thought this was a documentary, Zac,' he said. 'A warts-and-all exposé of education as it is in the 2020s. By law, I have to register each class before I begin. Elf n Safety and all that. So if the whole place is engulfed in flames, we know who to look for.' Maxwell used his more in sorrow than in surprise face; it rarely failed him and it didn't now.

'Oh, I see. Well, all right, then, carry on. We'll cut this bit.'

'Your programme,' Maxwell shrugged and as the director moved to the back of the class, promised him, 'The fireworks will come later.' He winked.

He finished his roll call, closed the laptop and stood up. 'Now, then,' he said, surveying the rather diffident faces in front of him, all of them tortured souls going through hormonal changes that no one had prepared them for *and without their phones*. Could there be anything worse?

'That,' Maxwell pointed to his laptop, 'and other gadgets in this room . . .' He was willing them to glance at the camera and nobody did. He could have hugged them all but that would have meant lawsuits and angry mobs and Fly's documentary would float noisily out of the window, '. . . are of our time; the twenty-first century. But today, people, we are going back to the fourteenth.' He scanned the room again. 'So what date is that, Tom?'

'Thirteen something, sir,' Tom piped up. Some were pleased that Maxwell had not picked on them. Others were furious because they knew that answer too. Tom was in seventh heaven.

'Spot on,' Maxwell smiled. 'You'll be an emeritus professor at Oxford one of these days. And, in thirteen something — thirteen eighty-one, to be precise — what were the peasants in England doing?'

'They were revolting!' The whole class reverberated with much laughter and banging on desks. Mel's sound needles were bouncing all over the place and Littleton was scratching furiously with his biro, to pass a note to Maxwell to tone it down a notch. You couldn't please some people.

'Now, the question.' Maxwell's quiet voice brought them all to order and Mel had to extend her hamster to pick him up at all. 'Is why? Was it because they'd left the EU?'

A few voices dissented.

'We hadn't won the Eurovision Song Contest — again?'

More voices denying that likelihood.

'Was it because boatloads of illegal immigrants kept turning up, for example, on Leighford's beaches?'

There was silence now. As far as Nine Aitch Queue knew, that was plausible. After all, hadn't it always been like that? Zac Littleton was scribbling furiously. He didn't care at all for where this was going.

There was a solitary hand in the air, not Professor Emeritus Tom this time but a rather quiet-looking girl with big glasses.

'Yes, Marissa?' Maxwell smiled at her.

'The government weren't happy, sir,' she said. 'They thought the peasants were overpaid so they hit them with the poll tax.'

Maxwell chuckled. 'Good girl,' he said.

Littleton scribbled down 'patronising bastard' but he didn't intend to pass *that* note on. It was a shame he wasn't watching the girl's face — her day was already made, patronising or no.

'That's absolutely right.' Maxwell was circling the class. He didn't really expect to find any rogue mobiles still in the possession of any of this lot, but you couldn't be too careful. 'And since you've brought up the idea of government, who are we talking about?'

'The king,' Professor Tom was into his stride now. 'The government was the king back then.'

'Absolutely,' Maxwell said. 'And who was the king in the year of our Lord 1381?'

There was some hesitation. 'Richard?' an uncertain voice came back to him.

'Number?' Maxwell asked, though he had no intention of turning this into a Maths lesson.

Three or four hands went up. 'The second,' somebody said.

'Right again,' Maxwell beamed. Nine Aitch Queue were on fire today. And he hadn't even primed them. 'How old was he?'

There were puzzled faces, even from Zac Littleton, although he pretended not to show it. Maxwell stopped at a desk alongside a rather angelic-looking boy. 'How old are you, Ahmed?'

'Fourteen,' Ahmed said, a little surprised to be asked.

'Well, there you have it,' Maxwell said. 'The exact same age as the king. Off you go, then.'

'What?'

'I've just made you king for the day . . .' he glanced at his watch, 'well, for the next twenty-five minutes.' Someone in the back groaned and without turning round, Maxwell said, 'I know, doesn't time fly when you're enjoying yourself?' He gestured to the teacher's seat. 'Take my throne, why dontcha? No, better yet, move all that crap off the desk . . .'

Littleton's biro was in overdrive.

'. . . and sit on it. There. How does that feel?'

Ahmed wasn't the most forthcoming of kids, but here he was, the king of Nine Aitch Queue, the king of Room 8, of Leighford High, of all England. And this was a day he would never forget. Mel Bright, adjusting her woofers and tweeters, smiled and nodded. In common with thousands before her, she wished that Mad Max had been her teacher.

'What shall we call him?' Maxwell asked.

'The king,' a wag called and there was general laughter.

'Witty as ever, Dennis.' Maxwell could cut anybody down to size. 'But if you were to greet the king, to be called to his presence, as they used to say, how would you address him?'

'Your Majesty,' Tom said, throwing away his Emeritus title with one careless word.

'Uh-huh,' Maxwell said. 'Kings before the Tudors were called "Your Grace". It was Henry VII who came out with "Your Majesty". Hell of a snob was Henry VII . . . So, Your Grace,' Maxwell bowed to the king of Nine Aitch Queue, 'what are you going to do about these revolting peasants, eh?'

* * *

'How'd it go?' Helen Maitland asked when Maxwell got back to his office at the start of break.

'I had Nine Aitch Queue, so a walk in the park. There are some worse ones down the line, but it'll be all right, I think. Is that coffee mine?'

It wasn't, but Helen nodded anyway.

'Because I don't really have time. I've got to go and see Gwen Harris about something.'

'Ooh.' Helen sucked in her breath. 'Really? Men have disappeared on that quest. Are you wearing a stab vest? Oh.' She was stricken. 'I . . . that's terrible. I didn't mean . . .'

'Don't worry about it,' Maxwell said. 'Though I like to think that every man's death diminishes me, I don't think that the dead man's colleagues are that cut up, so we don't need to tread on eggshells. Jacquie was saying . . .' he caught her eye, 'let's not talk about what Jacquie was saying, privileged and all, but anyway, long story short, don't worry. No one else is. Apart from the police, presumably.' He scratched the back of his head. This was getting in way too deep for his liking. 'I'm off to Gwen's lair, anyway. If I'm not back by afternoon school, send a party after me.'

'It'll be too late,' Helen laughed, glad that the atmosphere had lightened. 'She'll have eaten you by then. I hope you're not asking for anything major. She gave Maureen a thirty-minute lecture last week when she went for a lightbulb. Apparently, the Physics lab had a new lightbulb in 2017 and isn't due another one yet.'

'I'll be careful,' Maxwell assured her. 'Anyway, I'm just asking for a friend.'

* * *

It was, of course, impossible that the corridor leading to the site manager's office and storeroom was any colder, darker, danker or more spider-strewn than all the rest of the school. Maxwell told himself that by all the laws of logic, it should be brighter, cleaner and more arachnid-free, as the site manager was in charge of cleaning. And yet, he could almost feel the crunch of the bones of those who had gone before under his shoes and he was sure that he could see furtive eyes peering out at him from the shadows. He gave himself a shake. He was a senior teacher in the school and he was here with a perfectly reasonable request, so there was no need for such imaginary flights of fancy. He would knock on the door, state his business, she would agree and that would be that.

He tried her office first. Somehow, he felt, he was more likely to succeed in an office setting than in the gloom of a storeroom with boxes of rationed lightbulbs and jumbo vats of cleaning fluids looming over him. But she wasn't there and the cup of coffee on her desk had a skin on it, so she obviously hadn't just popped out. He'd learned that trick from an episode of *Morse* and it had come in handy as many times as this one.

He tapped on the storeroom door and got the immediate impression that a small noise that had been on the very edge of his hearing had suddenly stopped. He tapped again and pushed open the door. It was very gloomy in there, except for one light near the door, where Gwen Harris sat on a high stool, her legs tucked up onto the footrest to stop them dangling, a clipboard in hand, an open box of individual hand soaps open in front of her.

'Ah, Gwen.' He gathered all his available bonhomie together and let her have it, both barrels. 'I've come for a favour.'

She looked him up and down as if she had never seen him before, then licked a finger and riffled through some pages nail-gunned to the wall — when putting up notices, Gwen Harris played for keeps. 'History has had all its inventory for this financial year,' she said. 'And so has the sixth form. In fact, every department in the school has had their full allocation of everything. But you can still ask, of course. If you want.'

'It's not allocation,' he said, hoping to get on her good side, should there be one. 'It's about Mrs B.'

'Oh?'

'She's asked me to ask you if there is any way she can change her shift. She had a shock, you know, finding a body like that. A school is a scary place first thing in the morning.'

'She's off sick.'

Maxwell had an uneasy feeling that he wasn't alone. It was the feeling he got when Metternich and Bismarck wanted to go out on a cold winter's morning and they wanted to use the grown-ups' cat flap, not the fiddling little one. On those mornings, they would sneak onto the foot of the bed and stare until he woke up. They were so quiet that the lack of sound was somehow deafening, and so it was here.

'Do you have a cat?' It seemed like a crazy question, but he couldn't help it; he couldn't shake that feeling.

'No. There's one around, one of the dinner ladies encourages it in, but I don't.'

Somehow, Maxwell wasn't surprised. He couldn't let it lie, though. 'Is someone in here, then? Only, I just have this feeling . . .'

There was suddenly a rustle behind the nearest shelving and a small girl stepped out. It was his star from Nine Aitch

Queue, her anxious glasses turned up to him. 'It's us, Mr Maxwell.'

Surprised, all he could think to say was, 'Hello, Marissa. Who's us?'

In various stages of temper or fear, kids seemed to be stepping out from everywhere, all ages from Year Seven to Thirteen, all what he would call geeks. Mrs B had mentioned this, but he somehow hadn't expected so many. And . . . wait a minute — they all had mobiles. His thoughts were tumbling over each other. These children were not rule breakers. They wouldn't have brought in phones once they were banned. So . . . He turned to Gwen Harris, who was counting soaps as if nothing was going on behind her.

'Mrs Harris, if I may? What are all of these students doing here? And how do they all have phones?' He turned to the room. 'Are these your phones?'

A ragged chorus of 'No, Mr Maxwell' came back at him.

The woman shrugged. 'They miss their phones. They're . . . well, look at them. They get bullied, they rely on their phones. They calm them down.'

Maxwell looked at the growing huddle. One of them had switched a light on and a quick head count came to almost twenty. None of them, as far as Maxwell could tell, was a child with special needs. Bright, yes. Quiet, mostly. But they didn't need to hide in here with the site manager. He caught the eye of one of His Own, a clever lad even though he was doing sciences for A-levels. 'Matt, get them out of here. And come and see me in lunch break.'

'I've got work experience after morning school, Mr Maxwell,' the lad said.

'Tomorrow, then. First thing. Now, scat, all of you. And . . . don't let me find you in here again.' He stood to one side as they filed past, taking the phones from each one as they went. Most of the screens were dark but one or two woke up as he took them. All that seemed to be on them was games, mostly simple Solitaire, way below the interests of the students he knew them to be.

When they had all gone, he turned back to the site manager, who was now entering the number of hand soaps onto her list in tiny, neat writing.

'Can you have another go at explaining, Gwen?' he asked.

She turned to face him. 'Not really,' she said.

'You know I'll have to go to Ms Preddie, don't you?'

'I don't see where the "have to" comes in, but you will go to her, I expect, yes.'

Maxwell knew a brick wall when he was hitting his head against it. 'I'll wait until I have spoken to Matt tomorrow morning,' he said. 'But all that will do is decide the facts that I will share with Ms Preddie. It won't mean I won't tell her at all.'

'Yes, yes, I get it. And I suppose you also want me to change the shift for that annoying old bat you live next door to.'

'That's why I came down, but . . .'

'Tell her she can have the last shift. It's mine, so I can swap it over without bothering anybody else. All right? But it has to be tonight. I've already covered her this morning.'

'Can I check with her?'

'Nope. Take it or leave it.'

'We'll take it then, I suppose. What time?'

'It's twelve hours on, so seven to ten. I'll email her a list of what's needed.' She picked up her pen again. 'So we don't have much else to say to each other, do we?'

Maxwell looked at her sadly. He hated bringing trouble to anyone but he had no choice. All he could do was give her a stay of execution, as it were. He made his way back to the sunlit uplands of the sixth form block with a black dog on his back; he felt that he had turned over a rock expecting to find a woodlouse and had uncovered a rattler instead.

* * *

So deep in thought was he that he walked through the foyer without even noticing that the Long Riders were back in full fig, being given a thorough letting-off by Bob Roberts. Up in his office, it wasn't exactly conducive to quiet mulling either, as there was something of a crowd. Helen was sitting in her usual seat, cradling a cup of coffee. Opposite her, Mandy Proctor was mirroring her and Polly Allington was sprawled in his desk chair, wrestling with a KitKat wrapper.

Mandy craned her head round to see who had just come in and did a quick rerun in her head to think of who they had been gossiping about for the last five minutes.

'Oh, Max, it's only you. What a relief.'

He smiled wryly. 'I don't hear that very often. But you don't need to worry. I'm just here to grab a quick coffee if there's any in the pot; I have to go down and try to catch Arnie before she's off and gurning at a switched-off camera again.'

'Good news,' Mandy said, 'is that the teeth are no longer with us.'

'Thank heavens for that,' Maxwell said and meant it. In his memory they had grown larger and larger until they had reached epic proportions, somewhat similar to a *Spitting Image* puppet.

'Unfortunately,' Mandy said, putting her coffee down because she always became convulsed with laughter at this point in an already oft-told tale, 'some of the glue is still there, so her top lip keeps catching, like this.' She pulled an horrific face and Maxwell flinched. 'So, watch out for that when you go in. Don't react, though, will you?'

All three women laughed, Polly Allington flapping the air with her non-coffee-holding hand.

'One thing, though,' Mandy told him, 'she's got Diamond in with her. Giving him an earful at my last eavesdropping. Something about having been misinformed about the angle of the FOTWL programme. In other words, she's totally pissed off about you being the star.'

'Star? You wouldn't have said that on Friday, walking on the beach trying to make Joe Pargeter look intelligent.'

'Good luck with that,' Helen said. She was the only one of the three who had known Bernard Ryan and although he had often been a total pain in the neck, she felt a bit sorry for him. He had found the love of his life — a low-key news reporter on the TV once in a blue moon — and now was married to a rising celebrity with no discernible talent except for getting in front of any camera going. Although, as his agent, she supposed, Bernard had only himself to blame.

'He does seem to be a bit of a twerp,' Polly agreed. 'What's it like, working with the Telly Lot?'

'I don't honestly know,' Maxwell admitted. 'Being with them is like trying to catch farts in a colander, excuse my French. If I were to have to sum up, it would be selfishness, mild incompetence and dandruff.' He drained his coffee. 'Anyway, dears, I hate to gossip and run, but I must see Arnie before the bell goes. I promised Thingee Two I would have a word.' And with that, he was gone.

'Do the office staff mind?' Polly, as the newest member of staff in the room, asked.

Helen smiled. 'Do you mean the Thingee thing? They don't mind at all. He knows their names, their birthdays, their favourite colour for all I know. And as a term of endearment, I have known worse than Thingee, haven't you?'

Polly nodded. 'I . . . knew someone once who used to call me Bunch. I liked it until I realised he only did it so he didn't use the wrong name in the heat of the moment.'

'Not Jeremy, surely?' Mandy said, surprised. She had met him briefly in the car park one afternoon and had gone away with an impression of smoothness and a mind like a whip.

Polly laughed. 'God no. Jeremy never forgets a thing. Which is probably good, though it can get on your nerves when it's something you'd rather forget.'

Helen Maitland and Mandy Proctor exchanged covert glances. They liked Polly, but sometimes it could be a bit wearing when Mr Perfect was always hovering somewhere in the background. A little wrinkle on the surface was something to bear in mind, for later.

CHAPTER TEN

Maxwell tapped on the door of Arnie's second-best office, the one not at the back of reception. Even she had baulked at working in a room which had so recently had a corpse on its floor. Her precious rug, brought from home, had been taken by SOCO and so to all intents and purposes there was nothing to remind her of the carnage, but still . . . she could see that it would look insensitive, if nothing else, so she was using her other office, the meetings one.

He heard her rather hectoring tone stop mid-hector. Hearing her talking was no guide as to whether she was alone or not. She had no skill on the keyboard and had been delighted to discover from the IT department that there was such a thing as dictating emails, memos and texts. So her voice, flat and didactic, could be heard wafting from her office, whether or not she had anyone in there.

'Yes?' She sounded more testy than usual, which made Maxwell's heart sink more than a little. His morning had not exactly been a walk in the park thus far and so Arnie in a snit he could well and truly do without.

He gave his shoulders a bit of a shake and tweaked his bow tie so it was just so. He popped his head around the door and gave a smile his best shot. 'Ms Preddie,' he said, emphasising the Ms for all he was worth. 'I wonder if I might have a word.'

'Oh, come in, come in, for heaven's sake. Don't just hang around the door like Walter Matthau.'

'Goodness,' Maxwell said, slithering into the room. 'Are you a fan of *The Taking of Pelham 123*?' Perhaps the woman was human after all.

'Not really. But it's just an image that lingers.'

'Gesundheit!' Maxwell said and was startled to see a smile flit across her face.

'It was my father's favourite film,' she said, rummaging in a drawer to hide her expression.

'Good taste,' Maxwell said. 'I'm here on behalf of Britney.'

'Britney? Which one? We must have a dozen in the school in various year groups.'

Maxwell surreptitiously pinched himself. Could it be that Arnie was also up to speed with what was happening in her school, despite it having no direct bearing on her? Perhaps her snub from the Telly Lot had caused her to re-evaluate . . . He shook his head slightly. No, that was just crazy talk.

'The one in reception in the afternoons.'

'What about her?' She tried to shut her mouth but the top lip wouldn't obey.

'She's a bit worried that you will be angry with her. She was rather scared on her own last Thursday and I'm afraid I told her to go home. She . . . well, she is under the impression that she could lose her job over it.'

Arnie Preddie leaned over the desk and turned him to stone, or as near as dammit.

'Several things, Mr Maxwell,' she hissed. 'Firstly, you had no right to tell her to do anything. Auxiliary staff are none of your business. And secondly, I have to say, that I would have had no idea whether she had gone home or not, had you not told me. So . . . you've made it worse. Whether I act on anything we have just spoken of—' he noticed she didn't say 'discussed' '—will depend largely on my meeting with Mr Diamond who, rather unprofessionally, is running late.'

Or running scared, Maxwell thought.

'If, as I will be suggesting, the television company chooses to change tack and use more content involving the SLT, I will have no time to pursue Britney's transgression. If, on the other hand, they decide to keep on with this ludicrous idea of hanging this entire programme on you as a spokesman for the school and teaching in general, well . . . I can slot in a meeting with HR very easily.'

Through the door, Maxwell heard the bell and the concomitant thundering of two thousand feet with somewhere else to be. He gestured to it and she nodded sourly.

'We'll leave it there,' she said.

He was already halfway through the door. 'And so, will you take further action or not?' he asked for confirmation.

'In your hands, Mr Maxwell. In your hands.'

Maxwell turned in the doorway and cannoned into James Diamond, looking somewhat hot and bothered but, more importantly, late.

'Oh, hello, James. As you see, I'm just leaving. Best of British luck.'

Diamond gave him a wan smile and prepared to beard the beast in her lair. Maxwell dived into the press of humanity which in about ten seconds would have disappeared into various classrooms, leaving just a few bits of paper and smears of mud behind, to be removed by the endlessly circulating brooms and mops of the site management staff. It was like a magic trick and no one could see how it worked — perhaps the camera would capture it, but Maxwell doubted it. There were some feats of sleight of hand which would never be explained, and this was definitely one. No doubt the hopeful cameramen of the Victorian Society for Psychical Research had dreamed of catching fleeting ghosts in the same way.

Up one flight of stairs and second door on the left was his next port of call. This time, it was just him and the class — the Telly Lot were having a conflab in the minibus. Zac had had an email from head office, branded with the little red exclamation mark which he dreaded — there had been complaints. The parent company — so many levels away from FOTWL that Zac had never met anyone who worked there and wasn't even totally sure what country they were based in — had heard that there had been an 'unplanned death in service'.

Zac read this out and stopped, puzzled. Bevis filled the silence.

'I wonder what a planned death in service is?'

Zac was beginning to worry about Bevis's flippant attitude. Okay, so he was his assistant and as such a separate human being, but he had a sneaky feeling that head office might possibly be a few gigabytes of AI somewhere, allied to some accounting software. They probably wouldn't understand.

'I think, Bevis,' he said, rallying quickly, 'that what they mean is that it was sudden, unexpected, not following an illness or accident. Anyhow . . .' he flicked the screen to read on, 'they say . . . umm . . . blah-blah . . . they say that only one such incident is allowed per production or said production is deemed to have broken its contractual obligations . . . apparently, it's clause twenty-seven, subset m . . . by creating a substantively unsafe working environment.'

Reg broke in. 'This is mental. They're just using clauses put there to protect the workforce in unsafe conditions, not people being murdered! They haven't got the brains God gave sheep.'

Bevis agreed. 'He's right, Zac. You can't equate murder with . . . oh, I dunno, falling off a rig or getting electrocuted by faulty equipment. You have Act of God exceptions in your house insurance, surely the same thing applies when it's murder versus natural, albeit accidental, death.'

'Why are we worrying?' Mel piped up from the back seat. 'We're allowed one incident, we've had one incident, so . . . honestly, is anyone here really thinking there's going to be another murder? I know that everyone thinks that Gavin was a bit of . . .' She paused. Probably her word to describe him might not be theirs, so she hesitated to continue. 'Anyway, let's not speak ill of the dead. But I really think you're worrying too much, Zac. Let's just get on with this shitty job, which I think we all know is not going to see the light of day, and make the best of it.'

There were scattered murmurs of 'hear, hear' and she slumped back into her usual virtually comatose posture.

Bernard and Joe were sitting in the pull-down seats at the front, so they could face the rest, as behoved their status as they saw it. Not for them craning their necks round or raising their voices to be heard.

Bernard used a voice that Maxwell would have instantly recognised, rather tight as to larynx and rather more precisely enunciated than normal conversation.

'What exactly do you mean . . . Mel, is it?' Mel didn't answer, being by now busy filing her nails. 'Not going to see the light of day? Shitty programme? As Mr Pargeter's agent, I would like to point out that his contract states—'

'Oh, leave it out, Bernard,' Zac said, jumping up and sitting back down suddenly, having bumped his head on the handle above the door. 'This programme is shit, let's face it. You got your old buddy to okay it, it's the only way we would have got permission to film in a school. That meddling tart with the brief for a husband put the mockers on almost straight away, so we can't film the kids, we can't film most of the staff, we can't . . . and anyway, even if we could, what the hell *happens* here, anyway? The town puts the "sleep" in "sleepy". The kids are cute enough, I suppose, but not going-viral-on-YouTube cute, they're too old and spotty for that. But they're not knifing each other, either, are they? Any teen-age mothers? No. Any chess geniuses? Again, no. In a nutshell, all we've got going for us is a teacher with a bit of a way with words and crazy hair. It isn't enough, is it? Well . . . *is* it?'

Joe Pargeter smoothed his hair back with a practised hand and clutched his husband's arm with the other. 'I was brought onto this project to bring some *star quality* to it. Because you're absolutely right, this school has absolutely nothing going on. But unless something happens soon, then I am breaking my contract . . . no, Bernie, hush now. We don't need the money, after all, and this certainly isn't going to bring any exposure. So, Zac, Bevis, this is the bottom line. Bernie and I are going home for the night. We need our proper mattress, not that ploughed field that passes for one at the hotel you booked us into — five star? Don't make me laugh. Then, when we get back tomorrow, which may or may not be in the morning, it will all depend, I . . . we . . . want to see some changes around here. Something meaty for me to get my teeth into.' He glanced at Bernard Ryan as he spoke and something about the juxtaposition made Bevis start to laugh. Pargeter gave him a look that would sour milk and then left, his huff almost visible in the cold air that swept into the van.

After the reverberations of the slammed door had died away, Reg spoke. 'Come on then, guys, what's it to be? Pregnancy, chess or murder?'

'Bags I the murder,' Bevis said, and it didn't take a child genius to guess who he had in mind.

* * *

The bell had just gone for the start of the final lesson of the day when James Diamond walked into Peter Maxwell's office.

Maxwell had a free period and was jotting down some notes for the next day from a textbook from his personal stash above his desk. He didn't need notes, but there were such things as spot Ofsted inspections when the Stasi and the Spanish Inquisition arrived in unison and it paid to have something in writing. He looked up and then looked up at the clock.

'Blimey, James. That was one helluva meeting, wasn't it? You've been in there for *hours*!'

'What?' Diamond felt as if he had come in on his own conversation by mistake and didn't know what was going on. He thought back over the day. 'No, no, I haven't been with Ms Preddie all this while. I had to go back to County Hall, to liaise. She . . . well, she's not happy, Max.'

'Of course she isn't. She's doing a job that's well out of her comfort zone with a staff any of whom any number of staff who would happily shove her under a train. Why should she be happy?'

'Bob Roberts seems to like her,' Diamond suggested.

'Bob? Poor old Bob. He hasn't had an original thought since 1997 and that was one his mother told him about. No, really, James, she is never going to be happy, no matter what is going on. And yes, I know, the Telly Lot aren't filming her and she isn't the star and all the rest. But what did she expect? That if she stuck on some plastic teeth she got from some Chinese retailer on the internet that she would be an instant Insta star?'

Diamond's eyes widened. 'Sometimes, Max, and even after all these years, you surprise me.'

Maxwell chuckled. 'That I have heard of Instagram? James, don't underestimate a dinosaur. We have eyes and ears, you know, though I understand that most species couldn't see all that well. Nolan is by way of being a buff, though show me a small boy who isn't. I keep up, you know, so that I can rubbish things when I need to; otherwise, who would put these kids right? Not their parents, in the main. Anyway, you didn't pop by to marvel at my internetular acumen, I'm pretty sure. So, how can I help you?'

Diamond sat down and Maxwell left his desk to join him in what were laughingly called the comfy seats.

'I need—'

'Ooh, hang on!' Maxwell looked startled. 'My phone is doing something.' He fished it out from the inside pocket of his jacket. 'It's a WhatsApp.'

Diamond's eyes nearly fell out of his head.

'Oh, I wish they wouldn't send these. Apparently, my Amazon delivery will be at the house between 1642 and 1747. So, from the start of the English Civil War to the last time they beheaded a member of the aristocracy — Lord Lovat, should you be interested.'

Diamond looked wistful. 'I do actually find I miss you, sometimes, Max,' he said.

'Ooh. Wait, there's another. It's from Mrs B. Hold on a minute while I answer. I'll do it on the laptop, it's quicker.' He held up his hand. 'I don't seem to have prehensile enough thumbs.'

He stood at the desk and tapped out his reply and pressed send. There was a faint whooshing noise and he sat back down.

'Right, how can I help?'

Diamond spread out his hands. 'You can't. But I promised I would at least try and here I am. Ms Preddie, and now the powers that be, want you to cry off filming.'

Maxwell sat there. Then gave a small jump. 'Oh, sorry, James, I thought you were going to ask me to do something I was averse to. Is there something I need to sign? If so, lead me to it. Being filmed is a total waste of my time and more importantly, my A-level and GCSE students' time. You remember how I used to complain about how tight time got around now? Half-term. Easter. Labour Day. Whit. Any class which is mostly timetabled on a Monday hardly sees a teacher after the middle of February. So to have an idiot with his hat on backwards and a ton of hardware all around the room does not fill me with joy, James.'

Diamond sat back. 'Ms Preddie is under the impression that you . . . well, to quote her, well, paraphrase, perhaps, "Maxwell's got something on one of that Telly Lot. Otherwise, why should they make him their star?" I think Bernard would argue there, for him there is no star but Joe. The rest of us might think differently, but Bernard has rose-tinted spectacles where Joe is concerned.'

'He certainly seems devoted,' Maxwell said, carefully.

'I tried to tell her that you would certainly have no interest in bribing them and she suggested that you were blackmailing them.'

'Goodness.' Maxwell sat back in postural echo. 'It's always a bit of an eye-opener to discover how another person sees you, isn't it? Do I really come across as a blackmailer?' He was honestly flummoxed.

'Of course not! I was really annoyed with her and told her she was being an idiot. But she told me that I was bound to say that.'

'Don't tell me — because I have something on you.'

Diamond inclined his head with a smile.

'I think Ms Preddie is just yay close,' Maxwell held up finger and thumb almost touching, 'to having to have her bumps felt. Let's let this filming finish first, shall we? Not to mention the murder investigation.' He smiled at his erstwhile Headmaster. 'Do you remember we always used to find this term boring?'

Diamond nodded. 'We certainly did.'

'This year is certainly proving us wrong, don't you think? The easiest course for you, James — and I say easiest but it is by no means easy — is for you to circumvent Ms Preddie this time and report back to County that nothing would please me more than for the filming to stop. But in the end, I suppose, it will be down to contractual obligations, that kind of thing. I haven't signed anything. Polly Allington's husband advised those who didn't want to get involved to write a letter and I believe a lot of the staff have. For the kids, it's parental consent on a one-by-one basis. But long story short — yes, I am ready to hang up my five and nine as soon as I can. Do you know, they wanted me to have a haircut!'

Diamond was suitably outraged on his behalf, though it was true that he had longed for the day when Maxwell came in close-cropped for once. 'Ridiculous,' he said.

Maxwell looked at him. 'Off you bugger, then, James. Soonest done, soonest mended, and all that. I've got lesson plans to write.'

Diamond was yet again staggered. Was there no end to the googlies this man would bowl this afternoon? 'Really?'

'No, of course not,' Maxwell said, getting up and going back to his desk. 'But whatever I write this afternoon will look enough like one, come the day, to pass muster. But mostly, I am mulling over this murder and who might have done it.'

'No, Max, don't . . . that sort of thing doesn't always end well, does it? I've lost count of the number of times you might have been killed.'

Maxwell laughed and physically ushered the ex-Head out of the room. 'Pish,' he said. 'I'm immortal, didn't you know?'

* * *

When Diamond had gone, Maxwell fished out his phone. He was always mildly surprised to see messages he had sent from the computer were now also on his phone. The little elf that did all those shenanigans was a clever devil, to be sure. He reread the messages. First, Mrs B had written and he could tell she was grateful, because she had used whole words throughout and even some punctuation.

'Thank you so much Mr M that's more than she woulda done for me. 7-10. I'll check the buses.'

Then, a few minutes later, she continued, 'Theres a bus, so it won't be too bad. It'll be alright when the light nights come.'

Then, finally, 'Just for this week Mr M, could you come with me. Not the whole week prolly.' Maxwell grimaced — that damned word would be in the New Oxford before any-one knew it. 'But tonight would be nice, if you could manage it. If not, it's alright.'

He had no idea what Jacquie's plans were for that evening. He knew, without the detail, that the interviews of the weekend had done nothing except to confirm that what they already suspected was true — that almost anyone of any gender, age or profession south of the Trent would probably, given a small bit of encouragement, murder Gavin Masters. Some people, Jacquie had confirmed, were simply not very nice. But that was good, in a way. It meant that it was unlikely to be repeated, and so, once Diamond cancelled the Telly Lot, life could finally go back to normal. And if Jacquie wasn't home, then Mrs B would understand. So that was all lovely and it might be quite fun to actually see the school from a cleaner's eye. Mrs B might even let him use the gigantic floor scrubber that was kept under the stairs, nicknamed The Beast. It was unlikely, but a man could dream.

* * *

'Are you really going to clean the school with Mrs B, Dads?' Nolan asked. He was not quite as gobsmacked as his mother, but he ran her a close second.

'I'm not going to clean, no,' Maxwell said. 'I think you need special training of some kind. But she just doesn't want to be there on her own in the dark right now, that's all.'

'Mrs B isn't afraid of anything,' Nolan said. It wasn't an opinion, it was just a straight fact.

Maxwell had seen her see off spiders as big as a Yorkshire terrier with sheer force of will alone, so had no doubt this was true. But the fact was, the woman was spooked and a huge dark building had had a body in it once, so it could have one again.

'She isn't,' Jacquie said. 'But Henry and I have decided it would be a good idea for there to be someone else with her for the first time she goes back, in case . . .' She hadn't thought it through as far as this and handed over to her husband.

'In case she remembers something. Do you remember, last week she found the . . .' The Maxwells had not stinted when it came to keeping Nolan au fait with the matters of birth and death, but there was a limit as to how graphic they wanted to be.

'The dead guy,' Nolan breathed, as bloodthirsty as only a child could be. 'All my friends at school said it was so exciting, that my dad owned the school and my mum was the cop in charge.' He looked from one to the other, these two people who had brought him his brief moment in the light of notoriety.

Maxwell picked up his fork again and carried on digging into his spag bol. 'Well, there you are, then, matey. You know as much as we do. Mrs B just fancies some company.'

'Cool.' Nolan took in an almost impossibly large mouthful of pasta and applied the time-honoured suction method until it was all gone.

Maxwell looked at the kitchen clock. 'Oh, for the love of Mike,' he said. 'Look at the time.' He shovelled in the last few mouthfuls, Nolan style, wiped his mouth, kissed his people and was gone. 'Don't wait up,' he called as he barrelled down the stairs.

Nolan looked at his mother, eyes shining. 'My Dads is so brave,' he whispered.

'Indeed he is,' Jacquie said, keeping the ironical tone almost out of her voice.

'And if the murderer *is* there, Dads will get him in an armlock, won't he, Mums, and Mrs B can call the police; er . . . you.'

'That's right.' Jacquie wondered if it would be that way round, but it was fruitless to speculate.

Nolan finished off his pasta and wiped his mouth on his sleeve. 'Sorry, Mums. Forgot.' He looked at his empty bowl for a moment. 'You will let me know when he's home, though, won't you?'

Jacquie looked at her boy, a strange amalgam of her, his father and, inexplicably, two cats as brave as lions. She held out her arms and he scurried round the table and climbed into her lap.

'He'll be fine,' she whispered into his hair. 'They'll both be fine. Meanwhile, ten minutes of telly and then bath.'

'Twenty?'

'Hmm. Fifteen?'

'I'll set a timer on Alexa.'

'You do that, matey. And no cheating. She'll tell me if you do.'

Jacquie sat at the kitchen table and had a sudden thought. She took out her mobile and rang Maxwell's number. From a distant point at the bottom of the stairs, she heard it ring. She shook off a feeling of impending doom; he was with Mrs B, owner of the most up-to-date phone it was possible to have and never further from it than the thickness of her overall pocket. What could possibly go wrong?

* * *

Mrs B and Maxwell walked up to the bus stop in a companionable silence. She was wearing her usual cleaning uniform of sensible shoes, trousers a good half inch short of her ankle bone (to prevent slips) and an overall which was an inch longer than her coat. She knew she didn't look elegant but she was neat, clean and ready for anything. She had started off carrying her hefty bag with her own — illicit — chemical-packed cleaning products but Maxwell was inherently incapable of letting a lady carry anything and had taken it from her, after a small tussle. He soon regretted it, but didn't let it show. The effort of carrying the bag and walking uphill had a lot to do with his silence — panting was not a good look, especially when walking alongside someone as sprightly as Mrs B.

The bus stop was undercover but didn't give much protection against the cold. The days were getting a bit warmer — according to the Met Office rather warmer than the usual seasonal average — but once the sun went down, it was truly biting. At least it was dry. Maxwell perched on the flop-out seat with the bag on his lap and looked at Mrs B, who had an unaccustomed smile on her face.

He smiled back. 'What?'

She nudged him with a razor-sharp elbow. 'You,' she said, simply. 'I bet no one walking past here could guess your IQ. Or what you do for a living.'

He looked down at his chosen clothing proudly. 'I just thought I would dress down a bit, you know.'

'And you have,' the woman agreed. 'You look like a burglar. I think you could lose the willy hat, though. It . . .' She gestured to her head in a halo motion. 'You don't look like you with it on.'

'I was trying to be a bit incognito,' he said, pulling it down a bit further with his free hand.

'You're just to stop me having the ab-dabs,' she said, nudging him again. Maxwell made a note to self to sit on the other side of her on the bus. 'We're not burgling the place.'

'True,' he said, 'but my head's warm now, so it's staying on. I quite like it.'

'I can't believe you even have one,' Mrs B said, standing up as the bus approached. 'Ooh, good, look, it's the ninety-two. That goes direct. We'll be a bit early, so that's good. I can have a chat with Kelly. She does the shift up to seven and I haven't seen her for ages.'

Maxwell forbore to remark that if there was going to be someone there then Mrs B hardly needed a minder. It wasn't like her to show weakness of any kind and he had chosen to take it as a compliment that she had let him see her more vulnerable side.

'What do you want me to do while you're working? Do you want me to come round with you? Or shall I just go to my office until you're done? Actually, the wall charts in Room 8 could do with a freshen. One of them says, "Liz Truss for PM". I could do those.'

At the front of the queue, Mrs B flipped her bus pass at the reader and went down to the back to snaffle a double seat. Maxwell fumbled for change and joined her after a slight altercation with the woman halfway back whose shopping trolley got tangled up with Mrs B's cleaning accoutrements bag.

He sat down and she was talking straight away. She had been marshalling her answers. She did wish that he wouldn't ask questions in a string like that; most annoying. 'It's up to you, really. I don't mind. If you like. You're right, some of the Blu-Tack has come loose. And who's Liz Truss, when she's at home? That would be a good use of the time, yes.'

He looked at her and burst out laughing. She nudged him again and he realised that he was still sitting on the same side.

'Ow.'

* * *

Maxwell knew Leighford High School like the back of his hand and had been there in the evening often, for school plays, parent–teacher evenings and meetings. But he had never caught it asleep before. From the front aspect, it was dark, although he knew that somewhere in the bowels, Kelly would be wielding a duster or whatever her specific task was that day. It looked like a great beast, asleep on its low hill, with the muddy grass in front of it looking brown in the street lights and just one window, on the first floor, reflecting the sky. He pointed it out to Mrs B.

'Is that window open?' he asked.

'Oh, that. It's in the Chemistry lab. It hasn't closed properly for years. They don't seem to mind it and we've had it checked for security. No one can get in that way, so they haven't bothered to have it fixed.'

'Right. And . . . you go in through the front door?'

'Yes. It's a bit of a shove — it's a big door — but the keypad on the side door is broken so we have to go in this way. So, you can go in by the side door still, but then when you go out and reset the alarm inside, all hell breaks loose, because the building, y'see, can't work it out that someone is going out what hasn't come in.'

Maxwell was relieved to find that it was not only him who thought of the school as a person.

Mrs B tapped in the code and pushed on the door, which was stiff to start with, then opened smoothly.

'This door is a bit of a bugger,' she said. 'Once it's in motion it's all right, but getting it moving takes work.'

'Inertia,' Maxwell said.

Mrs B wasn't sure, but said it anyway. 'Bless you.'

'Thank you.' Maxwell could follow her thought processes like a shadow.

'Kelly will be in the kitchen,' Mrs B said. 'I'll just go and have a word and then get started. I'll be polishing this floor as soon as she's gone, so if you come down before I come up to get you, don't walk across, walk round.'

'Right ho,' Maxwell said. 'Am I likely to be done first? Will it really take you until ten?'

Mrs B rocked her head and her hand from side to side. 'Depends. If no one has made an unholy mess anywhere, it might be half nine, I suppose. You just carry on with your boards, Mr M, and I'll come to you. Probably best. You don't want to be wandering round in the dark.'

'I do know this school backwards, Mrs B,' he told her.

'It's different in the dark,' she said. 'So watch your step.'

He stood at the bottom of the stairs and watched her disappear into the dining hall and waited until he heard the double doors into the kitchen bang closed. He looked around him at what should have been such a familiar scene and had to admit that the cleaner was right; probably pitch dark would have been easier than this, with light coming in from outside and picking out certain things and swathing others in the deepest shadow. The open-tread staircase looked like an Escher drawing, with bars of orange light from the lamps outside casting the remainder into shadow. Looking up to the landing, he could see only black.

Once he had his foot on the bottom step, he felt more in tune with the flight of stairs and went up them fairly fast, being careful at the top to check that he was on the landing and not another stair. He had seen umpteen students — and colleagues — take a tumble, so he knew how easy it could be to make a misstep and regret it all the way down and even more at the bottom, where the foyer floor was particularly unforgiving.

Once up there, the landing wasn't totally dark either. Maxwell felt a little kindred spirit with the Count and the Chancellor, able to see far more than would immediately seem obvious. The unexpected thing was that he could hear things too, that he wouldn't during the day. There was a faint soughing of the perpetual draught that ran through the building, never ceasing, always there to chill the ankle and riffle papers. He could hear the thirty-seconds-apart clunk of the electric clock on the landing wall. Clocks in classrooms had long since been removed, being too much of a time-waster as kids (and often staff) would stare at the infinitesimally slowly crawling minute hand at the end of each lesson. So this clock — too big for the space, really, so the long-sighted had to lean back to read it — ruled the floor.

Doors ranged ahead, less clearly as they got further away from the window onto the road, which allowed the street light in. One at the far end glowed faintly, with the moonlight, a poor competitor, coming in through the skylight in the roof. Maxwell stood and drank it in. The silence was almost complete. Beneath his feet and a little ahead of him, he knew that Mrs B and Kelly were catching up on all that had befallen since before the start of the half-term holiday. He could hear the occasional reverberation as the big oven doors were slammed closed or when a particularly enormous baking tray was lifted from the stainless-steel sink. It was like listening to a very distant and rather slow steel band rehearsal.

As luck would have it, Room 8 was one whose door was in complete shadow. Still stepping gingerly, Maxwell made his way along the corridor, his fingertips just barely brushing the wall. He had fallen foul of Kelly's cleaning methods before, having once trodden into a discarded bucket and done a couple of steps which would have made Dick Van Dyke go green with envy before ending up head first in the stationery cupboard to the amusement of all. So, although her stamping ground these days seemed to be downstairs, he wasn't taking anything for granted.

The door to Room 8 opened smoothly and without so much as a squeak. He had to take his hat off to Gwen Harris, the probably soon-to-be-former site manager. She did do her best to keep the place in good repair, stuck-open Chemistry window notwithstanding. He switched on the light and blinked for a moment in the brightness. It never seemed quite as glaring in the day. He walked over to the teacher's desk in front of the whiteboard and looked with a dispassionate eye at the display boards around the room. The posters and other paper ephemera really did need replacing. The History Department shared the room with Geography and years ago, rather than pace out who had what square footage and which side of the room got the best light, they had decided to only decorate with subjects that applied to them both. Currently, it was exploration, which, of course, covered both disciplines superbly well. There wasn't really anything else that did it so comprehensively. But everything was looking a bit tired and faded; neither department really wanted to step up to the plate and redo them, so Maxwell decided to take the bull by the horns by stripping the walls and then someone would have to do something. He had a feeling that that someone would end up being him, but it wouldn't be tonight.

Room 8 had originally — back in the days before Leighford High School buildings had spread beyond anyone's wildest dreams — been the Domestic Science hub and retained wide work surfaces around three sides. Not particularly useful in a day-to-day sense, they were nevertheless a popular addition as there was masses of cupboard space beneath and the tops would hold an elephant, so anyone working on the boards had somewhere comfortable to sit. Maxwell himself often sat cross-legged here, ready to outflank a mutinous class if need be. In other rooms, it was a stepladder or — forbidden by Arnie on health and safety grounds, a rule mostly ignored — a couple of chairs and someone standing behind in case of a wrong step. So, for someone doing this job on their own in a darkened and largely empty building, Maxwell assured himself, Room 8 was definitely a sensible choice.

There was a tradition when emptying the boards in any room, but Room 8 had more scope, in that instead of just standing on a drawing pin, there was a strong likelihood that you could kneel on one as well. Maxwell was relieved to have done both within the first five minutes, so there was no need to worry about that any more. The repetitive motion of removing drawing pins and for once having the leisure to put the images together in rational piles instead of putting them in a random pile on the teacher's desk to be sorted later — teacher speak for 'never' — made the job strangely therapeutic. He was halfway down one wall when he heard Kelly call out goodnight and at the corner of the window wall when he heard Mrs B power up The Beast to give the foyer floor its weekly punishment. He stripped the left-hand board quickly and had moved over to the one on the right of the run of windows. He paused to look out. The windows which were such a draw during the day, with their view over the playing fields and then, distantly, the town and the lure of the sea, showed a very different world at night. The playing fields were ghostly under the moon which now was riding high in the sky and the town was a twinkling fairyland. Like many seaside councils, Leighford kept the lights up all year and made them do for Christmas, then for the summer trade. In some years, when the ruling party was greener than usual, they were switched off in between, but at the moment, the council seemed to be in spendthrift mood, so that Maxwell could plot the three main roads leading from the Dam down to the Esplanade and then the mile of seafront itself. He tapped the windowsill to break himself out of his reverie — there were worse places to live, that was for sure.

He had got halfway along the remaining wall when he became aware that the scrubber had been switched off and made an effort to go faster. He didn't want to make Mrs B wait and a half-undecorated board was not something he wanted to leave behind. He distributed his sheaf of images on the teacher's desk and was just climbing back on to the work surface — rather more slowly now than when he had begun — when the light went out. He half turned to see what was happening but never completed the movement. There was a sudden dull pain in the side of his head and then another as the other side hit the floor. He wasn't conscious for the kick in the ribs, but he would certainly know about it later.

CHAPTER ELEVEN

Jacquie was sitting in her favourite spot on the corner of the sofa when the phone rang. It was the landline, which took her a little by surprise, because hardly anyone used it these days. She picked it up quickly, so it didn't wake Nolan or Bismarck, who was sitting in her lap and tended to dig his claws in when woken suddenly.

'Maxwells.' She never gave the number and Maxwell rarely remembered it, preferring his usual 'War Office'.

'Oh,' a voice breathed, 'thank goodness. I wondered if you were in.'

'Mrs B?' Jacquie was instantly alert and brushed Bismarck off so smartly that he didn't have time to so much as flex a digit.

'I'm Up at the School,' the woman said, still speaking quietly.

'I know. And . . . Max . . . ?'

'He's . . . he's here as well,' she said. 'He . . .' Her voice faded as if she had turned her head. 'He's all right now. He's had a bit of a tumble.'

Jacquie was on her feet by now. 'A tumble? What do you mean, a tumble? From where? Not down the stairs, surely?' She was pacing.

'No, no, from about, oh, I don't know, three feet? But I suppose if he was standing up when he fell, well, that's nine foot, ennit? About nine foot?'

In the background, Jacquie could hear someone else talking. If it was Maxwell, that was good news. If it wasn't . . . then who was it? And Maxwell never fell over. He'd been in scrapes, by the dozen, but he wasn't a man who just fell over. She decided to try to retake the whip hand in this conversation. 'Is he all right, Mrs B? Is he . . . conscious? Can I have a word?'

''Course. Hold on, let me change to hands-free. There's some . . . blood. Just a little bit. Don't worry.'

Jacquie could hear Mrs B as she gave the phone to Maxwell. 'There you are, Mr M. Just hold it . . . Are you okay? Do you want to lie down for a bit?'

Lie down? Maxwell never lay down, not for any reason! Jacquie tried to engage non-panicking police person mode, but it wasn't easy. Finally, the voice she needed to hear came on the line.

'Hello, heart. Sorry to . . . sorry to give you a scare. I . . . Mrs B thinks I fell off the . . . thing . . . you know, that thing in Room 8. It's about . . . yay high. You know it?'

'By repute,' she said, trying to keep her voice light. 'How did you fall off?'

'I . . . didn't. I was climbing back on, I only had one knee up on there and . . . the lights went out . . . that's it. The lights went out.'

Jacquie heard Mrs B agree that, yes, the lights were out when she found him.

'Perhaps . . . is it on a timer, something like that?'

Mrs B's voice loomed nearer. 'No. Elf n Safety won't allow it.'

'Right. So . . . Max.' Jacquie was now back on the sofa, curled into a ball. 'Did you feel anything hit you?'

'Anything?'

'Anyone.'

'Both sides of my head are bleeding, if that helps.'

'You can't have hit both sides by falling, surely?' Jacquie was now picking up her mobile from the coffee table and scrolling through numbers. 'Is there anything nearby that could have hit you?'

'I . . . don't know.' Maxwell's voice died away and Jacquie shouted his name in panic. 'Sorry, I . . . bit dizzy. Mrs B? Is there anything that could have hit me?'

There was only silence.

'Mrs B?' Jacquie yelled. 'Mrs *B!*'

'I . . . I don't know how this got here,' the cleaner's voice came, quieter and less strident than usual. 'It's my handheld vac. It's . . . it's got blood on it, Mrs M.'

There was a silence and Jacquie could imagine the two of them locking gazes.

'I didn't do it, though. It was in my bag. I bring it for the corners, y'know. You can't do everything with a mop.'

Jacquie took a deep breath and pinched the bridge of her nose, for some clarity. 'Mrs B. Max. Don't touch anything. Max, if you want to lie down, do, but don't touch the surface you were climbing onto. Mrs B, I'm on my way. Just . . . just wait there, okay? Is the door open?'

'Kel would have locked it, probably. But you can come in at the side. It will play hell with the alarms when we leave, but you can get in that way.'

Jacquie swallowed hard on that small fact. She was pretty sure that no one at the nick knew that a main door to a building which had contained a dead body wasn't locked at night, but she thought that was probably something for later.

'What about . . . ?' Maxwell slurred to a halt.

'What about what?' Jacquie had already pressed call on her mobile.

'Nole.'

'Don't worry. I'm on it. See you soon. Lie down. Relax. Got to go.'

'Hall.'

170

Jacquie turned her attention to her mobile. 'Henry. I've just heard from Max. Someone has attacked him at the school.'

'What was— ?'

'Don't ask. I need to go and get him. Can you come over and sit with Nolan until we get back? Tell me if it's not convenient. Only . . . it will kill two birds with one stone, because you'll hear everything while it's fresh in everyone's minds. I'll get him checked out at A&E; I don't think they'll have to keep him in. He's talking. A bit. So . . .'

'We're on our way.' Henry Hall was a man of few words but they were almost always the right ones. 'We've just come in so we're literally in the hall. Ten minutes. Don't worry.' But Henry Hall *did* worry. If Peter Maxwell was only talking 'a bit', there was something very wrong indeed.

As the phone went down, Jacquie heard him calling to his wife and she breathed a sigh of relief. Sometimes, you didn't need that many people in your life. Just the right ones.

* * *

Jacquie didn't notice that Leighford High loomed on its low hill. She didn't notice how borderline spooky it looked now that the street lights had switched to power-saving mode and were largely out. All she noticed was Mrs B standing by the open front door, talking to someone behind her, someone who she was trying and failing to control.

Jacquie screamed to a stop at the top of the drive and was running up the shallow steps almost before the engine died. Mrs B held open the door a little further for her and stepped aside.

'I'm sorry, Mrs M. I tried to stop him, but you know how he is. He wasn't happy until he was down here, waiting for you.'

On the bottom stair, Maxwell was sitting leaning on the metal newel post, his head back and his eyes closed.

'For God's sake, Max,' Jacquie said, dropping to her knees in front of him. 'What were you thinking? How on earth did you get down the stairs?'

'"You put your right leg in",' he murmured. 'Crime scene. Had to keep the crime scene . . .'

'He come down a step at a time,' Mrs B said. 'I walked down in front of him and he kept a hand on my shoulder. He wouldn't stay up there.' She was beginning to show the strain and Jacquie held out a hand to her, which was quickly taken in a grip like iron — wielding a mop gave you very strong digits, she decided.

'Okay, okay, it's all done now, so let's not dwell. We need to get you to A&E, Max. And you, Mrs B. You've had a shock. *Another* shock, perhaps I should say. Ambulance or car?'

'Car,' Maxwell murmured. 'No hospital, though. Just home, eh?' His eyes suddenly flew open and he grabbed her arm. 'Nole!' he said.

'Henry's there. Henry and Margaret. He couldn't be in better hands. So we don't need to rush back.'

'But . . . I really just want to go home,' he said, his voice trailing away.

'In your dreams,' Jacquie said. 'We're going to Leighford General, I am going to flash my police credentials and we are going to be fast-tracked. *Then* we'll go home. Look,' she checked her watch, 'it's not quite ten. If we get a wiggle on, we'll beat the influx of drunks. Can you wiggle, darling?'

Mrs B had rarely heard out-and-out endearments between the two and she realised properly that this was serious. Without being asked, she went round to one side as Jacquie took the other arm and they gently got Maxwell to his feet.

'Oooh,' he said, smiling down at his attending women. 'Swimmy.' It was a perfect Don Estelle from *It Ain't Half Hot Mum*, but nobody noticed.

'Just wait a second, then,' Jacquie said. 'When you're ready. You're in charge here.'

'Damn straight,' he said. He waited a minute and then opened his eyes, checking. He nodded. 'All right. Let's try it. I assume that Christmas tree on the drive is your car, heart?'

Jacquie had left the door open and all the lights on, so the car was spectacularly easy to find.

'That's right,' she said. 'Let's just aim for the light.'

'Don't go into the light.' For a man with a concussion, it was a fair rendition of JoBeth Williams in *Poltergeist*.

Jacquie chuckled. There had been times — and she knew there would be more — when Maxwell had scared the life out of her, but when he could do film take-offs, how bad could things be?

While she wrestled him into the front seat, giving him a folded coat to put between his head and the front window, to support it, Mrs B went back to the school building and locked the door. The timekeeper would say that she had knocked off early, but that would be an argument for another day.

* * *

Leighford General was the kind of hospital that doesn't make headlines. It did everything passably well, it had had no homicidal nurses, or at least none that had ever been detected. Its recovery rates, its diagnostic stats and its waiting lists were all just on the good side of average. Its buildings were Nineties, a little bit worn but not yet crumbling. Its grounds were still not all given up to car parks charging a king's ransom for every hour a car was there. All in all, if you had to be rushed to hospital in the middle of the night with a head injury — no, make that two head injuries — Maxwell mused, you could do a whole lot worse.

Jacquie parked the car in the short-stay A&E section, which gave them both a moment of amusement — whoever thought that an A&E visit would warrant short-stay status? Mrs B went off to find a wheelchair, while Maxwell, protesting, struggled to get out of the car. Eventually, after sounds of distant cursing, she appeared pushing something more closely related to a Victorian bath chair than a normal wheelchair.

'What's that?' Maxwell muttered, climbing aboard. 'I feel like the Akond of Swat.'

'There's a sign,' Mrs B said, gratefully giving up pushing duties to Jacquie. 'Apparently, people kept nicking the fold-up ones, so now they have these. Shocking, ain't it?'

'Not as shocking as these wheels,' Jacquie said, as they careened into a gully at the side of the path. 'They're like the worst supermarket trollies in the world all rolled into one.'

'Let me walk,' Maxwell said, wriggling to show willing. 'I can, honestly.'

With difficulty, Jacquie applied the brake and went round to face him. 'I daresay you can,' she said, hands on hips. 'But think on this for a minute. I turn up with a mad old git under his own steam and say it's an emergency. Or I turn up with same mad old git in a wheelchair and say it's an emergency. Which mad old git gets seen this side of Easter?' She waited. 'Hmm?'

'Point taken,' he said, settling back down in the unforgiving plastic seat. 'That nice Mr Nye Bevan didn't mean it to be like this.'

'So,' Jacquie said, when they were negotiating the hair-trigger automatic doors into the department. 'What do we not say when they ask how we are?'

'The royal we already?' Maxwell said, with a trace of his old self. 'I might as well check myself in to Tiergarten 4 now and save everyone the trouble.'

Jacquie ignored him, but was secretly pleased that he had become a bit bolshie; this was more like Maxwell. 'And your answer is?'

'Fine. I won't say I'm fine,' he grumbled.

'Right answer.'

By now, they were at the desk, Mrs B an outrider behind Jacquie, ready to wade in, though she didn't think for a moment it would be necessary.

In the time-honoured fashion of A&E receptionists, the woman at the keyboard scarcely looked up.

'Name?'

Jacquie said, 'We're not booked in, we . . .'

Wordlessly, the woman slid a piece of paper and a stub of pencil across the desk. Jacquie slid it back, with her police ID on top of it. Startled, the woman looked up.

'Is this a victim of crime?' she said, not willing to give up the high ground without a fight.

'Is this?' Jacquie said acidly. 'Do you mean is this gentleman in the chair, a human being, a victim of a crime? Yes, indeed he is. As is this lady. So, I would appreciate being put in a room *with* a door and with a doctor the right side of it within five minutes. As for the piece of paper . . .'

Maxwell looked down and smiled at his lap while Mrs B held her breath.

'. . . I will be filling in my own paperwork later, of which you will get a copy. Now, which way, left or right?' She gave the woman a humourless smile.

The receptionist picked up the phone and murmured into it. Within what seemed to be a few seconds, two nurses appeared and one took Mrs B to triage while the other trundled Maxwell into a side room.

'Smartly done, immortal beloved,' Maxwell said, eyeing the bed longingly. 'Do you think I could . . . could have a lie-down?'

'We'd better wait,' Jacquie said. 'I expect there'll be X-rays and such.'

'The lights are so bright in here,' Maxwell said, shielding his eyes. 'Are the lights bright in here, do you think?'

Jacquie agreed. She could also do with something a little more ambient. In what she hoped would be just a few seconds remaining before the doctor arrived, she said urgently, 'Who did this, Max? Did you get any clue at all?'

'None. But I can say quite categorically that it was Gwen Harris.'

175

Jacquie was surprised. But perhaps it was the concussion talking. 'Any reason for that?'

Maxwell thought for a moment. There were any number of reasons, but they all needed more words than he could really be bothered to use right now. He settled for a very careful shrug. 'Just is. Tell you later.' He closed his eyes.

The door opened and closed again quietly, revealing a twelve-year-old in a white coat. Closer investigation revealed the age estimate to be a little low, but not by much. He held a clipboard.

'Right, now, Mr Maxwell,' he said, then, aside to Jacquie, 'that's the name the other lady gave for this gentleman. Is that right?' Obviously word had got round and politesse was the watchword.

'That's right,' Jacquie said. 'I'm his wife.'

The doctor's eyes unfocused for a moment. 'Oh, I . . . sorry, I was told you were from the police.'

'It is possible to be from the police and also married to someone,' she pointed out. 'Mr Maxwell has been attacked and then fell. He has a contusion on the right side and a rather worse one on the left. I think that the left side was caused by a blunt instrument, probably a handheld vacuum cleaner, and the one on the right was caused by falling to the floor, more or less from standing.'

The doctor stepped forward. 'It's a shame all spouses aren't police as well,' he observed. 'It would make our jobs a lot easier.' He pulled a small flashlight out of his top pocket and shone it into Maxwell's eyes, one by one. 'There is normal pupil reaction, so that's a good thing. Can you follow my finger, Mr Maxwell? Can I call you Peter?'

'Not if you want an answer,' Jacquie said. 'No one calls him that. He answers to Max when he wants to answer at all.'

The doctor stood up and looked at Maxwell properly for the first time. 'Are you . . . are you *Mad Max*?' he asked. 'My girlfriend goes on about you all the time. You were her teacher at school.'

Jacquie wondered if a day would ever come when they would not meet an Old Highena or one of their family. But this was probably a good thing, as Maxwell had often said when they had taken ten minutes to do a one-minute walk down the High Street. Usually, Maxwell would ask for names, but his eyes had closed again and the doctor bent back down and felt carefully at the sides of his head. Maxwell winced, but there didn't seem to be much more required so he didn't bother opening his eyes.

'Well, Mrs Maxwell,' the doctor said. 'I think what we have here is a mild concussion. There is no significant swelling and, more importantly, no depressive fracture, so what we have to conclude is that your husband here has a skull like a cannonball. If you want, for evidence purposes, we can do an X-ray, but clinically, I don't think it's necessary. He is sleepy, which is something we watch for, but then again, it is getting late and he has had a shock. Has he got worse, since he was found?'

Jacquie looked at her husband, dozing in his bath chair. 'No, he hasn't. He has improved if anything. Little bit of his sense of humour coming back, he knows where he is and why.'

'Could you take him home? Would there be anyone to stay with him for, say, the next twenty-four, forty-eight hours? It's just that if he gets difficult to rouse, hallucinates, anything like that, you may need to bring him back in.'

'I have to answer that with a question. Is the lady I came in with also okay to go home?'

'I didn't see her. Hang on, I'll go and see.' The slightly-older-than-twelve-year-old dipped out of the room for a moment but was soon back. 'She's ready to go home as well. She was in shock, but we did quick bloods and she's fine, oxygen levels all normal, pupils, all the rest of it. We offered her some Valium but she . . . she was quite sure she didn't want any.' Jacquie smiled. She would have expected no less. 'So, if she is part of your plan I would say, yes, he's good to go home.' He scribbled on a pad. 'He'll need painkillers for a day or two, rest of the week off work. A nurse will be in in a minute to do a dressing and just make sure the wounds are clean. Especially as one was caused by . . . did you really say a vacuum cleaner?'

Jacquie nodded and Maxwell, temporarily in the room, gave a low chuckle.

'There might be dust, fluff, all sorts in there then, so it needs a clean. The dressing will really be to make it more comfortable to lie down and also to remind him he has a head injury. Something he will need, if what Chantal tells me is true.'

'Chantal!' Maxwell said. 'How lovely. How is she getting on?'

'Very well,' the doctor beamed. 'She's in line for associate next year. We're getting married in the summer.'

'Wonderful,' Maxwell said, and the doctor left the room with a waggle of his fingers.

'You remember his girlfriend, then,' Jacquie remarked as they settled down to wait for the nurse and her bandages to arrive.

'Nope. No idea who she is. But he thinks I do, and she will and that's the main thing.'

Choosing her spot carefully, Jacquie bent down and kissed Maxwell's forehead gently. 'I do love you, Peter Maxwell,' she whispered. 'And I won't be letting you go out cleaning again any time soon!'

* * *

After what seemed a lifetime, Peter Maxwell was ensconced in his favourite chair in his favourite place on earth, home. Henry and Margaret Hall had dozed off but like good babysitters do, had roused themselves when the cavalcade arrived at the door. Henry had helped Maxwell up the stairs by the simple expedient of walking behind him at his pace. As he said, he was probably the only one present who could take the hit if he fell backwards. Metternich and Bismarck watched with big eyes as the man who seemed to think he was their master went slowly past them. The cats exchanged glances. Played right, this could be an opportunity to have a nice midnight feast. Henry and Margaret made going home noises but Jacquie stopped them.

'Margaret,' she said. 'Can I ask one last favour? Could I just borrow Henry for a few more minutes?'

Margaret Hall had not been a policeman's wife for a millennium without knowing the rules. She got up to go into another room.

'No, no, stay here,' Jacquie said. 'I know how it works. Anything you hear when Henry has his policeman's hat on, even if it's the casual one he wears at weekends and in the evening, is not to be shared.'

'If you're sure . . .' Margaret said. 'But even so, I will go and feed those lovely pussies of yours, if I may. They looked a bit hungry, I thought. Henry said not to listen to them, but . . .'

Maxwell chuckled. 'Margaret,' he said, 'those cats can spot a soft touch at a million paces. But yes, go and feed them, by all means. They've probably been worrying.'

Mrs B had subsided into the sofa and sat there with her feet planted like an ox in the furrow. She wasn't going anywhere.

'I'll make this quick, Henry,' Jacquie said. 'It's getting late.'

'Can I?' Maxwell interrupted. 'I was with Mrs B at the school, Henry, because the body last week was a bit of a facer, even for her.'

'I should think so,' Henry said, turning to the woman. 'I'm surprised you're back yet.'

'It's that Gwen Up at the School,' Mrs B said, with venom. 'Getting any sick leave out of her is like getting blood out of a stone.'

'I went to see her,' Maxwell said, 'Gwen Harris, the site manager, this morning . . . is it still Monday?'

Everyone except Maxwell checked their phones. 'Just barely,' Jacquie said.

'I promised Mrs B that I would see if she could change her shift and eventually, Gwen agreed. But she wouldn't give her a daytime one, she would only give her the last one, seven to ten, because she worked that one and the swap was easy to do.'

'Cow,' Mrs B muttered.

'When I was in her storeroom, I became aware of some students, literally hidden in the dark in the shelving. They were all on phones.'

'Of course they were,' Henry pointed out. 'Kids are always on phones.'

'Not at Leighford High they aren't,' Maxwell told him. 'Since last week, they have been banned. What with one thing and another,' Jacquie frowned at him — that seemed a rather disrespectful way to talk about a dead person, but she could see he wasn't quite himself, 'today was the first day it kicked in. Polly Allington and I made sure that none crept in first thing and I know that everyone was vigilant throughout the morning. And yet, when I went down to her bolthole, there they were, a dozen or so of the quieter kids, all on phones.'

'Have you reported it?' Henry said. 'It sounds . . . I don't know what it sounds, but surely, she shouldn't be doing that?'

'No, and I planned to do it tomorrow, when I had talked to one of the Year Thirteens who was there, but . . . I'll have to get Helen on it now, I suppose. My gaolers won't be letting me out tomorrow, if I know anything.'

Jacquie and Mrs B made generalised damn straight noises.

'Where was I?'

'Kids. Phones.'

'Yes, right. They gave them up without a murmur; they weren't their phones, they all belonged to Gwen Harris. And they weren't even doing the usual social stuff, as far as I could tell from the few with screens still up. It looked as if they were playing card games. I didn't know kids even did that these days.'

Margaret came back into the room, shutting the door quietly behind her. Back in the day, her boys had slept with one eye open and one ear cocked and she and Henry had spent what had felt like a lifetime creeping around like burglars after their bedtime. She had never really got her head around the fact that Nolan could have slept soundly at a brass band convention if he were tired enough.

'I expect they were playing those games where you win money,' she said, sitting down and looking from one to the other. Hall looked at her as if she had just produced a rabbit from a hat. She caught the look and laughed. 'Henry,' she said, 'I know I am not exactly a computer whizz, but I don't live down a well. Some of the ladies at the book club do it. It's a bit of fun, really, you don't win big money. Mainly, it's a way to drag people in and show them endless ads. Presumably, it's worth their while. But . . .' She looked puzzled. 'Did you say kids, Max? I don't know how they do that, then. Not kids.'

'You're right,' Mrs B said. 'You need a PayPal account and also you need to prove you're over eighteen. They couldn't play for money. Perhaps they . . . just like card games.'

No one thought that sounded likely.

'Or . . .' Maxwell said. Then he stopped. No one knew whether he had just had a recurrence of the concussion or whether he was still thinking. Then, 'Gwen Harris is signed in on all the phones, and the PayPal accounts are hers.'

'Can you do that?' Margaret said, secure in her innocence.

Mrs B snorted. 'I reckon I could teach anyone in this room to do it in minutes,' she said. 'And yes, Mr M, that means you. You just need . . .' she glanced at Henry who was beginning to look interested, 'a bit of knowledge of websites, and you're done. The trick is to use different keywords to log on, you can even use your own address over and over if you're careful. Use a name for one, a number for another, street name, town, nearby town — by the time you've used every combination, you already have a fairly solid foundation. Most sites will allow three or four email addresses per physical address; PayPal, you can add a debit card rather than a bank account. Ooh, there are loads of ways to beat the system.' Again she covertly glanced at Henry. 'Not that I would, of course.'

'But these games are scams, surely?' Jacquie asked.

'You'd have to play a lot and have some luck, but if that Gwen has got a load of kids playing every break and some of them probably after school as well, she's tipping the odds in her favour.'

'And if she doesn't pay them a cut, just lets them hole up in her storage room for breaks and such . . .' Maxwell chipped in.

'She could be on to a good thing,' Henry concluded.

'But, Max,' Jacquie said. 'It's a long way between being caught out in what is after all not strictly illegal and bopping you over the head with a vacuum cleaner.'

Margaret's eyes were wide. Her vacuum cleaner was the most enormous that Mr Dyson had to offer and she often had to ask Henry's help to get it up the stairs. This Gwen they were talking about must be built like a brick lavatory if she could hit anyone round the head with it.

Jacquie saw her confusion. 'It was a handheld, Margaret. But even so, it gave Max a nasty knock.'

'Where is it?' Hall asked. 'Did you bring it with you?'

'No,' Jacquie admitted. 'What with one thing and another . . . sorry.'

'Understandable,' Henry said. 'When does she get to school? Mrs B?'

'She's taken over my shift, so seven. A bit before.'

'I'll just get someone from the nick to be there at half six,' Henry said, reaching for his phone. 'See how Ms Harris enjoys being interviewed under caution.'

Maxwell was suddenly so tired he could hardly speak. He tried to turn his head to look around the room, but that seemed like an awful lot of work. Dimly, he heard someone ask someone else if they could help put him to bed. If he didn't nod, then he certainly meant to. And then, there was a cool pillow behind his head, and dark and silence.

* * *

Jacquie and Henry had a brief phone call the next morning, while she was getting breakfast for Nolan. It was brief because Henry wouldn't take any rubbish about Jacquie having Mrs B all lined up to do the morning shift of watching Maxwell. It was brief because he was about to go into Interview Room 3 — the one with the leak from the room above which dripped one single irritating drip once every forty-two seconds precisely — to interview the living hell out of Gwen Harris. And it was brief because, essentially, Jacquie Carpenter-Maxwell was out on her feet, having watched her husband sleeping all night, counting his breathing and occasionally having a little cry.

Eventually, she gave in gracefully. 'All right, Henry. I give in. But let me know as soon as—'

'When I know, you'll know,' he said. 'There isn't much doubt, though, is there?'

'I don't think so. Max was wakeful around four o'clock and said to tell you that the confiscated phones are in his drawer in his office. Helen will get them for you. Also, I've texted you a list of names of the kids. It's not exhaustive, but—'

'Yes, I've got that. With any luck, they won't be involved. Without her hitting him round the head, this would have been a storm in a teacup. She'd have lost her job, probably, but surely that's better than a custodial sentence. Because she's bound to get that.'

'Do you think she had anything to do with Gavin Masters?' The question needed to be asked.

'I'll let you know,' he said again. 'Now, get Nolan off to school and then *go to sleep*. I won't ring unless I really need to.'

'Henry.'

'Yes?'

'Thank you. You and Margaret, for last night.'

'You're welcome. Margaret is very chuffed she knew about those card games.'

'I know! It must be like living with Miss Marple.'

'But without the knitting. Must go, I think I hear site manager noises in the corridor. *Go to sleep*.'

Jacquie knew she was honoured to see the other side of Henry Hall, the side that wasn't all po face and blank glasses. Nolan was being super good that morning — one step down from tremendously good, which usually only happened in the run-up to birthdays and Christmas — and was ready without the usual ten times of asking. With loud music blaring just to be sure she stayed awake, Jacquie delivered him to school and then got back to the house, snuggled in next to her dozing husband and did, finally, go to sleep.

CHAPTER TWELVE

Both Maxwells woke at almost noon and looked at each other with a smile. In spite of the large bandage and two glorious black eyes, Maxwell was himself again. It all seemed like a rather Grand Guignol dream, with a touch of Stephen King, but in the daylight creeping in around the curtains, everything seemed brighter.

Jacquie leaned over and kissed him on the nose. 'How's the head?'

He reached up and encountered bandage much sooner than he expected to. 'This bandage is . . . big,' he said. 'But under it, I don't feel too bad. I don't remember everything. Do I have stitches, for instance?'

'Nothing so dramatic. You have some Steri-strips on the left-hand side, just an ordinary non-occlusive dressing on the right.'

'Hark at you, with all these medical terms.'

'The nurse was a bit of a sharer. But there's no need to go back, if you feel better. You are definitely off this week, though.'

'I'll be fine to go back tomo—'

'Forget it, sunshine. Apart from anything else, the nice infant doctor at the General—'

'I'm so glad you said that. I thought I had hallucinated a teenager.'

'Yes, he said that he would be sending a report to school. Because his girlfriend Chantal said you wouldn't stay home otherwise.'

'Dratted Chantal, whichever one she is. There was a bit of a trend about ten years ago, if you remember. We had to number them, in the end.'

'Max, please don't give me any lip.'

He put his hands up. If he were to be totally honest, he wouldn't mind a few days in bed. He didn't tell Jacquie, though, he knew she would only worry.

'I'll stay home. But I need to ring in, to give cover instructions. Is that all right, milady?'

'That, I'll allow. Meanwhile, I'm just going to check the phone to see if Henry has been in touch at all.'

'Perfect. And then, some lunch?'

'You're hungry?'

He looked thoughtful and licked his lips. 'I could just go some beans on toast, for some bizarre reason. Just half a slice and a small tin. Would that be doable?'

She smiled from the doorway. 'I'll have the other half and we can share a medium tin. Like old times.'

Maxwell cast his mind back. Sure enough, there were memories of midnight beans on toast, before and after Nolan. Neither of them ever ate them under normal circumstances, but today, when he was back from being murdered, it just seemed right somehow.

Jacquie was soon back, brandishing her phone.

'News?'

'They had her in. She immediately rang for her solicitor, who turned out to be that total Rottweiler who you read about in the paper all the while, getting dodgy businessmen off tax evasion, that kind of thing. Member of the Mafia Lawyers' Association.'

'I know him. Slicked-back hair. Awful pinstripe suit with really narrow trousers.'

'I didn't have you down for a fashion guru but — yes, that's him.'

'And?'

'Well, they didn't mention Gavin Masters, started with you. Brief immediately bounced in with the fact that you had gone to the storeroom to make advances to Gwen Harris.'

Maxwell's eyebrows disappeared under his bandage.

'When Henry said that they had a list of the kids involved, he backtracked on that and said that she was suffering from menopausal hallucinations and didn't mean that. What she meant was that you were obsessed with phones and stole some spare ones she had in her desk drawer. After that was blown out of the water, the final thing was that she didn't remember a thing, that she is a gambling addict who is also addicted to over-the-counter pain meds and cough mixture and she couldn't tell right from wrong.'

'And then.'

'Well, there is no "then". That turns out to be absolutely true. They did a blood test and sent it in. The results didn't take long, thanks to the usual police persuasion. She was totally off her face on a concoction of various painkillers and some bath salts nonsense that was all over the internet a while back. Add in the stonking overdraft and I think it's a good defence, as it goes. She's signed herself in to some rehab place in South London somewhere, and we had to let her go.'

Maxwell leaned back on his pillows. 'It's hard to believe she was just pottering around the place, counting soap and whatnot while all the time . . . she was Leighford High's answer to Fagin. How many kids were involved?'

'She wasn't sure. She had twenty phones in all and sometimes they were all in use, sometimes just some. She made a small profit over the week and there was a touch of vicarious gambling as well, I think.' She sat on the edge of the bed. 'I know she shouldn't go around hitting people upside the head . . .'

'Thank you,' he said, coolly. 'I'm glad of that.'

'You know what I mean. Of *course* she shouldn't. But I can't help feeling sorry for her, in a way. And you're all right, so I don't want to bear an unnecessary grudge.'

'I think you're too good for me, heart,' he said. 'What had Gavin Masters done to her?'

'She's not put her hands up on that one. Yet.'

'It seems a bit coincidental, though. He was all over the building, laying wires, staple-gunning anything that wasn't nailed down already. He could easily have rumbled her little game.'

'That's what we're working on. But she is adamant she doesn't even know him. To her, she claims, they all look alike. Apart from that one that looks a bit like Tom Hiddleston.'

Maxwell looked pensive, then smiled. 'If getting bashed round the head helps solve this, I'm glad. I don't know what this will do to the scheduling, though.'

'Ah, sorry, meant to say. I had a WhatsApp from Helen. Apparently, they've taken a new path with the documentary. They're concentrating on the SLT. The stresses and strains, etc. Arnie restuck her teeth and then Mandy walked in in a dress that she might as well have painted on and Arnie was nowhere. They even have Bob in a subsidiary role. He reminds Zac of the young Anthony Hopkins, so that's him sorted.'

Maxwell pouted. 'So my starring days are over,' he said, trying to sound as though he cared. 'Young Anthony Hopkins my arse, by the way.'

'By no means are they over. They are planning a sequel — which they don't call sequels any more, but that's what it is — for when they charge Gwen Harris with Gavin's murder and then you will be up front and centre. The One That Got Away.'

'Who?'

'You. Because, you know, you didn't die.' She was glad that she knew him so well, or she would have him back in A&E like a rat up a pipe, for relapsing.

'No, the one *who* got away, not that.'

'Oh, I see. It's a grammatical thing, with you lying there with concussion and a man dead in the morgue.'

'Grammar is important,' Maxwell said. 'Now, any chance of them beans?'

* * *

After lunch, it became increasingly obvious that Jacquie wanted to check in on the nick and Maxwell finally convinced her that he wouldn't immediately relapse if she left him for an hour or so. She had to get Nolan after all, so . . . he made shooing noises and gestures and eventually she gave in and went, but not before she made sure that he had his phone, suitably charged, in his trouser pocket. After a few false starts, he finally heard her car start up and drive away and he sat back in his chair and closed his eyes.

Despite the painkillers, he had an absolutely banging headache, as if a couple of small anvils were being beaten in counterpoint by two little blacksmith elves, standing on his ears. His cheeks ached with the swelling from his black eyes. His right shoulder hurt from where he had fallen on it and the rest of him hurt because he had spent a couple of hours climbing up and down off a waist-high surface. This being murdered game — it was for the youngsters, that was certain. He allowed himself to drift off and said goodbye to first the sinus pain, then the shoulder, and he was just about to see off the blacksmiths when the doorbell went. He briefly toyed with ignoring it. If it were Mrs B she would just let herself in. If it were anyone else — who actually cared? But when it went again, he levered himself up out of his chair and carefully made his way down the stairs.

'Max. How the hell are you?'

Polly Allington *had* been to 38 Columbine before, but that was at a New Year party and she could barely remember how she got there, still less how she got back. Jeremy always drove when they went out and his car had satnav so sophisticated it all but got out and rang the bell for you. This afternoon, the satnav on her phone was on the blink and she'd had to navigate old school, up past the Dam, left at the crossroads. It all began to fall into place. As soon as she got to the first road named after a flower — Artemisia Drive — she knew she was almost there.

NHS bandaging of the type they do in A&E is not a good look on anyone, but Maxwell was beyond caring. When he'd checked himself in the mirror earlier, he rather saw himself as Cyrano de Bergerac in the last, poignant scene in the play where (spoiler alert!) he dies of a head wound. Of course, he didn't have the nose for it. Nor the hair. Nor the poetic skills and swordsmanship. Other than that, he was a dead ringer.

'Polly,' he smiled, but that hurt, so he settled for a grimace instead. 'I'm doing it! I'm doing it!'

'What?' she frowned. Clearly the bash over the head was taking its toll on the old bugger.

'Year Eleven coursework. We've still got a few days to go, haven't we?'

'Good God, Max, I'm not here about that. I came to see how you are. My blessed double free of a Tuesday afternoon. It's not every day that the national treasure of my department gets bopped over the head. Can I come in?'

'Oh, God, sorry, Polly. Where are my manners? Of course. Watch the—'

She stumbled on cue.

'Threshold. It needs work, but don't tell Elf n Safety.'

He slowly led her up the stairs to the kitchen. 'Grab a seat,' he said. 'Coffee? Tea? Pint of champagne? I gather that's the new thing.'

'Coffee, please,' she said. 'Black. But let me do that, Max. You should be taking it easy.'

'My good woman.' He stood up to his full height, annoyed that it didn't quite match hers, particularly in his slippers. 'This is the twenty-first century. As the New Man of my time, I am perfectly capable of making a . . . now, where the hell has the Mem put those little poddy jobs? Ah . . .' His rummage in the cupboard paid dividends. 'Here we go. One lump or two?' He smiled at her and managed to do it this time with minimal pain. 'Or is that just my head?'

Polly had found a seat and slid Nolan's latest elaborate Lego creation to one side to give her room on the table. 'Is it *very* painful?' She was wincing for him.

'Well, it missed my brain by several feet, of course, so no harm done.'

'What's going on, Max?' She was suddenly serious.

'Up at the School, you mean?' He ferreted in the fridge for the milk.

'Yes, I do.'

'Well, you know, same old, same old. Those who don't learn from History are doomed to repeat it.'

'Max!' she growled at him. 'You know what I'm talking about.'

'Yes.' He was suddenly serious too as he handed her her coffee. 'The body in the library that turned out to be Arnie's office.'

'Well, bizarre doesn't describe it.'

'Agreed, but if you say "Things like that don't happen in Leighford" I'm going to risk bursting my bandages and scream until I am sick. Murder happens everywhere — it's no respecter of people or places.'

'All right,' she conceded. 'But even so. Look, I'm a relative newcomer around here. I don't pretend to know the ins and outs. And the television thing can't be a coincidence, can it? Everything's as you say, same old, same old until they turned up.'

'Why the school, though?' Maxwell was talking to himself, really.

'How do you mean?'

'If somebody had it in for Gavin Masters, for whatever reason, why not kill him at his home? In his car? In the pub? Why wait until he gets to Leighford High? So, obviously it's about the television people,' he reasoned, 'but there's another dimension, too, some kind of link with the school. Joe Pargeter's convinced it's nothing to do with his lot, which is pushing it a bit.'

'Joe Pargeter!' she snorted. 'He came across as a complete arsehole, I thought.'

Maxwell smiled. 'That's why you're Head of History,' he said. 'Summer-up of situations, grasper of nettles. Allowing for certain differences, you could be me in a frock.'

'Eughh,' she scowled. 'There's a thought. Then we come to Gwen Harris.'

'Indeed we do.' Maxwell felt his head spin again. 'You'll have to fill me in there. My memory of the last few hours isn't as clear as it might be.'

'I thought Jacquie would have filled you in,' Polly said, sipping her brew.

'Uh-uh.' Maxwell was about to shake his head, then thought better of it. 'We have an unspoken rule, the Mem and I. She tells me nothing until I've stretched her out over an anthill in the garden under a blazing sun. Only then does she crack and confess all — I could tell you things about Leighford nick that'd make your bogles dangle!'

'Seriously, though.' She raised an eyebrow.

'Seriously, Polly, Jacquie doesn't tell me anything — not nuts and bolts, anyway. Especially in this instance. If the whole assault thing becomes a court case, I'll be a witness. So Jacquie can't get involved in all that. Gwen's defence team would wipe the floor with her.'

'But she *is* under arrest, though? Gwen, I mean.'

'I don't think it's as simple as they make it look on television — although, my apologies, you must know more about procedure than I do, with Jeremy and everything.'

'He doesn't tell me anything more than Jacquie tells you,' Polly said. 'He's like a clam, is Jeremy.'

'As I understand it, she was taken in this morning—'

'Too right! The whole school is still agog!'

'And she was questioned. But, again as I understand it, she is now no longer at the nick.' Maxwell wasn't proud, but he could dissemble for England when he had to.

'They let her go?'

'Not so much "let" as had to, I gather. She had a very good lawyer. And again, you would know all about that.'

'The thing that none of us can understand, in the staffroom, I mean, is why? Why would a site manager try to kill a Head of Sixth Form? You didn't teach her, did you? Revenge being a dish best served cold, et cetera?'

'If I did, she is the one who got away,' Maxwell said, for the second time that day.

'I'm just kidding, Max,' Polly said. 'The point is, though, that in the space of less than a week, we've had one murder and one attempted murder. There has to be a link. And that means . . .'

'Yes?'

Polly shrugged. 'It's Gwen. Gwen did them both.'

Maxwell was shaking his head, slowly and carefully. 'Just between you and me, I caught a boatload of kids in Gwen's storeroom the other day.'

'Really?'

'Yes. I went there to . . . well, it doesn't matter. And there they were.'

'What, she knew about it?'

'Oh, yes. I told her I would have to tell Arnie about it, though whether I would have or not is moot. Being the class sneak isn't really my thing. And she knew I was on to her, so I'm sure it would have all died a death after that, anyway. No need to involve the Predator.'

'So . . . what if Gavin found out as well. Put a rather less generous light on it than you have. Would she kill him, do you suppose?'

'I don't know. I have heard that . . . well, I have heard that he wasn't a very nice person, so I doubt he would have baulked at, I don't know, blackmail? He had rather a cavalier attitude to women, or so I gather. That nice girl Mel, the sound engineer; you must have seen her . . . I got that from Mel herself, not Jacquie, by the way. But whatever the story is, I'm sure that Jacquie and her boss Henry Hall will have a take on it.'

193

'But you'll be the last to know,' she smiled.

'Exactly. You'll read all abaht it in the *Leighford Advertiser* before anything will pass my lips. Talking of which,' he held out a packet. 'Hobnob?'

She declined. 'Max, I couldn't help noticing. Were you in the middle of cooking, here?' She gestured to the vegetables laid out on the kitchen surface.

'Thought I'd surprise the Mem,' he said. 'I have to admit that this is not the first bump I've had and she does worry about me. I thought if I got the goulash going — you know, just the right amount of goul without making a hash of it.'

'For God's sake, man, let me do that. I'm Tante Marie trained.'

'A first-class degree,' his eyes widened, 'albeit from London university, an excellent teacher *and* you can cook. Jeremy's a lucky man.'

'So I keep telling him,' she chuckled and within seconds, she was dicing onions with a speed that made Maxwell's eyes water.

'I can never work out how you don't slice your fingers off,' he said. 'You don't seem to be looking at what you're doing.'

She laughed. 'Believe me, Max, I never let my eyes wander. It's nice that your knives are in good nick. Some people are very slack and wash them in the dishwasher and everything. Jeremy is a bit of a stickler for that kind of thing. I suppose being a perfectionist is what has made him top of his game. The Tante Marie was a wedding present from his parents. I need to be able to cook, for when he entertains clients and colleagues. It can get a bit posh in our house, sometimes!'

'I expect nothing less,' said Maxwell, still mesmerised.

'There,' she said, scraping it all into the pot, 'and Jacquie will never know.' A thought occurred to her. 'I wonder,' she said, looking into the middle distance of Maxwell's kitchen, 'if what's going on is more direct than that. That there's a link between Gwen and this Masters bloke. Knew him before, kind of thing. Didn't I hear he lived not far from here? Anyway, what if she was poncing for him? Something like that.'

Maxwell gave her a private ten out of ten for imagination. 'Blimey.' Maxwell swallowed half his biscuit. 'That's a *Sun* banner headline, right there.'

'Yes, it's probably not as dramatic as that,' she said. 'But . . . you didn't know the sound guy, did you? Another Old Highena?'

'No,' Maxwell said. 'No, I didn't. Why do you ask?'

'Well,' Polly wriggled back down in her seat, getting into full conspiratorial comfort mode, 'if you *had* known him, Gwen kills him for reasons yet to be named. *You* know why, because you know them both. And she knows you know. So you have to die too.'

'Except I didn't,' Maxwell said. 'And although I don't have the details, as I understand it, Masters was stabbed. I got clobbered round the head. Serial killers rarely change their MO. Gwen should have gone for me with a blade.'

'Let's hope,' Polly held her cup out for a refill, 'she won't get another opportunity.'

* * *

After Polly had left, Maxwell looked at the clock and calculated that he had about an hour and a half before Jacquie and Nolan got back. He didn't want to be like a dying duck in a thunderstorm around Nolan. It had been a shock to him to find his father swathed in bandages, though he had hidden it well, so Maxwell wanted to be as near to normal as he ever came when they returned. So a nap would probably be a good plan. Polly had let herself out, to his relief — the stairs were still something of a challenge. He had heard her talking to someone and braced himself for an influx of Mrs B, but it turned out to be Metternich, on his own for once; Bismarck was obviously out scouting for rats. Although they were amply provided with cat flaps, both animals preferred to have the door opened for them — less bother than opening one with their head and also, proof, should proof be needed, that humans were indeed their slaves.

Metternich was not a lap cat, unless the lap was Jacquie's, so Maxwell was surprised when he jumped up and made himself comfortable spread out along his thighs, his head on his forepaws lolling on his stomach. He purred briefly and Maxwell was quite touched. The old softie loved him after all. As though he could read his mind, the great beast flexed his claws, not quite breaking through the moleskin of his undress trousers but just to show he could, if he wanted, flay him alive like a vole.

Maxwell risked stroking him between the shoulder blades, his favourite place until it wasn't. With over a stone of cat on his lap, Maxwell knew that sleep was not likely so accepted that just a little downtime would have to suffice. Last night's events were running through his head anyway, so he started talking to his favourite sounding board.

'Sorry about the headgear, Count,' he said. 'I daresay it came as a bit of a shock, when I came home like this.'

Metternich didn't answer; it would have been hurtful to let the mad old git know that as far as he and Bismarck were concerned, an extra sachet each had taken away any shock. There were some things a cat just didn't share.

'It was bad enough, to be honest, to be bopped on the head and left for dead, but it's worse to discover you're one of a pair. Or was I? I'm having difficulty finding any links between me and Gavin Masters. He was not from Leighford, though he wasn't from far away, I suppose. So that might be a small tick in that box. He was a bit of a stinker, by all accounts, which I like to think I am not. He took advantage left and right and I can't say I took to him much on our brief acquaintance. He struck me as being the sort of bloke who would use anyone to get a bit closer to the money. Or power. Or perhaps some of each. He certainly seemed to think he would be climbing the greasy pole to directorhood any day now, whereas I am not the ambitious type.'

The cat raised his head and looked at Maxwell with just one sleepy eye.

'And you're right, of course. What do I have to be ambitious about? I have a perfect family, home, job and . . .' he paused to release the impending claw, 'cats, so I don't need to struggle against my peers. But to be fair to me, Count, and I know this will shock you, but in the days before you owned me, I wasn't ambitious either. So we have to think of other things.'

Maxwell became aware of an incipient cramp in his left calf. This wasn't going to end well because turfing Metternich off a lap before he was ready to go was not popular, as a rule. He carried on mulling; perhaps he could just talk the cramp away. What did his heartless old PE teacher say in the brave days of old? 'Walk through the pain.'

'His job involved his putting wires and mics in unlikely places. It's a smallish team, as I understand it, for this kind of filming, so he might have done other things as well. I did notice when they were filming me . . .' again, his interest piqued, the cat looked up, 'yes, I told you. We'll let you know when, if ever, it airs. What was I saying? Oh, yes, when they were filming me in Room 8, there were little bits of gaffer tape on the floor, angles marked out for the cameraman. Some kids haven't got parental permission, so they have to be careful they aren't in shot, that kind of thing.'

Metternich curled up and took some of the pressure off Maxwell's thigh muscle and the cramp in his lower leg began to subside, to his relief.

'But I don't see why he would have come into contact with Gwen Harris, except perhaps to ask for something like . . . well, I don't know, to be honest. A duster? A ream of paper? What sort of things do people ask a site manager for? And even if he went into her storeroom and saw her cohort of geeks, would that raise a red flag to him? Would he even suspect that that was not normal? If he did, she could fob him off if he tried to make anything out of it. Straight blackmail, would that be?'

He scratched the cat between the ears and got some more purring. He was being spoiled today, that was certain. Usually it was one purr a day, strictly rationed to a feeding experience.

'Would anyone kill a blackmailer after what can only have been one attempt at coercion? I know it's not unheard of for blackmailers to be killed, especially in the tales of the sainted Mrs Christie, but I just don't see it. No one would expect a site manager of a school to have enough dosh to make it worthwhile. And then, of course, we come to the means. Gavin Masters was stabbed extremely competently in the chest with a very sharp blade. I accept that Gwen would have access to those; she has spares of anything the school might need so she would have blades for the CDT department as well as the kitchen. But she's a bit of a short-arse — Jimmy Krankie meets Gimli — and I doubt he would crouch down obligingly to be stabbed. And then she hit me round the head with something that had fortuitously come to hand, no planning really for that. So, very different, Count, wouldn't you agree?'

If he did, he did it without moving.

'So I think all we can say for sure is that Gwen Harris had opportunity. She could come and go as she liked. She knew the place inside out. When Gavin Masters died, she was still working the late shift. Last night, I don't think there is much doubt that she had turned up to give Mrs B a hard time and was probably amazed to find me there as well. She was angry and scared of the consequences of my discovery of her gambling set-up and so she just lashed out. I like to think that she would have gone back to check on me later, but we'll never know that. Let's leave her with the benefit of that doubt, shall we?'

A sudden itch galvanised Metternich and their interlude was over. He jumped down and threw himself onto his side on the rug, chomping furiously at the base of his tail. It was all part of life's rich tapestry.

'Well, if that's all you can bring to the table, Count,' Maxwell said, 'we'll leave it there, shall we? Bottom line, we're still looking for the killer of Gavin Masters. Remember where you heard it first.'

* * *

Helen Maitland had been Mad Max's Number Two now for more years than either of them cared to remember. She was loyal and true and eminently sensible, neither of them non-sense-sufferers. It wasn't a sexist thing. Helen was just as likely to be found patting the arm of a troubled Year Thirteen lad as Maxwell was doing the same for a girl of like years. Neither of them kept their doors open, which was the advice from County Hall, and both of them belonged to a union just because it was more trouble not to. She would happily bring Maxwell his cocoa, wearing a duffle coat like all the Number Twos in the black-and-white naval dramas that Maxwell watched — young Dickie Attenborough to his Jack Hawkins. She was also happy to take the helm when the Great Man was away (which was rare), hearing his impeccable Duke of Wellington impression from Waterloo — 'Now, Maitland; now's your time.'

But what happened on Wednesday morning was far beyond anything Maxwell or Maitland could have expected. Helen was not a particularly early riser, but she was an early arriver, so it was nothing for her to get to the sixth form corridor ahead of everybody else, making coffee and trying to persuade Benny Goodchild and his ilk that the horrendous Mr Clifford, Head of Physics, was actually a lovely man who watched seabirds in his spare time. Occasionally, it was advice of a more personal nature, when Alyson Bristow had, yet again, gone too far with her boyfriend the night before. On these occasions, it was coffees all round and some straight talking — Mary Poppins meets Nanny McPhee. More often than not, it was messages on the answerphone — coursework issues, UCAS enquiries. Did anybody mention coffee?

That morning, however, was different. To begin with, there were no visible signs of cleaners. Usually there would at least be a mop or a duster, if only to prove to Gauleiter Harris that they were on song. Waving to Thingee One, opening up reception, Helen padded up the stairs past the not-half-bad A-level artwork as she always did, struggling with her laptop and wondering where she had stuffed her car keys.

Bugger! There on her desk was that dratted report, the feedback of Year Seven, that utterly pointless piece of bureaucracy that the government insisted that all schools fill in so that the Member (and never was there a title more apt) for West Sussex could answer truthfully in the House just how many students at Leighford High were taking A-levels which included Further Maths. It was one of those imponderables that the Chancellor needed to know; so had the War Office (the real one, not Maxwell's) and the Minister for Levelling Up back in the day. And somebody else; now, who . . . oh, yes, the Secretary of State for Education. Helen and Maxwell took turns year and year about to fill in the feedback to the report; after all, teachers didn't have much else to do.

She flicked on the coffee machine, helped herself to a Hobnob and thought of all those lazy so-and-sos Working From Home as she munched. They had Hobnobs in common, but there'd be no Peloton for her. Instead it would be Seven See Bee before morning break, wrestling with the literary complexities of Judy Blume. She wondered, as she bustled next door to Maxwell's office, how many of the little dears had read the book and how many had watched the film?

She didn't notice the wilting spider plant in the corner, nor Cuba Gooding Jr looking all mean 'n' moody on the *Boyz n the Hood* poster. All she saw was a woman's body sprawled in front of Maxwell's desk. Her eyes were open, staring at the ceiling, and one arm was bent across her stomach. Just above it was a dark red stain that spread across her blouse and ran onto the carpet on both sides. Helen may have been Mother Teresa to her sixth form, a calm oasis in their seas of trouble, but a dead body was a step too far. She ran back to her own office, scrabbling for her phone. When it came to bodies, surely she had people for that.

* * *

Leighford High School becoming a crime scene again was a somewhat déjà vu experience for most of the staff and pupils that Wednesday morning. Yet again, the drive was blocked with police cars with their blue lights mutely flashing. Yet again, constables were parked at intervals along the pavement, up the drive and in front of the main door. Yet again, the Telly Lot were ensconced in their minibus, but this time, their ranks were even thinner; and this time, Zac was curled into a small ball on the back seat, his coat over his head. Yet again, Arnie Preddie was having what was perilously close to a total meltdown in the foyer. At least it wasn't in her office this time; it was in Maxwell's and she knew from experience, good luck to him in getting the stain out of the carpet. Her world had turned upside down. Gwen Harris had disappeared. No one had swept the crumbs from her desk, again, although she had sent enough memos to kill several trees on that task alone. Helen Maitland was being stoic in the corner over by the dining hall, where the usual small cohort of breakfast clubbers were looking out through the wire-meshed glass with owl-like eyes. Thingee One was in reception making the same phone calls she had been making at almost that exact moment six days ago. All in all, Arnie Preddie wanted a good jolt of brandy and a lie-down in a darkened room.

What was annoying her more than somewhat was that no one at all was taking any notice of her. Surely, she asked herself, as headteacher she should be everyone's first port of call. She made a decision and walked on stiffening legs over to the police person who currently had her arms around Helen Maitland and was patting her back gently. How unprofessional was *that*? Arnie asked herself triumphantly.

She tapped Jacquie on the back.

'Excuse me,' she said.

Jacquie looked her up and down. Maxwell was right. The teeth really were quite extraordinary. 'Can I help you?'

'I would like to have a word, please. This is *my* school, after all, and so it is only right and proper that I should be interviewed first.'

Even in her distress, Helen Maitland, her face buried in Jacquie's shoulder, had a little smile to herself. This was going to be good, she could feel it in her water.

'Did you witness the murder?'

'No.'

'Were you on the premises late last night?'

'No.'

'Did you know the victim?'

'No.'

'Are you some kind of forensic expert or, God forbid, some kind of psychic with a message from the world beyond?'

'*No!*' Arnie was getting really cross now. This woman really was the end!

'Well, in that case,' Jacquie said, returning to her soothing ministrations, 'I really don't see how an interview with you could possibly help. You could go out front, though, and help the police turn away anyone attempting to enter. At least you won't have to deal with my husband this time, as he is at home still with his head wrapped in about a mile of bandage.'

Very few adults, outside of books, actually stamp their feet with rage, but Arnie Preddie did so now. Finding it got her nowhere, which most toddlers have worked out by the age of about two and a half, she went and got her coat. She stood in front of Thingee One to tell her the serious news that she was going home. However, Thingee One was in the middle of a phone call and simply flapped her hand at her. Swallowing her rage and almost her top set, Arnie left the building. It was only when she was in the car and weaving a path down the drive between the police vehicles that the penny dropped. 'My husband.' Bandages. God dammit, she had just been put in her place by Mrs Peter Maxwell.

At the end of the drive, her car gave out. She had forgotten to plug it in the night before and now it was dead as a badger in the fast lane. Arnie Preddie let her head drop back and she bayed at the late moon, hanging still visible in the light blue sky of spring. This murdering lark, she was going to have to put her foot down about it — it was totally ruining her school.

* * *

That evening, at 38 Columbine, the goulash leftovers had gone down a treat.

'Stew is always better the next day,' Jacquie said. 'That was delicious. Tante Marie, you say? I think we'll have to sign you up, Max, up your game.'

He flicked at her with a tea towel. 'In fact, heart of darkness, I googled it.'

She looked up at him, amazed.

'Yes, yes, you may look at me. But I can do things as long as I am left to myself to do it in my own time. And you might not be surprised to learn, they don't have prices. You have to apply.'

'Kind of, if you have to ask, you can't afford it.'

'That kind of thing, yes. So I think that our Jeremy is not only minted because he is what he is, but he also comes from Money.'

'How nice for Polly.'

'Money isn't everything, of course,' Maxwell said, wiping down the draining board. In his bandage, he looked a little like a Twenties housekeeper in her fashionable toque.

'It's the root of all evil, or so they say.'

Maxwell opened his mouth to correct her but decided that there was no need. She knew the correct quotation, it was just too cumbersome to bother with.

'We've been looking into poor Mel's finances, of course. See if it was a motive there.'

'And?'

'Not a bean, poor love. She had left her home and her husband with what she stood up in, more or less. Some standing orders were still going out of her account, which leads me to suppose she was not planning to leave forever. She probably was just having a break . . .' Jacquie reached for a banana and peeled it slowly. 'He seemed genuinely upset, the husband.'

'Well, he would, I guess. If it wasn't his idea, her leaving. Does he have an alibi?'

'Pretty cast iron, yes. We're going to see him tomorrow afternoon, though. Just to see if there is anything in her past that might help. The Telly Lot all know each other from other gigs — Zac knew Mel, for instance, from one fairly long-running series — but they don't *know* each other. They just circle round each other without taking any notice, really.'

'I don't wish Mel ill, of course, when I say this, but at least it proves Polly's theory wrong.'

'Polly's theory?'

'That Gwen Harris killed Gavin Masters. I couldn't see how that could make any sense, even before this second murder.'

'We never really considered it, but we did check. Gwen hasn't left her rehab since she checked in yesterday midday. She's fairly heavily sedated at the moment, even if it wasn't miles away. So, no, it isn't her. We briefly considered that this whole playing games for money might be some kind of consortium, but honestly, the money to be made is just not enough to interest the big boys. Gwen was desperate; only someone desperate would think of doing it to make anything, it averages out at pence, if that. I do feel a little sorry for her, actually, Dyson upside the head notwithstanding.'

'So we're back to everybody and nobody,' Maxwell said, twirling an invisible waxed moustache.

'We are. So, any contributions gratefully received.' Jacquie folded her banana peel and lobbed it unsuccessfully at the bin. 'Tell you what, that goulash really was delicious. I'm definitely signing you up for a course. I could pimp you out.'

Maxwell folded the tea towel, picked up the banana peel — as clear a case of an accident waiting to happen as he had ever seen — and ushered her out of her chair and into the sitting room. 'If you will allow me, milady, I will be in with the drinks trolley shortly, after I clean the silver and draw your bath.'

'Jeeves, you're a marvel,' she muttered, stretching and yawning.

'I rather fancy I am more a Bunter,' Maxwell said, being more of a Dorothy L. Sayers man, 'but Jeeves is good. I can do Jeeves.'

And for the rest of the evening, until she begged him to stop, he did.

CHAPTER THIRTEEN

Donald had only just finished typing up the notes from Gavin Masters' post mortem and had somehow squeezed in his daily tai chi routine. Any outsider would have assumed that Donald was a sumo wrestler going through his paces because a man of his build would dwarf most wardrobes. Because of his inner peace, however, he saw himself as a latter-day Nureyev, whose body was a temple and who turned heads wherever he went.

His recent empathy course had led him to tone down his attitude to his boss. He had learned at the knee of the great Jim Astley, late of Leighford parish, who was now pushing up daisies of his own. He occasionally still saw his widow around the town, but she consistently ignored him, so he had dropped the bonhomie.

Even so, in Donald's world, pathologists were inevitably older and wiser than lab assistants, yet the appointment of Alan Hargreaves had thrown Donald's life into disarray. The man was actually *younger* than he was. As to wisdom, it was difficult to say. Jim Astley was of the Sir Bernard Spilsbury school — this is what happened, how it happened and probably why it happened. Because he said so. As to who did it, that was a job for the police. Did Jim Astley have to do *everything*?

Alan Hargreaves was an altogether newer breed. The certainties of Spilsbury were long gone, to the extent that, in his darker moments, Donald wondered if forensic science wasn't actually going backwards. Because of that, he realised, before he went on his course, he may have been a bit pushy with Hargreaves, giving an opinion when it wasn't asked for; that sort of thing. So, of late, he had toned it down.

'Single stab wound,' he said, 'single-edged blade.' He caught the look on Hargreaves' face. 'Probably,' he added rather lamely and wandered off to rearrange some bottles.

Alan Hargreaves adjusted his mic. He was in his scrubs, as was Donald, peering through a magnifying lens fitted to his headgear. Shit! The obnoxious busybody was right — and he'd only just glanced at the wound.

On the slab in front of him lay all that was left of Melanie Bright. Her eyes were closed and Hargreaves was talking into the mic as he peeled back the sheet. 'Adult female,' he said. 'Mid to late thirties. Medium build. Medium height.' He'd get to the actual measurements later, but for now, he was just glad that Melanie wasn't a missing person — with a description as ho-hum as that, nobody would ever find her.

He opened the dead woman's mouth. 'Sound teeth,' he said, 'all present.'

'And correct,' Donald sang from across the room. Hargreaves paused. God alone knew what made the man tick. 'Slight bruising to the upper right forearm,' he lifted the shoulder, 'and shoulder. Bruises are pre-mortem,' he adjusted his lens, 'and I doubt we'll get any meaningful prints from that.' He pulled the sheet down further, exposing the woman's breasts and stomach. There was a vertical knife wound below the sternum, clean and single. He measured the opening. 'Wound caused by a single-edged blade, perhaps a kitchen knife or similar.'

He heard Donald's insuck of breath.

'When I measure the depth of the wound, I can be more accurate,' he said for the benefit of the tape; and for Donald.

'Bruising around the wound itself, probably because the knife's hilt hit the skin. This would have been a quick in and out. No hesitation. No guesswork. Whoever did this knows what he's doing.'

'He?' Hargreaves heard Donald's voice floating like his own conscience through the lab.

'Figure of speech,' he said. 'What pronoun would you prefer, Donald?'

Having been thoroughly empathised, Donald really wanted to say 'they' but that was probably a step too far. 'No, no,' he trilled. '"He" is fine.'

'Good,' Hargreaves muttered. He pulled the sheet off the body. 'No other signs of assault,' he said. 'Nothing obviously sexual. Do we know anything about this woman, Donald?'

At last, the lab assistant sensed his moment had arrived. He scuttled back to Hargreaves' side. 'She was a sound engineer, apparently,' he said. 'My old gran says you can't hear anything anybody says on TV these days and if she's right, it's the fault of people like her.' Then he remembered his empathy training. 'Lovely woman, though, I'm sure she was.'

'Have you got the police notes there? Anything from Henry?'

'No,' Donald said. 'From Jacquie.' The man actually glanced upwards as though he heard an angelic choir at that moment. Had Peter Maxwell been there, he'd have assumed that Donald had had an out-of-body experience involving Doris Day. Alan Hargreaves had no idea that Donald had always had a thing for Jacquie Carpenter-Maxwell and could never understand what she saw in the mad old duffer from Leighford High.

Uncertain of himself as he always was, Hargreaves made the mistake of asking Donald to read the notes to him. Empathy be buggered, Donald thought. This was his moment. He almost turned the angle of the lamps so that the spotlight was on him. He cleared his throat and lifted his chin.

'Melanie Bright: age uncertain as she lied about it on her application to FOTWL.' Donald read it out as separate letters — he had enough acronyms in his day job to last him a lifetime. 'She had, according to colleagues, recently left her marriage which they suspected may have been at least coercive, possibly violent. We are currently confirming alibis but it looks unlikely that this has a bearing. From a previous interview with her regarding the death of Gavin Masters, it transpires she had a brief sexual encounter with him.' Donald beamed at Hargreaves. Jacquie was so kind and discreet. He could only imagine how some of the animals they had notes from sometimes would have worded it. 'She was to have met him on the night he died, but again, alibis check out. There was a change of plan, which they both might have been glad of. Sorry to not have more info for you, Alan,' Donald bridled, 'I'll let you know if and when we get more.' Donald waited for the metaphorical applause to die down in his head. 'So, there you have it,' he said. 'Are we any the wiser?'

Hargreaves looked at him. Was that the royal 'we' or an inclusive 'we'? With Donald, you could never tell.

'There has to be a pattern,' the pathologist said. He pointed to the rows of steel doors, the cubicles of the dead. 'Over there we have Gavin Masters, sound engineer. Here we have Melanie Bright, sound engineer.'

'It'll be the cameraman.' Donald was modestly proud of his deduction.

'Really?' Hargreaves had turned his mic off. Oddly shaky on forensic grounds though he was, in terms of logic versus conspiracy theories, he surrendered to no man.

'Stands to reason.' Donald was busying himself with weighing scales, saws and knives for the use of. 'I took part in a documentary once.'

'Did you?'

'Yes. Dear old Jim Astley . . .'

Now *there* was a name Alan Hargreaves hadn't heard for at least half an hour.

'. . . Dear old Jim was standing where you are . . . Oh, no, come to think of it, it was the old lab. And *South Today* were doing a piece on police work. The camera loved old Jim, of course. He was a natural.' He paused in mid-laying out of utensils. 'And this is where it gets interesting. The cameraman and the sound guy were at total loggerheads. At one point, the sound guy, of all people, made a noise, scraped his cables or something, and the cameraman said, without taking his eye off the lens, "Any kind of red wine, then, Tom, you stupid shit."' Donald glanced at Hargreaves to make sure he was still listening. 'Because, they have this kind of thing, you see, that if anyone interrupts filming, they have to buy everyone wine.'

'Yes,' Hargreaves said, sardonically, 'I guessed that might be it.'

Donald ignored him. This was his story. 'And it went downhill from there.'

'Surely we can't assume that all TV companies have people like that?' Hargreaves reasoned.

Donald snorted. 'Don't you believe it!' He laughed. 'It's like the farmers and the cowboys in *Oklahoma!* that the Leighford Players put on last year. They *always* hate each other.'

'Like musicals, do you, Donald?' Hargreaves was almost afraid to ask.

'Love 'em,' the assistant said. 'Take part whenever I can.'

'Ah, and who were you in *Oklahoma!*?'

'Old Jud,' Donald announced proudly.

'Yes,' Hargreaves sighed. 'Knew you would be.'

And, to the rather incongruous jangle of an a cappella range-rider from Donald's barely recognisable repertoire, both men went about their business.

* * *

Maxwell was getting a little fed up with being at home but also with his bandage. He loved it that Jacquie was so solicitous for his welfare; he appreciated that she had been given instructions in A&E (or 'Casualty' as he still preferred to call it) but this morning as he looked in the mirror, even he could see that it was beginning to look a little disreputable.

He could take it off on Friday, he had been told. Friday and not a moment sooner. So he tried to ignore it, with its bits of random sticking plaster for places where it was coming loose and an annoying thread that always seemed to hang down and get in his ear. At least he no longer needed a babysitter and Mrs B had been gently weaned off her habit of checking on him hourly. He had unearthed some cookery books from under the stairs in the hall and was leafing through one called, rather over-confidently, *What Every Cook Should Know*. It had chapters on basic techniques and he was about to go upstairs with it and give it a shufti when the bell went.

He glanced at the clock in the corner. It was a grand-father, the only family heirloom he had and one which he sometimes regretted keeping. Its chime had been silenced for years, but its slow and sonorous tick could be heard all over the house in the quiet of midnight. It also lost (or sometimes gained) half an hour a day on a good day. But, with a little bit of leeway given, Mrs B wasn't due for a check-in yet. He opened the door, therefore, ready for anything.

Mandy Proctor stood there, in all her splendour. He liked Mandy anyway, she was efficient and pleasant and, sadly quite rare in the teachers he knew, actually seemed to like children. But her main skill was that of just being Mandy. She wore what she wanted, said more or less what she wanted and did what she wanted. He happily put his book down on the hall table and welcomed her in.

'Oooh,' she said, picking it up again. 'That looks inter-esting. I can't cook to save my life. I lost quite a pleasant boyfriend over that, back in the day. I think it was the con-stant indigestion did for us in the end. Do you do a lot of cooking, Max?'

'I dabble,' he said. 'But Polly was here on Tuesday and she has done a cookery course and I could tell that I just don't have the dexterity. I need to read up on it a bit.'

'I know what you mean,' Mandy said, taking off her coat in a waft of Jo Malone and hurling herself onto the sofa. 'I used to do all sorts of courses, back in the day. Riding, I did, one year. Fencing.' She mimed a quick parry in quarte with a languid hand. 'That was with . . . ooh, can't remember. Mario, I think.' She turned back to the book. 'Lots to keep you amused here, though, till you come back. When are you coming back, btw?'

Maxwell smiled. 'Btw? Are you texting me, sitting on my settee? Lol.'

Mandy put the book down and smiled. 'It's a habit. Did you know that illiteracy is growing in the under tens but they can all text? It's shocking. I have actually been headhunted by an illiteracy group.' She stopped and reran the sentence in her head. *'They're* not illiterate, of course, they are trying to combat it.'

'And are you going? We'll miss you.'

'Nah, you won't. Bob runs the school. Just because he never speaks, don't be misled. I haven't so much as looked at a timetable plan, and I mean *ever*. He does it on paper, too. No algorithms for Bob. Anyway, I guess you haven't heard about Arnie?'

'Don't tell me she's illiterate?'

Mandy laughed until she almost cried. 'Functionally, more or less. But, no, she got in such a snit with your missus yesterday she dashed out of school and hasn't come in today. When you ring her number, some woman as old as God answers and says she is indisposed.'

'So, her mother is real, then.' Maxwell had never known which of the hundred rumours about Arnie's private life to believe. The living-with-her-mother one was so boring that hardly anyone ever mentioned it these days, but it seemed to be true. He had hoped it might be more like the stuffed mother in *Psycho*, but he had always known that that was unlikely.

'Apparently. Anyway, I can't leave Bob on his own, so I am going in to the charity office this afternoon, to see if I can cox and box for a while. You know me, Max, the original rolling stone that gathers no moss.'

'We'll be sorry to see you go,' Maxwell said, meaning it. 'But surely you haven't come here to tell me that.'

'No, of course not. Although rumour has it, you have stood in for the Head before now.'

Maxwell shook his head, making his bandage wobble. 'Yes, and, before you ask, no. James Diamond is at a loose end. You should ask him.'

She narrowed her eyes. 'Is that a serious idea? I've heard things about the old days with you and him.'

'Take no notice. We were like two little birds in the nest. So . . . why are you here, except for my beautiful blue eyes?'

She leaned forward. 'More black and blue, actually. Although that one,' she pointed to her left, 'has started getting that sort of yellowy-green thing you get with bruises. I am here, in fact, to reunite you with something you have lost.' She sat back, hands folded, waiting for him to explode in gratitude.

'Um. Marbles. Mind. Plot. You'll have to help me here, Mandy. We have a saying chez Maxwell. Nothing is lost, we just don't know where it is. And in this case, I don't know what it is, either. So please, just tell me.'

'Well, that was disappointing,' she said. 'Usually when you say to someone "I've found your phone" they almost wee themselves with delight.'

'You've found my phone?' He was puzzled. He didn't know exactly where it was, as per the family saying, but he was pretty sure it was in the house somewhere.

'Yes, look.' She ferreted in her bag. 'Here it is, look. It's got your initial on it and everything.'

'My phone doesn't have my initial on it,' he said. 'It's just . . . well, it's just a phone. Silver. Rather outdated but does the job. You know. A phone.'

'Oh.' Mandy was a tad deflated. 'I was sure it was yours. I . . . well, I feel a bit silly, now. Someone at Leighford High is probably looking for it as we speak. I can't even bring up the home screen, because the battery is dead. Most people have a picture of the family, so we could fine down the search that way.'

'Well, I have the answer for that,' Maxwell said. 'Mrs B will have a charger.'

Mandy looked at Maxwell fondly. Bless his little cotton socks! He thought there was only one kind of charger. He intercepted the thought.

'Mrs B is by way of being a phone whisperer,' he told her. 'She actually tests new designs for all the big manufacturers but apart from that, she has a real affinity with technical things. And don't ask, like most people do, why she is therefore not a Silicon Valley millionaire. It's because she simply prefers being Mrs B. So, hang on a minute, I'll give her a shout.' He raised his voice and spoke into the corner of the room. 'Alexa. Drop in on Mrs B.' While he waited, he lowered his voice a little and spoke in Mandy's direction. 'I've only just learned how to do that,' he said proudly. 'It doesn't always work, because our Alexa is going a bit senile, we think, but usually—' He was interrupted by a ping and Mrs B's disembodied voice came through loud and clear.

'Are you okay, Mr M? Not dizzy or anything?'

Mandy smiled. Virtual nursing.

'No, no, I'm fine, Mrs B. I've got Mrs Proctor here, with a dead phone we need to wake up. She's found it Up at the School and doesn't know whose it is.'

'Well, that's easy. Can you bring it round, Mr M? I've got a rapid charger here and also some . . . software we can use to get round the security. See you in a minute. Alexa, dismiss.'

Mandy Proctor was wide-eyed. 'Mrs B is a *hacker*?' she breathed.

Maxwell chortled. 'She doesn't like the "h" word,' he said. 'But, in essence, yes. Where did you leave your coat? It's not far, but it's still chilly.'

* * *

Mandy Proctor wondered why Maxwell didn't just step over the low hedge that separated his front garden from that of the house next door. However, without saying anything, she solemnly followed him down his path, through the front gate, through the front gate next to it and then up the twin garden path to where Mrs B was waiting in her open doorway.

'Oh, come in, both of you, out of this wind. It's chilly.' She more or less ignored Maxwell, as she always did when anyone more interesting was around. She didn't want him to get big-headed, think he was important. She held out her hand and Mandy Proctor gave her the phone. 'Come through,' she said, leading the way, to Mandy's surprise, into what seemed to be the garage. Inside, it was like the Tardis. It was painted bright white, with halogen lights flush with the ceiling every few feet. The entire room, including in front of the never-opened door, was fitted out with cupboards with kneeholes every now and again and a cool off-white work surface. Just above that, trunking ran around the room, with sockets every foot or so.

'Blimey,' Mandy said. 'This is amazing, Mrs B.'

The cleaner beamed. 'It's took me a while, ain't it, Mr M? But I think I've got it how I want it, now. Let's have a look at this here phone, then.' She turned the phone over in her hands. 'Hmm. Initial just scratched on. That usually means somebody has to hand it in sometimes.' She looked at Maxwell. 'I suppose that could mean one of the kids, what with the ban and all.'

'But they wouldn't think of that, would they? They would only bring a phone if they thought they would be undetected. And anyway, M? How many kids with the initial M do we have? If you count both names, it must be dozens.'

'That's true. Well, perhaps that's got nothing to do with it.' While she was talking, she pulled out a bundle of chargers, looking like a rather dour bunch of flowers. 'Lemme see . . . it's an iPhone 7. So, Mr M, if you're doing your Miss Marple thingy, that probably means someone not that bothered about tech *or* somebody without much money. You can get one of these for just over a hundred quid online, probably less down the market. Or perhaps it's someone's spare phone, you know, the one you don't want the missus to find.'

Mandy Proctor was in awe. Who was this woman pretending to be Mrs B?

'So, let me recap, Mrs B,' Maxwell said. 'It's either a cheap phone, a spare phone, a secret phone or . . . what was the other one?'

'A non-techie's phone,' Mandy said, to prove she was listening.

'My money's on a cheap phone,' Mrs B said. 'It's . . . where did you find it, Mrs Proctor?'

'Well, that was the strange thing. I was doing some photocopying in reception this morning and it was down behind the bin.'

'Hmm. It could have been there weeks,' Mrs B said. 'That Frankie, she does reception and she never met a corner she couldn't ignore. On a written warning, she is.'

'So another non-clue, then,' Maxwell said. 'Have you got a bit of paper here, Mrs B? So I can jot these down.'

'There's a Scribe there,' she said, pointing. 'Just tap it to wake it up. The pencil's on the side.'

'Oh, I don't . . .'

'Don't be chicken, Mr M,' she said. 'Nolan uses it all the time for his homework. You'll do fine.' She looked at the phone and said, 'Right, it's not got much battery, so we'll leave it plugged in, but there's enough to open it up. Right, monkey, let's see what . . .' She pressed the circular button on the bottom and a screen came up. 'Ah,' she said, without emphasis. 'You don't often see that as a home screen.'

Mandy Proctor and Maxwell went round to look over her shoulder and they both echoed her 'Ah'. A rather badly lit picture of an erect penis filled the screen.

'What we need,' Mandy said drily, 'is a banana for scale.'

Mrs B chuckled. 'Chaps don't like giving the scale, though, do they, Mrs Proctor?'

Maxwell suddenly felt horribly outnumbered.

'I was hoping we would be able to . . . well, identify someone from the home screen,' Mandy said, moving away. She had no objection to penises per se, but that one just seemed a little bit too pleased with itself.

Mrs B gave another throaty chuckle. 'Depends who's looking at it, I s'pose,' she said. 'Although this one doesn't seem to have any real identifying marks, does it?' She turned it round so that Mandy could have another look. 'Anyway, never mind, I'll just get into the gubbins.'

Maxwell nodded to his colleague. 'Technical term,' he said.

Mrs B unplugged the phone and took it over to a PC in the corner, which was rigged up with three screens. She reattached it and sat down, hitching the chair nearer.

'Can we watch how she does it?' Mandy breathed.

Maxwell had often watched but had never got the sense of a pattern emerging. 'I think,' he said, quietly, 'that it wouldn't help you. She puts in fake moves to put you off the scent. She is,' he said with all the pride of a parent whose child has just won a gymkhana riding an ostrich, 'something of a guru when it comes to this kind of thing.'

Over in her corner, Mrs B chuckled. 'Guru,' she muttered. She loved it when he called her a guru.

On the left-hand screen, rows of small green letters, numbers and symbols were tumbling over one another scrolling down as they went.

'This is just the basics,' Mrs B said. 'Every phone, every technical thing, has got this. Even my new oven is Smart. Not that I ever feel the need to ring it up, but I could.' She looked at the numbers and tutted. 'Whoever this phone belongs to hasn't updated the software for ages. It should be running on 16.1 but this is . . . oh, dearie me, this one is 15.5. Still, if we're right and it's just a spare . . .' She tapped a few more keys and rubbed her hands together. 'Okay, Mr M., Mrs P. Watch the middle screen. You'll get the recent messages there, texts, WhatsApps, all that. On *this* screen,' she pointed to the one on the right, 'you'll get images, that kind of thing. It might take a while. Let's see . . .'

She spun round and looked Maxwell up and down. 'That bandage is looking a bit manky, Mr M. Tomorrow it comes off, is it?'

'Or tonight,' Maxwell said. 'It's beginning to itch.'

'Well, it will . . .' Mrs B stopped. She was looking at Mandy Proctor, who was looking at the screens, transfixed. On the right-hand screen there were some images of wires stapled to walls, of microphones hidden behind plant pots. But before them, there was a picture of the late Melanie Bright, her hand held out to try to stop the photographer. She appeared to be caught in the act of pulling on her knickers. But it was the middle screen that had really stopped Mandy in her tracks. In between a few schedules and some messages from Mel Bright begging him to delete the picture, was a message with an attached image. The focus wasn't wonderful, the wallpaper was a little garish, the bedclothes tumbled. But, unmistakeably and in all her glory, the woman grinning into the camera and displaying her perfect naked body to the photographer was Polly Allington. And the face grinning at the top left-hand corner, getting in on the act in more ways than one, was clearly Gavin Masters.

The three were speechless. They had had no real pre-conceptions of whose phone it might be. Thinking about it rationally, the place it was found made it not unlikely that it belonged to Gavin Masters. It didn't look too good for the SOCO who should have searched reception, but mistakes happen. The thing — apart from the photo, which still had them transfixed — was the message that went with it.

I'm assuming you won't be wanting Mr Basildon KC to see this. If I'm right, better meet me tonight at the school. Bring a grand with you in cash and we'll talk about setting up a DD. Lol.

Mandy was the first to find her voice. 'God, Max, we need to get this to the police.'

'We do,' Maxwell said. 'But I don't just want . . . look, ladies, I know this needs to go to the police, but it has to be the *right* police. We don't want them going in bull at a gate and just . . . well, Leighford's been through enough in the last week or so, hasn't it?'

Mandy gave him a spontaneous kiss on the cheek. Only Maxwell could find a murderer and not want to upset Eleven Gee Eff just before their GCSEs.

'I'll go to the school,' he said. 'Mrs B, can you save all this? Has it damaged the . . . wotsit?'

'Data.'

'That's the chap.'

'No. I've just accessed it. Nothing is wiped.'

'Right, then. If you could . . . whatever . . . save it, onto a . . . thing.'

'USB.'

'If you say so. Or email it or something. I'll get up to the school and . . . I just want to know, you see.'

'How will you get there?' Mrs B said, anxiously.

'On Surrey.'

Both women put anxious hands to their heads.

'What? Oh, it's just a bandage. I don't even notice it any more.'

'I'll take you, Max,' Mandy said, already reaching for her car keys.

'No. You have your appointment. You can't put your life on hold because someone has done something horrific. When Mrs B has done . . . whatever she has to do . . . if you could drop her off at the nick, that would be splendid. But don't tell anyone anything, not before you hear from me. Is that all right?'

Both women nodded, reluctantly.

Maxwell dashed off to put on a coat and his bicycle clips. Just because he had a murderer to catch didn't mean he wanted chain oil on his trousers! While he was struggling into his windcheater, he tried Jacquie's number, but it just was ringing off the hook. It wasn't like her not to answer, but when she didn't, Maxwell knew she was otherwise engaged. He didn't have a personal number for Henry Hall so he rang Leighford nick. A voice he didn't recognise picked up.

'Leighford Police Station. How can I help?'

'This is Peter Maxwell.'

Nothing.

'As in DI Jacquie Carpenter-Maxwell.'

'Oh, yes.'

'I'm her husband.' Maxwell rattled through a list of names and faces he knew among Jacquie's colleagues. If he knew them, they knew him and yet whoever was on the other end seemed woefully ignorant.

'Oh, yes.'

'Is she there?' Maxwell asked. 'I need to speak to her urgently.'

'I don't believe the DI is in right now,' the voice said.

'Henry Hall, then,' Maxwell said. 'Get me the DCI.'

'Who did you say you were again?'

'Oh, for Christ's sake.' Maxwell was doing something he hardly ever did; he was shouting down the phone. 'Is there anybody from CID there? A detective? You know, a bloke — or a woman, of course — in plain clothes?'

'I don't think you need to adopt that tone,' the voice said. 'May I ask the nature of your enquiry?'

'Murder,' Maxwell said.

'You what?'

'Look, who the hell are you?' the Head of Sixth Form was at the end of his tether.

'I am not at liberty to divulge . . .' the voice said.

'Oh, I see.' Nobody did a sarcastic smile over the phone like Peter Maxwell. 'I'm sorry, I didn't realise we already had AI automatons on switchboards just yet. And there was me, fully imagining I'd be talking to dear old Sergeant Dixon of Dock Green, not Mr J.O.B.S. Worth. Thank you so much for your inestimable help.'

'I'm afraid . . .' the voice began.

'Afraid as well as stupid,' Maxwell broke in. 'I can't help but feel you're in the wrong job, sunshine.' And he hung up.

* * *

White Surrey was waiting patiently for him as he always did, propped up against an old cupboard with one empty paint pot and a strimmer in it. Now he was actually about to mount the thing, he felt a little less sanguine. He had got into the coat all right, of course; the cycle clips had been a little more of a challenge and had meant sitting down and carefully looking dead ahead and doing it by touch. The bicycle helmet, which he always wore unwillingly anyway, wouldn't go anywhere near the bandaged head and so he left it off. If he was arrested, he was arrested and at least it might get him a step nearer to speaking to his wife. There were times in the Great Man's life when he'd imagined mounting the destrier of King Richard III, all sleek white coat, shining with chamfron and metal plates, the gilt-embroidered leopards and lilies of the horse bard sweeping the ground. Today, however, in the reality of a head wind and a steady drizzle from the sea, White Surrey looked incredibly like a battered old Raleigh. It was probably the last bike in England to have a basket on the front and the bell needed work too.

Maxwell had left Jacquie a hurried, scribbled note on the hall table. '*Up at the School. 3.26. Love M xxx*'. Both his signature and the kisses looked like something Guy Fawkes might have attempted after torture, but time was of the essence. In just over twenty minutes, the damn bell sans merci would sound and Leighford High School would be a ghost town, without even a site manager to police it.

Why, Maxwell wondered, did it hurt his head every time his foot pressed down on the pedal? He made a mental note to have extra padding glued to Surrey's saddle before his next excursion, but at least he now knew why the Bradley Wigginses of this world wore padded Lycra. He had known he had bruises — it just seemed ridiculous, almost three days later, to be discovering new ones.

He pedalled down Columbine and did his best to tackle the hill that led to the Dam. He always prided himself on his careful cycling, stopping at red lights and zebra crossings and never, *ever* using the pavement. But today was an exception and he had to cut corners. He saw himself in the dock, up before the beak. 'I'm sorry I bowled over two old ladies and a Pekinese, your honour, but I was trying to catch a murderer.'

'That,' His Lordship said in his head, 'is what they all say!' The gavel crashed on the desk. 'Take him down!'

And down Maxwell went, crashing through the bracken at the bottom of the dip in the Dam, narrowly missing the improvised swing that some kids had dangled from the old oak there. He hurtled out onto the cycle path, momentarily legal again, and dashed diagonally across the road. He heard the blare of the horn of the HGV at his back, but not the expletive that followed it and swung to his left, bouncing over the kerb so that his teeth rattled in his head and every bone in his skull grated against every other.

What with the exertion, the wind in his face and the throbbing in his head, Maxwell's eyes were burning with tears, as he swung a right across the traffic onto the Esplanade and down Mill Street.

'Lycra lout!' he heard somebody yell and glanced back, briefly. Either it was an ancient lady in tweeds who looked like Vera's mother (which was unlikely) or it was the Highland terrier padding alongside her.

CHAPTER FOURTEEN

Bugger and poo! School was out already, despite his death-defying ride. Along with Paul Revere, Dirck and Joris, he had galloped like a maniac, but time, the uncompromising bastard, had beaten him again. He saw the yellow buses snarling up to the layby outside the school gate and the first skirmishers snaking out along the road, suddenly free of the hells of education and on the way home, via a spot of smoking, shoplifting and vandalism on the way. He caught sight, briefly, of Cynthia Gregory, school bag already open to collect various unpaid-for goodies from the Poundland in the High Street.

He barely noticed the fact that everybody was looking at him as Surrey scythed through them.

'Out of the way, people,' he bellowed. 'Teacher coming through!' It wasn't just that he was going in the wrong direction — they'd all seen heroes in disaster movies doing that, on their way to fight Godzilla or whatever — it was the fact that it was Mr Maxwell, with a white bandage on his head and with two black eyes. Was it any wonder they called him Mad Max?

He half fell off Surrey at the school steps and, rather ungraciously perhaps, threw the bike onto the verge. The crowds were thicker here because the bell had well and truly gone and only the geeks who would inherit the earth were staying behind for Chess Club.

'Is there actually going to be any filming, Mr Maxwell?' he heard a voice call. He half turned, cost him pain though it did, sending the stars turning in their courses, to see Darcy Quincy and his caballeros, all twirling their canes, hoping to catch a cameraman's eye.

'What do I know?' Maxwell called back. 'I coulda been a contender.'

But nobody south of the Head's office had ever heard of Marlon Brando and *On the Waterfront* was where the kids all gathered on Friday nights for a piss-up and a doner kebab.

Then it was up the stairs — who the hell invented those? Maxwell wondered. As an historian, he should know, but hey, nobody was perfect. He turned right, along the corridor where Magna Carta stared at him from inside the glass frame and famous women in history quietly disapproved of him as he passed.

He didn't bother to knock on her door, but barged straight in.

'Max?' She looked up. 'Is it too much of a cliché to ask what you're doing here? I thought the doc had said "Take the week off."'

'He did, Polly,' Maxwell said, closing the door, 'but then I wouldn't have caught me a killer, would I?'

'What?' she laughed, putting her pen down. 'What are you talking about?'

He sat down on her sofa, facing her across her desk. 'I didn't want to be right,' he said, bracing all to shake his head. 'God knows, in this job, you need all the friends you can get and I thought you were one of them — one of the good guys.'

'Well, that's very sweet of you,' she smiled, making for the phone on her desk. 'I'll just give the hospital a ring, shall I? I'm afraid the blow to your head—'

'Put that down,' he growled. And she did.

For a moment, there was silence, then she relaxed and leaned back in the chair, folding her hands across her stomach and interlacing her fingers. 'Suppose you tell me what's going on?'

'As a preliminary to the chats you're going to have with Jacquie and Henry Hall, you mean?'

'Oh, there won't be any chats, Max,' she laughed. 'You forget what my husband does for a living.'

'Ah, yes, the "no comment" brigade.' Maxwell was glad to rest his head against the wall and was finding it easier to focus by closing one eye. 'And Jeremy is what this is all about, isn't it?'

'Is it?' Polly was listening intently now.

'I haven't googled him,' Maxwell said, 'or whatever you young people say. I'm not sure he's *quite* in *Who's Who* yet, but it can only be a matter of time. He's Harrow, isn't he? Followed by Tit Hall, Cambridge?'

'Trinity Hall,' she corrected him, on her dignity.

'Not in my day, it wasn't,' he smiled. 'London circuit, of course. Temple and all that. Did a stint, I think you told me, at Lincoln's Inn. And now, of course, silk and a KC. All very impressive.'

'What's your point?' she asked.

'My point, Polly, is that "Brutus says that Caesar is ambitious". And so, I suspect, is Jeremy. And to stick with that play, someone like Jeremy must be like Caesar's wife, above suspicion.'

'So?'

'So, not only must *he* be squeaky clean, but those about him must be too. If not, there goes his impending "K", cosy chats with the Lord Chief Justice, appointment to the Supreme Court. Hell, there goes his "KC", his licence to practise law and no doubt, the obscene hourly rate that he commands.'

'I don't see—'

'You, Polly,' Maxwell said quietly. 'You are the fly in the ointment, rather than on the wall. Because Polly Allington and squeaky clean don't quite gel, do they? Because you killed Gavin Masters. And you killed Melanie Bright.'

Polly laughed. 'What am I, Max? The Harold Shipman of Leighford?'

'No, no, in terms of body count, you're *way* below him. No, you only intended to kill Masters. Poor Melanie was an afterthought, a bit of collateral damage.'

She changed position, leaning forward now and resting her chin on her hands, elbows on the desk. 'Well,' she said, 'I'm intrigued. One of Jeremy's many specialities is slander law, so do say on.'

'It was just one of those things, really. We've all got pasts, Polly. My first family died on a wet road. It was nobody's fault, but it happened. In your case, along with the excellent degree and the dazzling teacher credentials and all the trimmings, you fell for — and married — a complete arsehole.'

'Tut, tut,' she scolded. 'And here's me thinking you liked Jeremy.'

'Oh, I do,' Maxwell said, 'but I'm not talking about Jeremy. I'm talking about Gavin Masters.'

There was no comeback now. Polly sat in stony silence.

'You were married to him, but it didn't work out, did it? I don't know whether he was abusive or not, but I think it's clear from what other people have said that he was a manipulative, greedy and lazy skirt-chaser. I don't know who walked out on whom, but the whole thing collapsed.'

'Such things happen,' Polly said.

'They do. But there was no actual divorce, was there? No actual untying of the knot. You drifted apart and along, belatedly, came Mr Right, lightly disguised as Jeremy Basildon. It was love at first sight or something like that, but you neglected to tell Jeremy that you were, in fact, still Mrs Gavin Masters. It was,' he leaned forward, 'and I'm sure you've told yourself a thousand times over, a stupid thing to do.'

'In theory,' she said.

'Always,' he smiled. 'All well and good. Until FOTWL came calling. Whether you knew Gavin was with them or you were just afraid he might be, you spoke out against the whole thing, remember, at that INSET staff meeting. You even got Jeremy to give us chapter and verse and the legal codswallop about why it couldn't go ahead. But it didn't work. A fatal combination of James Diamond, Bernard Ryan and Arnie Preddie had already done that deal. Tell me, where and when did you first clap eyes on Gavin? I like to dot eyes and cross tees.'

He had expected no answer, but he got one, 'If you must know, it was in the playground, the north one. I was on outdoor duty and there he was. He just grinned and said, "Hello, Mrs Basildon, although that's not quite your name, is it?" I took him behind the bike sheds — Christ alone knows what assorted members of Year Ten must have thought — and we had it out, though not in the way they might have expected. He told me he'd watched my career with interest. He knew all about my Leighford appointment and had specifically got his agency to give him this gig. He knew all about Jeremy, too, and he had a proposition for me.'

'Blackmail,' Maxwell said.

Polly nodded. 'Quaint, isn't it? The sort of motive that went out with Agatha Christie. Who the hell blackmails anybody these days? If the whole bloody Cabinet were up on child molestation charges, they'd just lie their way out of it, hire expensive lawyers like Jeremy and ride it out. But . . .'

For a moment, he saw her lip tremble and her composure crack. 'I couldn't take the chance. Not with Jeremy's career. It wouldn't have been fair.' She breathed in. 'And in a practical sense, it would never have worked. We have joint bank accounts and although sometimes the amounts going in make me blink, Jeremy always knows exactly how much there is. He was brought up with money, you see, and his family have always been known to be canny. Some great, great, however many greats it is to take you back to the Industrial Revolution . . .' She ran her hands through her hair. 'Oh, God, Max, I used to know that stuff before . . . before . . .' She breathed in, karmic, calming breaths. 'Anyway, long story cut short, they have more money than God and so do we, but he would still notice a regular grand or so going out. Because, for God's sake, Max, the little weasel wanted a direct bloody debit. A *direct debit*. It's a wonder he didn't want to use PayPal or something. Anyhow, I got Gavin to a more secluded spot than the bike sheds and begged him to call off his plan. He refused, point blank, told me I owed him. I didn't see it that way.'

'So, you killed him.'

'Yes. Oh, I'd like to say that I met up with him in Arnie's office to try to talk him out of it, offer him my body, whatever. That when that didn't work, I lost my cool and in a fit of hysteria, stabbed him with whatever was handy. But that's not how it was.'

'No?'

She shook her head. 'I was carrying cash in my handbag, not enough for Jeremy to be alarmed about — the handbag I was carrying it in cost more than the wad of money, after all — and certainly not what Gavin had asked for. I know common sense would dictate that I should have brazened it out, but it was that picture he sent. It was the day we were married and . . . well, let's say.' She stopped. 'Have you seen it?'

Maxwell nodded.

'How embarrassing for you. Anyway, we were young, I thought in love, and we got very drunk. The other pictures are rather more graphic and worth a lot more money to the weasel. So, along with the money, I was also carrying a knife.' She suddenly slid open a drawer and a blade gleamed in her hand. 'Viz and to wit, this one.'

Maxwell sat up. He hadn't seen either body in the morgue but he'd seen what the woman could do to a bunch of unsuspecting onions.

She smiled. 'I must admit, I toyed with the body thing. He'd told me, of course, where he'd be, that he'd kicked that moronic little Mel off the schedule so we could be alone. He demanded I turn up, really, but if I hadn't it would have made no difference. He was going to hound and hound and hound me until he bled me dry. I came on to him, just a little bit, you know, teasing. He must have thought when

I reached into my handbag that I was rummaging, Year Eleven-style, for a condom. The look on his face when he saw the knife was priceless.'

'And what about Mel?'

'Yes.' She toyed with the weapon, pricking random daisy patterns on some paperwork with its razor point. 'I *do* regret that. I know that she and he had had a little something, however brief, and I suddenly thought, what if he'd told her? I didn't know how much pillow talk had been involved, but I couldn't take the chance.'

'It was five minutes up against the wall in the gents'.' Maxwell found himself getting very angry on Melanie Bright's behalf.

'Oh. That's a shame, then. I didn't know. But at the time, she had to go. I left her a note under the windscreen of the van. I signed it from Doug Harvey, made it a bit irresistible, if you know what I mean, and she fell for it. She was waiting for me when I got there and it was over in seconds.' She paused. 'I know what you're thinking. Who would agree to meet Mr *Saturday Night Fever* in a darkened school, but she was a bit needy, poor old Mel.'

Maxwell swallowed his anger. Even without a bandage the size of a small wallaby on his head, he would have probably been no match for her and her knife, so tackling her across the desk was not an option in any universe, but he had never wanted to do it so much, ever. Not even during Bernard Ryan's most insane excesses.

'You had, of course, sorted the CCTV in advance.'

'Of course. Anybody can override sections of the system — well, anybody but you, Max. And, of course, that side door has been dodgy since I got here. Anyone who has forgotten anything nips in that way and there isn't anyone to know. Also, of course, you don't have to cross that perfectly polished floor, so no footprints for the men in white paper suits to find. Perfect. Now,' she put down the knife and stood up, 'this can go one of a number of ways. You can get on your bike, go home and we'll say no more about it.'

'Or?'

'Or I can fillet you like a haddock, deny all knowledge, adjust the cameras again and you'll look like just another victim of them Telly Lot. Why you? Because Arnie Preddie hates your guts and is jealous as Hell. *She* wanted to be the star and you stole her thunder, just like you did in that assembly when you told the whole school about the TV thing in the first place. Oh, it wouldn't stick, but your darling wife and the old fart she works for would spend weeks chasing their own tails.'

'Or,' Maxwell gave her a third option, 'you and I can go to Leighford nick right now and you can cough to everything we've talked about. In the interests of justice, you'll tell Jeremy where to stick his legal advice and you'll sing like a canary. I'm sure the *Daily Mail* would love to do a podcast on you.'

She looked at him for a moment and he thought that common decency had won. But he should have known, it rarely does.

'Nah,' she said. 'I'm going for Option Two,' and the knife was in her hand and she was sweeping round the table. Maxwell, trapped against the wall, hadn't a chance.

The door flew open and Darcy Quincy stood there. 'Mr Maxwell, Mrs Allington, I'm sorry . . .' Then he saw the knife gleaming in the woman's hand. 'Jesus!' he hissed. Polly pulled back, slashing the air in Darcy's direction and heading for the door. But Quincy was younger, faster, tougher. He twirled the cane and hooked the curved end of it around Polly's ankle. She stumbled, before falling headlong in the doorway.

Maxwell and the boy were on her like a flash. 'This is completely against my public-school ethos,' Maxwell said, 'to lay hands on a woman like this, but needs must. And now,' he hauled her upright while Darcy secured the knife, 'I'm going to exercise my medieval right and effect a citizen's arrest. As they used to say in *The Sweeney*, before your time, either of you, but I daresay it's available on YouTube,

"You're nicked, dahlin'." And, Darcy, if I ever tell you about carrying that cane to school again, you will tell me where to stick it, won't you?'

* * *

When Maxwell thought back on that hour of insanity later, several things would stay with him. He couldn't remember any shouting, which surprised him. After all, he and a seventeen-year-old armed with a cane had physically subdued a senior member of staff who had killed two people. You would think that that kind of thing would bring people running and then send them into hysteria, but no. A few people had ambled past and most had stayed to watch. Don from Maths was one and he very laconically went into the room and replaced Maxwell on the floor holding the sobbing and furious woman down. Maxwell had gratefully got up, with the help of several chairs and another passer-by and started to make phone calls.

The other thing was time. It hadn't passed in a proper regulated way, tick, tock, one second after the other in the appointed fashion. Some things had taken ages, such as the moment when Polly Allington had swiped at Darcy with the knife. To Maxwell, that threat to one of His Own was so much worse than when she had threatened him. Time had slowed to treacle speed when he was toiling up the Dam, when he was climbing the stairs and even opening the door to the office of the Head of History. The conversations, on the other hand, though never to be forgotten, passed in a flash. But the details of what she said, the almost casual way that this woman who he had chosen to bring to Leighford High School with such hope for the future, had spoken of removing people who would otherwise have threatened her comfortable life. He put the thought aside to ponder later — was he really as good a judge of character as he had thought?

And then, everything had suddenly pinged back to normal. The room was full of police, particularly his favourite one of all, enveloping him in a hug so tight he could hardly breathe. She then held him at arm's length and looked at him intently.

'You got here quickly,' he said at last, when she didn't speak.

'We were on our way,' she said. 'Mrs B was at the nick when we got back in from interviewing Mel's husband and . . . well, the USB was a bit of an eye-opener. She said you were on your way here and so Henry and I just jumped in the car and . . . Did you *really* wrestle her to the ground, you total imbecile?'

'Not by myself. Darcy helped as well.'

'Is that the lad in the duster coat?'

'That's him. If he wants to wear fancy dress from now until he leaves the place, he's welcome. Are the Telly Lot here still?'

'They've gone. I don't know whether that's as in "gone for the day" or "gone forever and sorry they ever tried". I must say, though, for a fly on the wall outfit, they have managed to miss almost every exciting thing that has happened here since they arrived. What have they got down as yet? A walk on the beach and a lesson.' She looked at his downcast face. 'No doubt as scintillating as always, but even so, not exactly BAFTA stuff, is it? We'll be tracking them down, though, just in case they can shed any light. And, of course, Kirsty Daniels, Masters's ex, will be helping. She knew Polly way back, although obviously they weren't on chatting-like-chums terms.'

Maxwell put his hand to his head. It felt different. His bandage, from being an albeit manky helmet, was now more of a loose swathe. He patted it ineffectually, but it didn't help. 'I feel like Gloria Swanson,' he said, though the resemblance was hard to spot.

Don from Maths, filling in a constable with the bare bones of his involvement over in the corner of the office, leaned round. '"Ready for my close-up, Mr DeMille,"' he said, with a thumbs-up.

Maxwell smiled and began to unravel the bandage. He only had the one film quote to bring to the table, but my word, that man had timing.

Henry Hall appeared in the doorway. He looked at Maxwell as the pile of unravelled bandage grew on the desk in front of him. '"You will not remember what I show you now, and yet I shall awaken memories of love . . . and crime . . . and death."' It was a more than passable Boris Karloff and everyone stopped what they were doing and turned around. Hall gave one of his rare smiles, shrugged and walked away.

Maxwell's voice filled the silence. 'Well, I didn't see that coming.'

* * *

That evening, Maxwell stretched out on the sofa, at Jacquie's insistence. Mrs B had googled head injuries and the rule for the moment was rest, no alcohol, no stress and no excitement. As the first two had already got big black lines drawn right through them, that left rest and no alcohol. Even so, it was nice to be home and safe after what even Maxwell had to admit was a rather more than exciting couple of hours. They had kept everything low-key for Nolan and the cats — it wouldn't help to make them worry. Nolan was now in bed, Metternich was stretched across as much of the hearthrug as he could take over and Bismarck was smugly ensconced on Jacquie's lap. A bowl of hyacinths on the side table were breaking bud and the scent was subtly bringing a hint of the long-awaited spring into the room. It was quiet. It was peaceful. They had promised each other not to talk about the case for a while, to detox for a bit. It was Maxwell who broke the promise.

'You should have seen Mandy's face when those images started coming up on the screen,' he chuckled. 'I'd always had her down as unshockable but apparently I was wrong.'

'Mrs B wasn't shocked,' Jacquie laughed. 'She just said she had never understood how men could think women

233

wanted to look at their willies all the time. "After all, Mrs M, they ain't exactly pretty, are they?"'

Maxwell gave her a nod to acknowledge a rather good Mrs B impersonation.

'A few heads are rolling in SOCO. Not finding the phone practically signed Melanie Bright's death warrant. And if it weren't for the M and Mandy thinking she was doing you a turn, that phone could have ended up in the bag of confiscated mobiles and never seen the light of day.'

'Serendipity, eh,' Maxwell said, thoughtfully, reaching for a glass of Southern Comfort that wasn't there. 'Do you think she would have killed anyone else, if we hadn't nabbed her?'

'She's having a psych eval,' Jacquie told him. 'Her brief insisted upon it.'

Maxwell's eyes opened as wide as the swelling allowed. 'Not Jeremy, surely?'

'The same. He isn't going for not guilty, which was a surprise, honestly, because he's got worse than Polly off scot-free. But he waltzed into the nick like an avenging angel and stopped everything in its tracks. His wife, he said, was under extraordinary mental strain and was not responsible for her actions. He hardly blinked when Henry reminded him that she wasn't his wife because she had still been married to Gavin Masters when they went through the motions in the beautiful little parish church where he and his forebears had been hatched, matched and despatched for centuries. He didn't even pause. He's a sharp one. And cold.' She shivered at the memory. 'If this hadn't happened, they would have become the perfect power couple with no doubt two perfect satanic children. Twins, I'm thinking . . . yellow eyes . . .' She gave another shudder. 'Sorry, went off at a bit of a tangent there.'

'Quite understand.' Maxwell had always thought *Village of the Damned* had been a good chance wasted, but didn't like to say; as long as she had enjoyed it, who was he to argue? 'But, to answer, what do you think? Sociopath? Psychopath? I can't believe I didn't spot it sooner.'

'But you don't, do you?' Jacquie pointed out. 'What's the stat that everyone bandies about when a case like this comes to the fore? About 4 per cent, they reckon, or something like that. I know it isn't quite how it works, but that means that three of your colleagues and forty of the kids are on the ladder.'

Maxwell put his head back and closed his eyes.

'You're working out who they are, aren't you?' Jacquie asked after a moment.

'Ssh. I'm counting.'

'Well, you've got one less now. Make sure when you choose the next one that they aren't smooth, beautiful and convincing. It's the one with the purple hair and one eye in the middle of his forehead you should be going for. They're usually okay.'

'True. True.' He raised his head. 'But what about Henry, eh? Who'd have thought that he was a Boris Karloff buff?'

'It was pretty impressive,' she agreed. 'But Henry has hidden depths, you know that.'

'Polly called him an old fart.'

'Well, there you are, then. A sociopath to her fingertips. Actually, one thing has been bothering me. Why did Darcy Quincy — what a name, by the way—'

'Mother a Jane Austen fan, apparently, though a very nice woman in all other respects.'

'Why did he come into your office at that very moment, do you know?'

Maxwell sat up and looked at her, the alternative ending to the afternoon's events suddenly flashing before his eyes.

'Do you know, I have absolutely no idea. I'm just darned glad he did.'

THE END

THE JOFFE BOOKS STORY

We began in 2014 when Jasper agreed to publish his mum's much-rejected romance novel and it became a bestseller.

Since then we've grown into the largest independent publisher in the UK. We're extremely proud to publish some of the very best writers in the world, including Joy Ellis, Faith Martin, Caro Ramsay, Helen Forrester, Simon Brett and Robert Goddard. Everyone at Joffe Books loves reading and we never forget that it all begins with the magic of an author telling a story.

We are proud to publish talented first-time authors, as well as established writers whose books we love introducing to a new generation of readers.

We won Trade Publisher of the Year at the Independent Publishing Awards in 2023 and Best Publisher Award in 2024 at the People's Book Prize. We have been shortlisted for Independent Publisher of the Year at the British Book Awards for the last five years, and were shortlisted for the Diversity and Inclusivity Award at the 2022 Independent Publishing Awards. In 2023 we were shortlisted for Publisher of the Year at the RNA Industry Awards, and in 2024 we were shortlisted at the CWA Daggers for the Best Crime and Mystery Publisher.

We built this company with your help, and we love to hear from you, so please email us about absolutely anything bookish at feedback@joffebooks.com.

If you want to receive free books every Friday and hear about all our new releases, join our mailing list here: www.joffebooks.com/freebooks.

And when you tell your friends about us, just remember: it's pronounced Joffe as in coffee or toffee!

www.ingramcontent.com/pod-product-compliance
Ingram Content Group UK Ltd.
Pitfield, Milton Keynes, MK11 3LW, UK
UKHW030828310325
5233UKWH00028B/159